CW00447411

SOMETHING HIDDEN

SOMETHING HIDDEN

Nick Blackstock

First published in Great Britain in 2009
by Picnic Publishing
PO Box 5222, Hove BN52 9LP

All rights reserved
Copyright © Nick Blackstock, 2009

The right of Nick Blackstock to be identified as the author of this work has been
asserted by her in accordance with the Copyright, Designs & Patents Act, 1988.

A catalogue record for this book is available from the British Library.

ISBN: 9780955861376

Printed and bound in Great Britain by CPI Antony Rowe
Designed by SoapBox, www.soapboxcommunications.co.uk.

All rights reserved. No part of this publication may be reproduced or
transmitted in any form or by any means, electronic or mechanical including
photocopying, recording or information storage or retrieval system, without
the prior permission in writing of the publishers.

This book is sold subject to the condition that it shall not by way of trade or
otherwise be lent, resold, hired out, or otherwise circulated without the
publishers' prior consent in writing in any form of binding or
cover other than that in which it is published and without a
similar condition being imposed on the subsequent publisher.

To Margaret.
For her continuing patience, advice, support and encouragement.

CHAPTER ONE

'DAMN!'

The driver looked round, automatically waiting for Harry's question, but his fireman hadn't heard. It was hardly surprising, for unless the engine was coasting normal conversation had to be shouted rather than spoken. In any event the other figure was too busy shovelling, the sweat on his brow reflected clearly by the glow of the fire. Another curse died on his lips. It wasn't important, and certainly shouldn't delay their arrival at Bristol unless they had signals against them. The driver turned again and looked out of the tender's window. The October fog had abandoned the hollows and wraith-like fingers were starting to invade the meadows. Almost automatically he pressed the whistle.

This time a startled Harry did look across to his driver. 'What's up, mate?'

'Just checking. It's getting a bit foggy out there.'

The fireman paused in his exertions and looked ahead up the line. 'Nothing to worry about. Besides, we'll be in Bristol in under an hour.' He glanced at his companion to see if he wanted to make conversation. 'I won't be sorry to see Temple Meads; it's been a long night. Still, back in Leeds tomorrow.' He couldn't resist a little dig at his driver who was not only a southerner by birth but also as near as damn it a teetotaller. 'Back to some decent beer.'

Jim Thornton only smiled; he was used to Harry's little ways. Then the smile died as he remembered the cause of his unease. Fog was always a problem, particularly when driving an express with responsibility for the lives of hundreds of people – not that there were so many on this one. He could remember almost every individual who had boarded at the interim stops since he had started at Leeds. There had been more than he expected at Birmingham, presumably with through connections. It was impossible with the crowds during the day, but on night expresses he had got into the habit of memorising faces and counting them off at their various destinations: he found it was easy to do while he waited for the guard's signal, and it helped to pass the long hours. Thinking about it brought back memories: 'A photographic memory, Sergeant Thornton. That's what you've got.' Even now he could recall the excited, high-pitched voice of Lieutenant Smith as, once again, he reassured the officer about the positions of their support companies, where the dead ground lay between them and the positions they had to take. Not that it had done the lieutenant any good. If only he had known it – less than a month to the Armistice. Jim looked at the fog again. Maybe that was it: too many memories of dawn attacks. Still, that was ten years ago. The fireman looked up from his labours as his driver shook himself and took a deep breath.

'Meldon coming up.' It was Harry's way of reminding Jim of the signal just the other side of the station. The driver shut down the regulator, slowing the express to virtual walking pace as it trundled past the bare platforms. A couple of workmen, huddled into their collars, looked up without curiosity: they would be waiting for the first stopping train, which was not due for another half hour. Jim noticed there were others in the waiting room, and wondered idly why the men on the platform hadn't joined them. It must be cold out there.

'It's red!' Harry saw the signal first. The train came to a gentle stop as Jim applied the brakes and closed the regulator right down. Harry switched on the injector, blowing off excess steam. They were silent as they waited for the signal to change. Somewhere, back towards the station, there was a shout. Jim looked back, straining his eyes, but it was not repeated and he could see nothing.

'Time to go.' Harry's acknowledgement of the signal change wrenched Jim's attention away from the train and back to the track ahead. The engine pulled away smoothly as he delivered his verdict. 'The last thing we wanted, another five minutes' delay.'

'We'll make it up.'

Glancing again at the fog shrouded fields the driver couldn't share his fireman's optimism. 'Not in these conditions we won't.'

Harry felt the need for conversation. 'I hear the company's hoping to change over all the rolling stock to electric lighting in two years.' There was no response but, doggedly, he pursued the subject. 'If they've got that sort of money to spend I can think of a lot better ways to spend it. After all, gas lighting works fine . . .'

'It's a question of safety, Harry.' There was an air of finality both about the statement and the way the driver turned to peer through his window.

Harry was not put off. 'Come on, Jim, surely it's a question of priorities . . .'

The comment seemed to galvanise his workmate. 'Yes, it *is* a question of priorities. Look – there've been far too many crashes turned into disasters by gas.' The fireman started to interrupt, but Jim overrode him. 'Not only crashes. Sometimes just a little shunt, then . . . woomph . . .' He stared hard at his companion. 'I can tell you that once we're rid of gas I'll be a lot happier. It'll be something we won't have to worry about any more.'

Harry decided to change the subject. 'We'll be coming up to the Eastmead distant signal soon. How's the fog?'

'Could be worse. There'll be no problem with signals unless we run into a bank of the stuff or it collects in a cutting.' He paused a moment. 'But to be on the safe side we'll both check it.' He crossed the cab to stand on the footplate behind his fireman, a move that served only to trigger slight feelings of anxiety in both men.

It was Harry who saw it first. 'There it is. The distant. It's green.'

There was no audible sigh of relief but for some reason both felt it. Then the green halo of the main signal appeared. The track was clear. Jim opened the regulator and the engine responded, gathering, thrusting, hurling itself forward – irresistible, unstoppable. The main signal flew past, then the station itself, a ribbon of platform, billboards and light temporarily banishing the pre-dawn gloom. Just as suddenly the darkness returned, and both men strained once more to make out details of the track ahead. As the driver had thought the fog had gathered in the cutting, but beyond he could just make out the bridge. His eyes were beginning to adjust, and he waited expectantly for the patch of lighter grey underneath it. But he could see nothing: it must be darker than he thought. Half-turning, he was about to shout across to Harry when an awful thought occurred. Could there be something else in the tunnel? But there couldn't be: both signals had been green. It must be a trick of the light.

Automatically Jim shut off the steam, even as Harry's scream echoed in his ears: 'Brakes, Jim. Brakes!' Frantically he sought to screw down the brake handle, but even with muscles and sinews stretched to their limit he was no longer the master of this screeching, shuddering monster. By now the patch of darkness ahead had translated itself into a shape, a shape that was beginning to take on an unmistakable form. It was a goods – a stationary goods – and on their line. There was no way of avoiding a collision, but he was slowing; all the time he was slowing. Please God might it not be a disaster.

'Oh Jesus, Jim! The up line. The up line. There's a goods on the up line!' Harry's despairing wail registered even over the tortured scream of metal on metal. Almost before Jim could take in the implications of this new catastrophe the dark heaving mass of the other engine was alongside, and for one frozen moment he glimpsed the horror-stricken face of the other driver. But it was travelling fast: it might even get clear before the other two trains collided.

When it came the impact was deceptive. The engine reared but, even as Jim was hurled upwards and backwards it seemed just possible for a moment that the express – his express – would stay within its own rails. That this would be an accident that did not turn into a disaster. That the upward goods would get past and clear. But it was not to be. As the last of the goods wagons thundered past Jim's engine slowly toppled into their path.

He regained consciousness to the sound of moans. At first he thought they were his own then, little by little, he realised they were Harry's. Pulling himself onto all fours he crawled to the other side of the cab where his fireman lay. Then the hiss of escaping steam sounded a warning bell in his mind. The boiler might rupture; he must get out of here. Pulling Harry behind him, Jim half-clambered, half-crawled over the twisted metal until he judged they were clear of immediate danger. It was only then that he looked back up the track. Back to where carriages were piled as a child might pile a toy train when he had finished playing. Like a man possessed Jim staggered back towards them screaming at the top of his voice. To an observer he would have seemed like just another victim of shock, but he was one of the few not only to have smelled the gas but also to know the inevitable outcome . . .

CHAPTER TWO

'CHARTERIS!' THE BELLOW was totally ignored by senior reporters, deep in conversation having put the paper to bed. It scarcely disturbed the two remaining secretaries as they helped each other on with their coats. Even the office boy, scurrying between desks, looked up only momentarily. But in a small alcove at the very far end of the office it registered loud and clear with its intended recipient.

'Shit!' The man stopped typing and stretched his shoulders. 'I don't know how he does it. It's like a foghorn. You know him better than me, George. Wasn't he supposed to be gassed in the war?'

The occupant of the other desk gazed towards the source of the noise. 'He was, Ron. He was. But if it affected anything it was his temper, not his vocal cords.' Ron pushed himself out of his chair and George looked at him sympathetically. 'Any idea what it's about?'

'Expenses.'

'Expenses! For God's sake, he's the deputy editor not the accountant.'

'They're fairly substantial.' The laconic reply masked Ron's anxiety.

'Oh, the train crash.' George tried to sound reassuring. 'I know you've been out on the story longer than most, but we all put in hefty claims.'

'The trouble is I've been concentrating on those kids.'

'Well, to a certain extent we all have. It's national news.' His interest aroused, George looked hard at his companion. 'Have you got somewhere?'

'No, no one's got a clue about either of them, and it's been three weeks now.' Ron sighed. 'I've had no option but to concentrate on the cops. Of course they're not releasing anything officially – at least not to us local boys. So I've had to sniff around, picking up whatever I can from whoever.' His pretence had dropped now and he looked worried. 'You know them as well as me, George. The crafty sods all hint they know something, but about three pints later you discover most of them know sweet FA.'

'I see.' George's sympathy was genuine.

'Exactly. A bloody big expense claim but not a lot of copy to show for it.'

'Now, where was it?' Querulously Albert Gent raked through the pieces of paper scattered about his desk until, with a little gasp of triumph, he found what he was looking for. 'Advance expenses – thirty pounds!' He brandished the offending document. 'You know the maximum is fifteen.' His voice ended on a squeak of incredulity as he examined the document more closely. 'And this signature. It looks like Curtis. Who the hell is Curtis?'

Ron became defensive. 'He's in accounts. If you remember, he took over when Sanderson was on holiday.' He took a chance. 'I explained why I needed that much, and you'll find that every last penny is accounted for.'

'I don't doubt it, and that's part of the problem.' Once more the deputy editor scrabbled among his mess of papers. 'There's this.' He picked up a receipt, was about to hand it over, then checked again as if unable to believe his eyes. 'Two pounds, fourteen shillings and sevenpence.' He enunciated every syllable, as if to emphasise the enormity of the figure. 'And what was it for?' He checked the expense sheet and proceeded to answer his own question. 'Food and refreshments at the Royal Oak.'

Despondently Ron regarded the figure opposite. Anyone hearing that voice would have expected a big man, but Gent was small, very small – indeed almost mouse-like. Sometimes that fooled newcomers, but after their first taste of his ferocious disposition they generally learned better. Rumour had it that in addition to his wife and kids in Yate, to the north of the city, he also had a fancy woman set up in a flat in Clifton. Ron reflected that if this were true it might account for his temper. Belatedly he realised that his answer was still awaited. 'That would be the police.' It sounded lame, and he hurried on. 'There was an inspector and two sergeants. We had quite a few sandwiches and . . . and . . . beer.'

The response was almost silky. 'And did this . . . feast . . . produce anything?'

'Well . . . I was able to confirm quite a few things and discount some others. It was the basis for a lot of that article I did last week.'

'Yes, that article.' Gent seemed to drift off, then recovered himself. 'Quite well written, interesting even – if you hadn't been reading the nationals. As it is, there's absolutely nothing new there.' He antici-pated Ron's impending interruption and brushed it aside. 'Now, we're the second paper in a provincial city. It's part of our stock-in-trade to regurgitate quite a bit of what the nationals push out.' His voice was rising towards some sort of climax. 'But for Christ's sake, man, we can do that sitting on our arses in the office, not visiting every bloody bar in Bristol to wine and dine the local police.' He was brandishing receipts again. 'Do you realise, Charteris, that this one bill is nearly a week's wages for a labourer?'

He paused, whether to catch his breath or gather himself for a fresh assault Ron didn't know, but he took his chance. 'I might not have got anything new but I do know there's something very funny going on.'

'Funny! Of course there's something funny going on! Two kids have been killed in a railway crash and three weeks later nobody has come forward to identify them. That's why the nationals are inter-ested. That's why we're interested.'

'No, it's more than that. Look, I've been with the police a lot. I'm positive they're steering away, or being steered away, from certain areas.'

'Oh come on. You're not on that hobby horse about them being the offspring of very important people, like that article in the *Daily*

Herald suggested.' Gent's tone was more weary than angry now. 'Let me put you right on this, Charteris. First of all the *Herald* has a political agenda. And second this is 1928 not 1828. Nobody, and I mean nobody, could hush up something like that.'

'All I know is that one of the inspectors I talked to considered it to be one of several useful lines of investigation, until about a week ago.' Ron paused, the better to make his point. 'Now it's just not under consideration. Not only that, no one will even talk about it unofficially. The inspector got quite shirty when I persisted. If they're really pushed by the London papers the agreed line seems to be that it's all fanciful speculation that detracts from the real investigation.'

Gent looked dismissive. 'Which is probably the genuine reason.'

'Maybe, but I always thought the police didn't arbitrarily abandon a line of investigation until they were absolutely sure it was leading them nowhere.'

He hesitated and Gent again became irritable. 'Come on. Spit it out.'

'Well, the inspector didn't want to venture onto that territory. Easy to understand, really. You know – "if you're hoping to be a super some day"; that sort of thing. But a sergeant I know was much more forthcoming in a negative sort of way.'

'Negative sort of way? For God's sake, lad, we're a newspaper! We don't publish inferences – at least not if we want to keep out of the libel courts.'

Ron persisted. 'What he did was give me a warning – not a threat or anything like that. Now I know this particular chap: believe me, he's genuine. His words were, and I quote, "Whatever you do, don't dig in that particular midden."'

Gent got up and gazed out of the office door. He didn't often do that: Ron supposed it was because he was sensitive about his height. Eventually he seemed to reach some sort of conclusion. 'You don't have anything we can publish – or are likely to have, come to that. Even if you were able to prove that the Romanovs didn't all die in 1917 and instead a couple of them met their maker on a London

Midland train we still couldn't use it.' He returned to his desk and glared his reporter. 'Now listen to me. I've had a word with Jarvis.' He was referring to the editor. 'We're going to run with the accident for another week and then review the position. In the meantime what we want from you is copy we can publish. On time, mark you, and without treading on the toes of senior police officers. And above all,' the receipts were brandished one more time, 'positively no more mass entertaining of His Majesty's constabulary!'

Ron caught sight of himself in a shop window and paused hurriedly to straighten his tie. The effect was far from ideal, serving mainly to highlight the fact that everything else about him was dishevelled. Despairingly he tried to smooth some recalcitrant strands of hair that were flopping over his forehead. It was no good. What a day to run out of Brylcreem. Behind him a local clock chimed the hour. He glanced at his watch, took a deep breath and marched, with as much confidence as he could muster, through an imposing portico, the sign above proclaiming that this was the National Provincial Bank.

'Yes, sir?' A top-hatted figure regarded him enquiringly.

'I've an appointment with Mr Surtees at twelve. My name's Charteris.'

'If you wouldn't mind waiting here, sir.' Top Hat glided away.

Ron watched him go feeling more depressed than ever. He hated banks: they always gave him a sense of inferiority. A little suburban branch wouldn't be too bad, but no, Dorothy's father kept going on about 'doing him no harm at all' to have his account at the Bristol head office. It had been weak of him to give in.

'This way, sir.' Top Hat had returned. Ron followed him along a corridor. Eventually Top Hat paused, knocked at a door and, in response to a reply that was almost inaudible, opened it. 'Mr Charteris to see you, sir.'

'Sit down, Mr Charteris.' It was the first time Ron had met the manager, who in normal circumstances was probably far too important to worry about the sort of paltry account he represented. Once again he fingered the letter in his pocket. Some of the phrases leapt to mind: 'unauthorised withdrawal' was the one that fixed itself in his consciousness. 'Mr Ronald Charteris, isn't it?'

'Yes.' There was a pause as he sought for something else to add. 'I work for the Echo, as a reporter.'

'No doubt very interesting work.' The manager sounded as if he didn't really believe it. 'If you don't mind me asking, how old are you?'

Ron did mind, but judged that this was not something to die in the ditch for. 'I'm twenty-six.'

'And not married?' Once again his hackles rose, and once again he subdued the urge to give a tart reply. 'I hope to get engaged next summer. She's the daughter of Mr Laidlaw, who introduced me to the bank.'

'Ah, James Laidlaw, the solicitor.' The manager nodded and his posture relaxed. 'A long-standing and valued customer.' Ron could feel his own tension relaxing too. Wherever his peccadillo ranked in the hierarchy of banking sins, it seemed that now Laidlaw was in the equation he was to be dealt with leniently. Perhaps he should take the initiative.

'I wanted to explain about going overdrawn. I've been involved in reporting on the railway accident at Eastmead. Normally we can draw advance expenses, but with all the irregular hours it hasn't always been possible . . .' He spread his hands. 'I'm afraid I just miscalculated.'

'I see.' There was a shuffling of papers across the desk. 'Normally we take a serious view about something like this. After all, the amount overdrawn wasn't trifling.' He glanced down. 'It was six pounds fourteen shillings – so in the circumstances you can consider yourself lucky your last cheque was honoured.' An exhalation of breath signalled that the lecture was over. 'However, as the account is now in order I'm prepared to overlook it on this occasion. Needless to say, you mustn't expect such leniency if it occurs again.' They shook hands at the door. 'Goodbye, Mr Charteris. Remember what I've said. A young man with marriage in prospect can't afford to get into slack habits as far as money is concerned.' Despite everything, the fixed smile on Ron's face didn't slip.

'What's so pressing, Gerald?' Summoned by an urgent phone call, Ron leaned on the counter of the local police station and tried to read the features of Sergeant Thomas. 'You going to reinforce that warning you gave me the other day?'

The face opposite broke into a grin, then suddenly became serious. 'Not exactly, Ron.' The sergeant leaned over in turn and lowered his voice. 'Inspector Maguire would like a quiet word with you.'

'Maguire? Here?'

'Keep your voice down.' The sergeant looked alarmed. 'But don't worry – he's not around.'

'Why does he want to see me?' Ron was genuinely puzzled. 'Isn't he in charge of the whole investigation?'

'More or less, although officially there's a superintendent at the top who's supposed to be co-ordinating everything.'

'Why me?'

The sergeant shrugged his shoulders. 'That's something you'll have to ask him.'

Ron rested his chin on his hand and tried to work it out. 'I suppose he wants me to meet him at the Royal. Isn't that where he usually entertains the press?' Ruefully he remembered his expense claim. 'Or should I say where the press entertains him?'

The sergeant shook his head sorrowfully. 'Now you're being cynical. As a matter of fact he suggested the Four Aces café on the Gloucester Road.'

'The Four Aces?' Ron was genuinely startled. 'Hang on – that's miles away. Isn't it right at the far end of Gloucester Road?' He gave Sergeant Thomas a hard stare. 'This isn't some sort of trick, is it? Because if it is, I can tell you that my sense of humour's wearing thin.'

'It's completely straight.' The sergeant pretended to check a file in front of him. 'But it's up to you whether you take him up on it or not.'

'What about a time?'

'He's pretty busy, so I'll telephone you with a day and a time.'

'Can't I telephone him myself?'

'No. He wants everything to be done through me.' Thomas closed the file decisively. 'You'll just have to take it or leave it.

The waitress brought over the teapot. 'Any scones and jam?'

Ron tried hard to avoid looking at the stained tablecloth and grubby ashtrays. 'Er . . . no thanks.' The girl sniffed her disapproval.

He glanced at the rest of the café. What a place to choose. He had met Maguire before, of course, but always as part of a group and, being a relatively junior reporter, hadn't spoken to the man directly. What on earth could he want with him? And to meet him in this place . . . The hole-in-corner manner in which the meeting had been arranged made Ron vaguely uneasy. He had even toyed with the thought of asking a colleague – George had sprung to mind – to pose as a nearby customer, but had rejected that idea: if there was a story he wanted it for himself. Besides, Maguire obviously wished the whole thing to be kept quiet. Why else would he choose a scruffy café miles from his regular stamping ground?

Ron poured another cup of tea and checked his watch. Ten to six: he was twenty minutes late already. His thoughts turned to Dorothy. They weren't getting on the way they used to. Probably it was his fault. He tried to say as little as possible about her father, but she must surely sense his feelings. God, the man was a pompous little name-dropper and puffed up with his own importance. How could a girl like Dorothy have a father like him?

'It's Ron Charteris, isn't it?' Maguire had arrived unnoticed and was standing beside his table.

Ron stood up and they shook hands. 'Would you like some tea?' It was a malicious question, but he couldn't resist it.

'No, thanks. Just finished my flask up the road.' Maguire smiled. 'I don't always have time for a proper break, so I always carry one.'

The faint aroma told Ron what was in that flask: the thought occurred that perhaps he had it in him to be a detective too.

Momentarily there was an awkward pause and he decided there was nothing lost by being direct. 'I was surprised that you wanted to see me.'

'We've been reviewing the case and, not to put too fine a point on it, there's a feeling that perhaps we haven't given the local press boys a fair crack of the whip.'

Ron tried to put on his best non-committal expression. 'I'm flattered. So I've been selected to represent the local press?'

'You know you haven't.' Just for a moment a faint smile flitted across Maguire's face. 'But you've been making a bloody nuisance of yourself.'

'I don't know what you mean.'

'Oh yes you do. All this probing about these kids being well connected. I've had complaints from quite a few of my officers.'

'I'm doing no more than a lot of national reporters.'

'True – but they're losing interest now. Other stories are taking over.'

'So what's so terrible about me pursuing a line that the police were interested in themselves a week ago?'

Maguire leaned forward and spoke with feeling. 'Because it's not true.' He sat back. 'I know that. More to the point, if these stories persist all that will happen is that we'll be distracted from the real leads we have.'

'Real leads?'

'Yes. Real leads.' Like a seasoned fly fisherman Maguire allowed the lure to rest on the surface for a few seconds before flicking it away. 'Of course, I realise that you might want to stick with your preferred fiction.' For a moment he sounded genuinely regretful.

Ron knew he was being manipulated, but the hint of disclosures to come drew him on. Even so he risked a little sarcasm. 'You really have some leads?'

Like sun going behind a cloud, Maguire's demeanour changed and his tone took on a slight hint of menace. 'Let's cut out the bullshit, Charteris.' Ron didn't reply and, satisfied he had made his point, Maguire continued. 'This is not something I would have chosen, but the deal is this. I'll fill you in on the background stuff about certain avenues we're pursuing. No names or anything like that, but what you'll get is enough to make a good story. A story, I might add, that will be interesting for your readers and helpful to the police.'

'And in return?'

'You'll lay off this wild goose chase once and for all.'

Shoulders hunched against the rain, Ron shuffled down the queue and climbed on board the trolley-bus, then collapsed into a seat just as it lurched forward. 'Tickets.' Ron fished in his pocket but found only half a crown. 'Nothing smaller?' He shook his head. The conductor looked disgruntled and grudgingly counted out the change.

He stared out of the window at the glistening pavements and few scurrying pedestrians. Of course Maguire had a car. No wonder he suggested a God-forsaken place like the Four Aces for a meeting. Ron went over the events of the past hour again. He didn't believe for a moment any of the bilge that had been used to justify the meeting. Obviously someone higher up had decided that speculation about connections with the high and the mighty had to be knocked on the head. He tried to be dispassionate. This didn't necessarily mean there was anything in his particular theory. The well connected always had a great deal they wanted to hide. Posses of journalists digging into the family lives of the rich and famous might come across all sorts of things.

The trolley-bus glided to a halt. It was getting near the city centre now and many more passengers boarded. 'Do you mind if I sit down?'

Guiltily Ron edged towards the window and the woman made a great production out of perching on the outside seat. As she stowed her umbrella she managed to transfer much of the rain it had collected onto his shoes. He grimaced and tried to shuffle a little further towards the window. Then he remembered his notebook and what was in it. Maguire had delivered on his promise – nothing specific, no chapter and verse, but enough to write a very good article. If Gent would wear it there could be a series of articles – two or three anyway: it could do him no harm at all.

It had already been reported that the children boarded the train at Birmingham unaccompanied: the driver had confirmed this. According to Maguire, the poor sod was likely to be blamed for the accident – and once that happened there was the further likelihood that he would face manslaughter charges. One of the theories that the police were working on was that the children's parents had packed them off to relatives and then committed suicide or had an accident. Accordingly they had asked forces throughout the Midlands to advise them about suspicious deaths.

The bell rang, and Ron's involuntary companion departed together with her umbrella. He looked out of the window again; it would be his stop next.

The police were also looking into the theory that the kids might be orphans, on their way to who knows where. It was a long shot, but they were contacting as many orphanages as they could. Another suggestion was that they might be Irish – yet another lead they were following up.

As the trolley-bus approached his stop Ron stood up, bracing himself against the seat. Whatever happened, he had enough material to write an article angled any way he wanted. As for the other theory, he would let that lie for the moment to keep Maguire happy. But this didn't mean he had rejected it completely.

CHAPTER THREE

ELLEN THORNTON STARTED awake from a deep, deep sleep. At first she thought it was the wind. The west wind that, blowing down from the Pennines and curling its way between streets and alleys, could sometimes make windows creak and groan even here in the centre of Leeds. Slowly the room came into focus: the wallpaper with its small repeating pattern of spring flowers; the chest of drawers with the washbowl on top; and beside it the framed photograph of Jamie in his sergeant's uniform along with his platoon. Even in her half-sleep she smiled at his little foibles, for it was the photograph that he obstinately wouldn't countenance having on display on the dresser downstairs. Then suddenly she was wide awake. It wasn't the wind making the noise: it was Jamie. Frantically she turned to the tossing, moaning figure beside her. 'Jamie. Wake up. Wake up.'

Jim Thornton sat bolt upright in bed. 'It's no good, Harry! We've too much speed.' The words were wailed rather than spoken.

Ellen held him to her, rocking her husband gently. 'It's all right, Jamie. You're having a nightmare.' She stroked his face, desperately trying to release him from his horrors by her sheer physical presence.

He gave a shudder, but then started to breathe more deeply and easily. Eventually he slowly disengaged her arms. 'I'm all right now. Truly.'

She lay back beside him. 'You must try not to brood about it. Didn't the union man say they haven't really got a case?'

When he replied his bitterness was palpable. 'The police feel they've got a case and they have the best lawyers working for them.'

He turned towards his wife. 'The union will do their best, but they can only afford young, inexperienced barristers. I mean, look at that fellow Gregory who's defending me. You were there when we had that meeting. He can't be a day over twenty-six or twenty-seven. What chance has he got of getting me out of a life sentence?'

Ellen closed her eyes, the better to ward off the terror that was in danger of overwhelming her. If she wasn't positive what chance was there for Jamie? 'But he said the manslaughter charge was just a technicality, didn't he? He said that once the inquest reached a verdict of negligence, then all the rest – the trial and everything – followed on automatically. It was just a case of your word against that of the signalman.' There was no response. 'Jamie, everyone believes in you: the union, the people at work.' A thought struck her. 'Even the management in Leeds thinks you weren't to blame.. You said yourself that normally you wouldn't get a penny until the case was settled. They must think a lot of you to suspend you on half-pay.'

He put his arms around her and she could feel the release of tension. 'You're right, love. You're right. Everyone thinks there's no case to answer, but they're not in my position.' They lay quietly for a while until it suddenly burst out. 'If only Harry could have been called as a witness.' She felt the tension returning. 'The fireman's testimony would have knocked this nonsense on the head once and for all.'

'You know he can't. His memory's a blank about everything a week either side of the accident. The doctors say it might come back, but they can't say when.' Ellen deliberately changed tack. 'Do you know what that detective inspector from Bristol wants to talk to you about tomorrow?'

'No idea. It can't be about the charge, as everything's done and dusted on that until the assizes. Gregory told me the only contact I'll have with the police is checking at the local station once a week, my bail condition.'

Ellen grew alarmed. 'Then should you be seeing them at all?' Her thoughts outran ran her words. 'I mean . . . supposing . . . you said something that . . .' She sought desperately for a coherent sentence. 'Jamie, please go to the union office in town before you see the police. They'll be able to give you advice.'

'No. I've got nothing to hide. Nothing to be ashamed of.' Jim had the bit between his teeth. 'If it's help they want they'll get it. I'll go and see this fellow tomorrow with my head held high.'

Despite his brave words to Ellen, Jim Thornton felt a sense of foreboding as he approached the main Leeds police station in Milgarth. He didn't like police stations: it was in a police station in Bristol that he had been charged with manslaughter. That had been by far the worst moment; even the committal hearing hadn't been as bad. He took a deep breath and reminded himself that today's meeting had nothing to do with the charge he was facing.

'Can I help you?' The tone of the desk sergeant was brusque and to the point.

'Yes, my name's Thornton. I have an appointment to see . . .' He realised he had forgotten the name and fumbled in his pockets for the letter, much to the annoyance of the sergeant. At last he found it. 'It's a Detective Inspector Maguire from Bristol.' He added as an afterthought, 'At eleven o'clock.'

'Oh, the Bristol chap.' The sergeant regarded him with renewed interest. 'Well, take a seat on that bench over there. I'll check if he's ready for you.' He disappeared into a back office, and Jim fixed his gaze on the various posters behind the desk. He noted that the most prominent cautioned against pickpockets in the city centre. Instinctively he felt for his wallet, only to let his hand drop. The ten shilling note it contained would hardly tempt any self-respecting pickpocket. The sergeant reappeared. 'Right. Follow me.' He strode briskly up a corridor, and Jim meekly followed in his wake. The knock on a door was peremptory, almost impatient. Not receiving an immediate reply, the sergeant opened it and stuck his head round to announce without ceremony, 'A Mr Thornton to see you.'

'Nice to see you, Mr Thornton. I'm Detective Inspector Maguire.' The middle-aged man who advanced across the room to shake his hand was affability itself compared with the desk sergeant. 'Although of course we've met before.'

'Have we?' Jim was startled.

'Yes. It was about two days after the accident. Mind you, one of my sergeants did most of the interviewing.' Jim was still puzzled, but Maguire was sympathetic. 'I expect you were still in a state of shock. It was in the stationmaster's office at Temple Meads station.'

'Oh yes.' Jim did remember. It was during those hours of questioning, first by the railway investigators then by the police. In a rather vague way he was beginning to place Maguire's face. 'Didn't you ask me about those children?'

'I did.' The policeman seemed delighted at Jim's returning memory. 'Actually, that's why I wanted to see you today.'

'But I told you everything at the time.'

'I'm sure you did, Jim, I'm sure you did. By the way, you don't mind me calling you Jim?' Maguire's face indicated that he didn't mind whether Jim objected or not; in any event he took the lack of response for assent. 'You must have read in the papers that we still haven't been able to identify those children.'

'To be honest I haven't been following the papers much, especially anything to with the accident. You know I've been charged with . . .'

The inspector intervened swiftly. 'Of course I do, and if I was in a different position, wearing a different hat as it were, maybe I'd have views about it. As it is,' Maguire shrugged, 'I'm sure it's best that we don't talk about that aspect.' An expression of mild impatience flitted across his features. 'But let's get back to the children. Quite a few passengers remembered – or thought they remembered – seeing them on the train.' He gave a deep sigh. 'The trouble is a lot of the statements are contradictory. It could be that they did notice them, or that they saw other children and mistook them for the ones we want to identify. The point is, Jim, that of all the statements yours is the only one that carries conviction. You had a clear view when they got on in Birmingham and you described them very well.'

He leaned forward. 'What I want to do is go over your original statement. See if we can dot a few more I's, cross a few more T's, that sort of thing.'

'I'll do my best.' Jim sounded uncertain.

'I'm sure you will.' Maguire opened the file in front of him and was silent for a moment or two as he scanned a sheet of paper, then took out a notebook and pencil. Eventually he looked up. 'Now you say here that you saw a boy of about ten or eleven in a dark blue raincoat and he was with a girl a year or two younger. She was wearing,' he checked the paper again, 'a red coat . . .'

Jim interrupted. 'A bright red coat – and it was too big for her – just as well, really. It was a cold night and she only had ankle socks on. In fact apart from their coats I don't think either of them was dressed for the weather.'

The inspector looked thoughtful. 'Are you sure, Jim? I mean, I'm a trained police officer, I'm trained to observe and remember, but I'm not sure details like that would have stuck with me, especially under the circumstances.'

'I've got a good memory, and on night runs I used to try and remember where people got on and off. Anyway, at every station I looked back along the platform for the guard's signal.'

'Did you see anyone with them?' Jim shook his head. 'Or who might have been?' Maguire stared intently across the table as if trying to read the engine driver's mind.

'No . . . I can't think of anyone who seemed directly connected, as you might say.'

'What about other people who were around?'

'At that end of the platform, you mean?' The other man nodded. 'Well, there were a couple of middle-aged women. I remember them because they had massive suitcases.' He searched his memory for more details. 'There was a young fellow in a dark suit with a brief-case. I took him to be a commercial traveller.' As he jotted down notes Maguire continued to nod encouragingly. 'Oh, and there were a couple of sailors – I assume they'd been on leave and were going back to Plymouth.' He breathed out heavily. 'You know, I can remember quite a lot but I'm not a performing memory man.' Jim didn't care if it sounded querulous.

Maguire didn't take offence. 'You're doing fine. Just fine.'

Jim continued to dredge his memory. 'There were four or five other men, but they all seemed to be travelling separately.'

'Can you describe any of them?'

'One was tall. Really tall. And he had a moustache. I just glanced at him, but I took him to be ex-army. You know, the officer type.'

The inspector looked interested. 'Why was that?'

'His shoes were shiny and polished.'

'But so are mine.'

No, I mean really polished.' Despite Jim's stammered apology Maguire looked hurt. The awkward pause that followed was finally broken when Jim continued, 'That's it. I can't remember any more. They were all just average, apart from the clergyman.'

'Clergyman?' For the first time Maguire raised his voice. 'You didn't mention a clergyman before.' He brandished the witness statement. 'There's nothing about that in here.'

Well, he might not have been a clergyman. I just thought he looked like one.'

'Did he have a dog collar?'

'He might have. I couldn't see it.'

'Then why do you think he was a clergyman?'

'I don't know. He just looked like one. A dark hat, a black coat with the collar turned up.' It was becoming an interrogation and, irritated, Jim's voice rose. 'I'm just telling you what I saw.'

Maguire softened his tone. 'Was he . . . I mean . . . could he have been with the children?'

'Not that I saw. Anyway, he might not even have got on the train. The last passengers were boarding and I was checking ahead for the outward signal. When I looked back for the guard's flag all the doors were shut.'

The interview went on for another half-hour, with Maguire going over his notes again and again, trying desperately to squeeze out the last drop of information. Finally he gave up, stood up and shook hands. 'Well, thank you for coming, Mr Thornton.'

His reversion to a more formal tone did not escape Jim. As he walked back to the front entrance he tried to work out exactly what Maguire wanted to know. This was certainly not about the children. Most of the questions had revolved around who might or might not have been with them.

'Enjoy your heart to heart with our southern colleague?' The desk sergeant's tone was significantly warmer than when he had come in. You're Jim Thornton, aren't you? The driver involved in that Bristol accident.' Jim nodded bleakly and the sergeant lowered his voice. 'Strictly between ourselves, a lot of us feel you've had a bad deal.' His voice brightened. 'Still, you're not hanged until you're through the trap door.' He smiled at his little witticism. 'Anyway, I hear the Bristol fellow only came up to try and get information about the kids who were killed.' He gave a conspiratorial wink. 'Now why on earth do you think they sent a senior detective inspector all the way up here to do a job any junior constable could do as well?'

CHAPTER FOUR

AUTOMATICALLY RON MOVED to the side as the clatter of feet behind him on the stairs warned of someone in a hurry. 'Charteris. Glad I caught up with you. I wanted a quiet word.' The panting figure alongside was his editor, Arthur Jarvis. For a moment he leaned on the banister rail, chest heaving; finally his gasps subsided. 'Just wanted to congratulate you on last week's articles on the Eastmead crash. The circulation manager tells me we've been shifting an average of an extra two thousand copies since then.'

Ron was very pleased indeed, but he felt a show of modesty could do no harm. 'Nice of you to say so, Mr Jarvis, but I can't take all the credit. After all, there's that new fashion competition.'

'Don't be modest, lad. Don't be modest. It revived the whole story.' The editor peered at him quizzically. 'You must have some good contacts.' Ron smiled disparagingly but didn't reply directly, hoping to convey the impression of a great many irons in the fire. 'But that's by the way. I happen to know that Rhodes at the *Mail* has been blowing his top.' He was referring to the editor of their competitor. 'Apparently he's been hauling everyone over the coals for letting us steal a march.' The broad grin on Jarvis's face indicated that this was a state of affairs he was very happy with. It was hardly surprising, as there had been a steady erosion of circulation over the last few months. Moreover, from what Ron had heard the proprietor had been making his displeasure plain. 'What I've suggested to Gent is that unless they solve the mystery of these children we do some follow-up articles. Do you think you'll be able to cover that?'

Ron let out his breath sharply. 'I suppose so. But it really depends on the police. If they make some progress – and it's a big if – then I might be able to ferret something out.'

He received a clap on the shoulder. 'Good man. See what you can come up with, then take it up with Gent.'

Jarvis mounted the stairs, a great deal more decorously than he had come down. Ron paused to think over what had been said, and as he did so nagging worries began to surface. He had agreed to the proposition automatically, but for the moment he had no clear leads or any new sources. Maguire had made it abundantly clear that what he had delivered was very definitely a one-off. Of course Gerald Thomas, his police sergeant friend, might have something – but the trouble was he was only on the peripheries of the investigation. The assize court hearing would provide some copy, though. It was due to start in a fortnight's time, and now that Jarvis had taken a personal interest in the reporting of the case he might be able to persuade the deputy editor to let Ron cover that. But this didn't take him much further: Gent was sure to want something by the middle of next week.

'Good God. You still here?' One of his colleagues rushed past, obviously on his way to catch a bus. He paused long enough to throw a remark over his shoulder. 'There's a letter just arrived in your pigeon hole. 'Stinks of perfume.'

Ron shouted his thanks to the rapidly departing figure. Should he go back upstairs and collect it? His articles had already attracted half a dozen letters, most of them from cranks: the likelihood was that this was another. But the last remark settled it. How could he leave it after a description like that?

Back in the office Ron fished out the envelope. The way it had been described was certainly apt, although he wouldn't have used the word 'stinks' himself; as a matter of fact he was rather taken with the perfume. Who on earth could it be from? He opened the envelope to find a couple of pages of closely written script. The address was in Taunton and the signature at the end was that of a Rose

Metcalfe. Rose Metcalfe? He was sure he didn't know anyone of that name. Intrigued, he started to read. Miss Metcalfe – somehow he was sure she was a miss – had read his articles. Her father had been a stringer for the *Mail*, the *Daily Mail* that is, but had died the previous year. He read on. A letter had arrived for her father, which she had opened. It was signed with a *nom de plume*, but she judged it was from one of her father's old contacts who was unaware of his death. The letter had made several assertions about who the children might be, and although she didn't wish to commit any of these to paper she felt 'someone' should know about them. She had seen the local police but they had been dismissive. Since the *Echo* was obviously interested in covering the case, did anyone wish to meet her to see the letter?

Ron sat back in his chair, mulling it over. It could be a hoax; or Rose might be genuine, but had been hoaxed herself. He held up the letter again and breathed in the scent. He was tempted. He didn't have time to visit Taunton during the week, of course, but he could see her on Saturday. There might be nothing in it, but he would curse himself if there was. Besides, it might be interesting to meet Rose. He and Dorothy seemed to argue all the time now – and he was beginning to doubt if she would ever tear herself loose from her father's influence. Ron quickly pulled out a sheet of notepaper and scribbled a reply. He would garner whatever he could from the police, and then see what Rose came up with on Saturday.

'Can't you see that job will get you nowhere?' Ron didn't answer, instead breaking off a piece of bread from his sandwich and tossing it towards the sparrows, which were gathering around their feet. 'Are you listening? Dad talked to me last night. He wants you to make your mind up about taking a job in his office. He says that if you put your mind to it you could be earning five hundred a year within six months.'

The sparrows ventured ever closer, only to scatter in alarm at his sudden outburst. 'Dorothy, when will it sink home? I'm a journalist! That's what I want to do. I'm grateful to your dad, but no thanks!'

Her cheeks flushed with anger. 'So all that talk about getting married is just that. Talk and nothing else.'

'You know it isn't.'

'And how do think we'll manage on what you get now? What is it? Less than two hundred and fifty pounds a year.' Her points, once marshalled, rolled out inexorably. 'Don't forget that once I'm married I won't be working. In fact you're lucky I'm working now and can manage to save up.' Suddenly Ron felt deeply, deeply depressed. What he was hearing was not so much Dorothy's own arguments as a regurgitation of her father's views. If this was in any doubt her next remark confirmed it. 'It wouldn't be so bad if you were working on the *Mail*. At least they have connections to the Jessop Group.' She mentioned the name of a big finance company.

Ron knew she didn't have the faintest idea who or what the Jessop Group were. It was unfair, but he couldn't help himself. 'And how would connections to the Jessop Group help?'

'Well, it would mean . . . you might have the chance . . . they're a big financial concern.' She broke off, confused and angry.

He put his arm round her shoulders and spoke to her gently. 'Dorothy, I do wish I could find out what you feel yourself – not what your dad thinks you ought to feel.'

The reaction was instantaneous; she shrugged his arm away and jumped up. 'Are you saying I can't think for myself? If that's what you believe then maybe it's as well we found it out now rather than later.'

'Please, Dorothy, calm down.'

'Calm down?' Ron had never seen her so angry: this was a side to her he hadn't even known existed. 'We don't agree on much, do we? It might interest you to know that although I don't see eye to eye with Dad on everything, I'm beginning to think I have more in common with his view of the world than with yours.' She picked up her bag. 'If you feel like apologising for what you just said then you can telephone me at work.' He could see she was nerving herself up for the conclusion to this argument. 'Otherwise I can't see there's any future for us.'

He watched her stalk along the path. It still wasn't too late. Even now he could run after her and make it up. But he didn't. Something held him back. Perhaps she was right; perhaps there wasn't a future for them. Perhaps it was the time for a clean break.

The counter was crowded at the police station; it was a busy night. Ron caught Gerald Thomas's eye, only to have him lift his police issue fob watch and indicate he would be a while. After ten minutes or so the counter was clear.

'A lot of business for a Wednesday night, Gerald.'

Thomas finished the notes he was making before looking up wearily. 'I've seen it worse. What can I do for you, Ron? Is it what I think it is?'

Ron was apologetic. 'It is. Any new developments?'

'Well, I'm not involved in the investigation now. Most of us are back on normal duties.' Thomas gestured towards the last of that night's customers being led towards the cells. 'As you can see.' Just then a man in civilian clothes emerged from a back office. 'Hang on a minute. You might be able to persuade Ferguson there to give you a titbit or two. He's a detective constable and still on the case. I'll introduce him, and then it's up to you.'

'Yes, Mr Charteris. What can I do for you?' Ferguson was wary and rightly so. Ron had heard that several junior members of the investigating team had been called to account for speaking out of turn.

'We're trying to keep the case in the news, but it's difficult with such a lack of information.'

Ferguson stonewalled. 'I'm sorry, but you'll have to rely on the official statements, the same as everyone else.'

Ron decided to play the local card. 'You know the nationals seem to have sources of information that the press down here don't have access to.' He tried to gauge the detective's reaction, but Ferguson was impassive. 'The point is the nationals are moving on and losing interest. That can't be good for the investigation.'

'It isn't. Especially at this stage.'

'This stage?' Ron's interest was roused. 'Look, I can promise you all I want is general background stuff. No crown jewels or anything like that.' He tried to lighten the mood. 'Not that I would refuse them if they were offered.'

A faint grin flickered over Ferguson's features. 'Well, it might be helpful.' He had obviously reached a conclusion. 'I'm off duty now and I can spare', he checked his watch, 'a quarter of an hour or so, but not here. There's that Italian café across the street.'

Ron sat down to wait. He was glad to see the café was much more cheerful – and cleaner – than the last one he had been summoned to, but it was too near the station for the likes of Maguire to visit in company with a reporter. It was strange, though, how the police had taken to using cafés rather than pubs. Perhaps someone high up had issued a warning about being seen too often with pints in their hands. Still, it ought to have a beneficial effect on his expenses claims. Ron's musings were interrupted by the arrival of the detective. The proprietor must have recognised Ferguson and followed him over to take their order himself.

Ron offered his hand. 'I do appreciate this. By the way, the name's Ron.'

Ferguson looked a little embarrassed, obviously uncertain as to whether he should be on first-name terms with a reporter. Eventually he muttered, 'Bill.'

'Well, thanks anyway, Bill.' Ron opened his notebook. He realised that at first he would have to make the running. 'Has there been any progress on unusual deaths in the Midlands?'

'No. There were two murders. They've got somebody for the first; the second was a robbery in Leamington Spa. The locals seem confident it's just a matter of time before that one's cleared up.'

'What about the people who were on the train? Have you traced them all?'

'More or less.' Now that the ice was broken Ferguson started to relax a little. 'We've plans of every carriage and where everyone was sitting. At the moment there are only about six or seven people unaccounted for.'

'And you're hopeful that anything we publish might help to fill in the gaps?'

'Yes. And by the way, one thing we do know for certain is that those two children were definitely not connected to anyone who died.'

Ron felt it politic to inject a note of sympathy. 'I suppose that helps by eliminating one area of uncertainty?'

Ferguson nodded. 'The problem is that another area, as you put it, has opened up. We don't know for certain, but it's a possibility that someone got on at Meldon.'

'Meldon?' Ron was puzzled. 'But that's a tiny station – way up in the Cotswolds. The night express never stops there.'

'Well, this one did.' Ferguson sighed deeply, no doubt thinking of all the extra work that this entailed. 'It stopped because the signals were against it.'

'Ah, the signals . . .' Although he could only remember visiting it once, Ron tried to visualise what the station at Meldon looked like. 'But surely that happens all the time. It doesn't mean anyone got on.' Another thought occurred. 'Especially at, what, five thirty in the morning.'

Ferguson still looked worried. 'There were some workmen waiting for the first stopping train to Bristol. They weren't certain, but they thought someone might have boarded.'

'More than one person?'

'They couldn't say definitely.'

Ron moved on, sensing that the detective was unable or unwilling to discuss the topic further. 'And what about orphanages, and the possibility they might be from Ireland?'

'No progress there either, I'm afraid.' Ferguson looked glum. 'Ireland's difficult. If the children were from there, then they could have come over to Glasgow or Liverpool at any time. But we're making enquiries into a couple of Birmingham orphanages.' He indicated that the Church authorities who ran them were not being as co-operative as the police would like. He noticed Ron's raised eyebrows and explained. 'Probably they've cut corners on adoption procedures – a lot of them do.'

Ron finished his notes. 'Well, if you're happy I'll mention the points you've mentioned, and we'll include the bit about Meldon in the next article. The Echo has a fair circulation, and there must be a chance that whoever was waiting for the stopping train will contact us.'

Ferguson looked brighter. 'If anyone does it would be a help.' His face clouded again. 'Mind you, it doesn't move the main mystery any further forward. We're absolutely positive that the only two unaccompanied children who were on that train got on at Birmingham.'

The weather in Taunton matched Ron's mood: it was pouring down and blowing a gale. He turned the corner and huddled gratefully behind a garden wall. The respite was only temporary, and served only to turn his thoughts back to that morning. There had been no word from Dorothy, so despite his doubts he had gone round to see her. It was her father who answered the door and his manner had been dreadful. Ron had thought about calling it a day but, fool that he was, he had persisted. When Dorothy appeared she was even worse. 'Did she have to spell it out?' 'Couldn't he take a hint?' The phrases cascaded through his mind. He remembered the last one especially: 'There is absolutely no point in continuing this acquaintanceship!' Acquaintanceship. Words were his stock-in-trade, not hers, yet effortlessly she had deployed this wounding description of their relationship. Perhaps it was just as well it had come to this. Ron screwed up his face: the wind was making his eyes water. At least he thought it was the wind. Oh, to hell with Dorothy and her whole family!

He dug the letter out of his pocket and checked the address again. She lived at number twenty-three. This was sixty-five, so somehow he must have passed it. God, it was back into the teeth of the wind again! What a way to spend a Saturday afternoon! He tugged the collar of his raincoat as high as it would go and gritted his teeth against the blast to come. For a while he had been holding the trilby to his head, but now he gave up the unequal struggle, clutching it to his side. Normally he didn't wear a hat, but for some reason had brought one today. True, a hat helped him to conform to the stereotype of a reporter – but that was only a help with older people, and Rose didn't sound old. How could he be so sure, though? There was no clue in the name. Rose was timeless: any girl over the last century could have been called that. He decided it must be the perfume; somehow he couldn't imagine a mature woman using that sort of perfume. He paused and squinted against the elements; surely twenty-three must be hereabouts. At last! He finally spotted the number as it came into view, partly shielded by the gale-tossed branches of a clematis.

The face that appeared in response to the bell was pleasant enough, but definitely of mature vintage. He had been wrong. 'Miss, er, Mrs Rose Metcalfe?'

For a moment the face looked blank. 'No, I'm Mrs Metcalfe. It's my daughter who's the Miss.' She called over her shoulder. 'Rose!' Then she turned back to him. 'And you're Mr . . . ?'

Before he could say anything another face came into view. This time a face with pleasant, regular features, framed with dark hair in a fashionable bob; all in all a face much more in keeping with the image he had been conjuring up. 'You must be Mr Charteris. Come in, please.' Ron followed them into the hall, pausing slightly guiltily to wipe his feet. The room they entered had comfortable-looking armchairs and a blazing fire. As if to remind him of the weather he had left outside, a frenzy of rain hurled itself against the windows.

He suddenly realised he hadn't formally introduced himself. 'By the way, it's Ron Charteris.'

'Please call me Rose.' They shook hands, and he noticed she wasn't wearing an engagement ring. 'Have you had to walk all the way from the station? You must be soaking.' She sounded solicitous and gestured to an armchair next to the fire. 'Here, let me take your coat and I'll make a cup of tea.' Ron slumped into the chair and his eyes followed the dark hair and trim figure as she took his coat back to the hall. Suddenly he felt better – very much better.

'Will you excuse me, Mr Charteris?' He started, realising that her mother was still in the room. 'Only I'm in the middle of a letter and I know it's Rose you want to speak to.'

Awkwardly he half rose. 'Of course not. I hope this isn't inconveniencing you.' She smiled and shook her head. Ron subsided and glanced round the room. It was spacious and unfussy and there were two large bookcases. He could make out some of the titles: there were quite a few Conan Doyle's – probably belonging to her late father. But he could also see two Somerset Maugham novels, and one of them had only just come out. Those certainly weren't Father's choices. He was becoming more and more interested in Miss Rose Metcalfe.

'It's an awful day. I half-expected you not to turn up.' Rose poured the tea and passed it over. 'Mind you, I'm glad you did. This letter is intriguing to say the least.'

She was good looking but, if the Somerset Maughams were anything to go by, not just a pretty face. Mentally Ron pulled himself up short. He was jumping to a great many conclusions – probably far too many. Besides, his real reason for being here was to see if there was any worthwhile information. He decided to try and get some background. 'Rose, you said your father was a stringer for the *Mail*. Did he do quite a bit in that line?' She looked uncertain. 'I mean, most stringers – even if they work for the nationals – usually do quite a lot of other work.'

'Oh, I see what you mean. Well, he did do a lot of writing for magazines and local newspapers and he had a few short stories published.' She glanced wistfully at the bookcases. 'He tried his hand at novels but wasn't successful, I'm afraid.'

He was diplomatic. 'It's a difficult business to get into.'

She volunteered more information. 'I think he was quite successful as far as the *Mail* was concerned. Most weeks he had something in the paper.'

'So he had quite a few connections round about?'

'You could say that. Of course he met most of them away from the house, but people were always turning up. Sometimes it was a bit of a nuisance.'

What she said was interesting, indicating to Ron that anyone in the immediate area who had a story would know whom to contact. 'Do you have this letter?'

She handed over two sheets of foolscap paper and he could see writing covered both sides. Rose sounded aggrieved. 'I took it to the police station, but they didn't even read it.'

'Don't be too hard on them. When a case like this comes up they're inundated with letters from all sorts of . . .' He was about to say 'cranks', but thought better of it. 'Well, let's just say people with a fixed point of view.' He looked at the signature. It was unoriginal: '*pro bono publico*'. 'Do you mind if I go through this?'

'No. You carry on.'

He settled back and began to scan through it. The correspondent had, it seemed, been at Taunton station on the morning of the accident. There were a few people waiting for the express, either to board it themselves or to meet friends and relatives. As news of the accident spread he had started to chat to people to find out why they were there. Obviously he had scented a potential story – several in fact – and Rose's theory that he had been a past contact of her father seemed to be borne out. The writer had spotted a vicar from Dorrington and his wife, whom he knew vaguely. Ron looked enquiringly at Rose. 'Dorrington?'

'It's a small village in the Quantocks, near Nether Stowey. You know, the place where Coleridge lived.'

He returned to the letter. In talking to the vicar and his wife. '*Pro bono publico*' felt that both were somewhat evasive. It struck him as odd even at the time, although only later did it assume any significance: it was some time before he made any connection to the unidentified children. Two weeks after the accident he saw an advertisement in a local paper seeking a girl to work at the vicarage in Dorrington. The work involved general household duties and, from time to time, looking after children. The 'time to time' bit intrigued him, so he checked up. Local gossip indicated that children stayed there for short periods: it certainly wasn't advertised, but it appeared they were bound for Australia, the vicar having connections to one of the Commonwealth emigration societies.

Emigration societies! Ron sat bolt upright. They dealt mainly with orphans. Orphans! Orphanages! This was one of the lines of investigation that Maguire was following. He wasn't even aware of speaking out loud: 'You know, that could be it.'

Rose responded eagerly. 'You think there's something in it?'

Instinctively he was cautious. 'Possibly. Just possibly. One thing you learn in the newspaper business is to check and double-check your sources.'

'So you'll need to go out to Dorrington and confirm all this?'

'Yes.' The thought came like a bolt from the blue. Of course it was a bit underhand and he would be mixing business with pleasure, but instinctively it burst out. 'Would you like to come out to this village with me – say next Saturday?' Rose looked uncertain, and for a moment he thought he had overplayed his hand. After all, she might feel it premature; or she might be involved with someone else. Ron found himself gabbling on. 'I don't know the area and you can be my guide. I think I can borrow a car from a friend for the day.' Anxious now he faltered to a halt, but his fears proved groundless.

'Thank you. I'd love to come.'

CHAPTER FIVE

'IT'S GOOD OF you to see me up here, Mr Gregory.' Jim Thornton stared anxiously at the barrister, who was deeply engrossed in the pile of papers on the desk. 'To be honest, we – the wife and I – are a bit hard up at the moment. I don't think we could have managed to come down to London.'

Still mulling over the papers, Gregory answered absentmindedly. 'Oh don't worry about that. After all, your union has loaned me this office for the afternoon.' His voice dropped to a murmur, almost as if he was talking to himself. 'Here it is. Out of order as usual.' He straightened one of the sheets of paper and looked the other man straight in the eye. 'We received the last of the court papers on Friday and I went over everything at the weekend and made some notes. Then on Monday I checked out one or two points with a colleague.'

Jim drew a deep breath. 'Is it bad news?'

Gregory let a thin smile cross his features. 'I suppose in a way it's neutral. You see, it's your word against that of the signalman. Usually, in the absence of collaborative evidence, that would be it and no case would be brought.' He was obviously thinking carefully about how he phrased his next comment. 'That's the good news.'

'So what's the bad?'

'I must be frank. I suppose it's the fact that it has been brought at all.' He saw Jim's look of perplexity. 'As it is, any decent prosecuting counsel would know there's no chance of a conviction. So we must be prepared – however unlikely it is – for new evidence to be brought forward.'

'New evidence? What new evidence?' Jim's voice rose in anger. 'There can't be any new evidence. Everything came out at the enquiry.'

'Gently, Mr Thornton. Gently.' Gregory paused for a moment or two; it had the required effect. 'I'm not suggesting there is anything; I'm just not ruling it out.' Sensing the temperature rising again, he pushed on. 'I think it's much more likely that this prosecution was decided upon because of the number of deaths. There's also the business of those unidentified children, which is keeping the whole thing in the news. So it's a political decision with a small "p".'

'All I read about is those children. All anyone seems to be interested in is those children.' Jim rocked back in his chair. He appealed to the barrister. 'I'm not heartless. It's dreadful that two kids can be killed without anyone coming forward. But what about me? What you're saying is that the trial's going ahead only because the mystery is keeping the whole business in the headlines.'

'It's a possibility – no more than that – and one of many.' Gregory came round the desk and clapped Jim on the shoulder. 'Now I don't want you to become upset. At the trial we'll all need cool nerves. And by the way, I want to put you in the witness stand. Do you think you'll cope?'

Jim bridled. 'Of course I'll cope. I want to put my side of the story.'

'Good man. Now I'm going to go over the likely course of events and the main arguments that are likely to be pushed. I want you to put any questions to me if you're unsure about anything.' Jim listened intently for the best part of half an hour as his barrister went over the details. The session only ended when one of the secretaries offered them tea.

'So you say it's likely to last three days?' Jim put down his cup. 'When it's going on will I be held in prison . . . or anything?'

'No. I can guarantee you that. You'll still be on bail.'

'But I really can't afford accommodation . . .'

'Mr Thornton, you mustn't worry yourself about costs. Or certainly not now. I understand your union will fund modest bed and breakfast accommodation for both yourself and your wife.' He saw Jim's relief. 'Actually, that brings me to another point. As you know, your union is covering the legal costs, but last week we had a very intriguing letter delivered to our chambers. It contained two hundred and fifty pounds in fivers.' He raised his eyebrows. 'Perhaps I ought to add they were used fivers.' Before going on, the barrister stole a sidelong glance at his client on the off-chance there would be some reaction. Jim's obvious mystification carried its own message. He continued. 'There was a letter with it – on good-quality notepaper – stating that the money was to be used to help your defence as, and I quote, you 'had been made a scapegoat'. It was signed 'a well-wisher'. Now that leaves us in something of a quandary. We have no evidence of illegal activity and there's no law against anyone contributing to a defence. Obviously we've informed your union and the money will be used to offset costs. But I have to ask, do you have any idea who this mystery benefactor might be?'

Jim looked stunned. 'No . . . that is . . . No. I've absolutely no idea.'

'It was postmarked Knightsbridge.'

'That's London, isn't it?'

'Yes. West London and quite fashionable.'

'Sorry.' Jim shook his head.

'Ah well, no matter.' The barrister slowly rose and offered his hand. 'You'll get an official letter informing you of the trial date. Whatever you do don't worry. I'm sure it'll work out all right.

He stood by the window, watching Jim as he left the office and crossed the street. Presently he was joined by the union branch secretary. 'I caught that last remark. Are you as confident as you sound?'

'On legal grounds yes, but . . .' He looked ruefully at the official. 'Have you heard that music hall monologue by Stanley Holloway?'

'Which one?'

'The one that ends, 'Someone had got to be summoned, so that was decided upon!'

'I never realised what a difference it would make, you being on half pay.' Ellen checked her purse again. 'No. That's it, Jamie. All our worldly wealth.' She became conscious of the absurd conjunction of the word 'wealth' with the three pounds fourteen shillings and fivepence spread out on the kitchen table. She tried hard to smile but didn't quite succeed.

Jim put his arms round her and gave her a hug. 'It doesn't matter, love. Truly it doesn't.' She tried to protest, but he brushed it aside. 'For heaven's sake, Ellen, I don't need new shoes. There's a cobbler in the next street and a new sole won't cost any more than half a crown. A bit of spit and polish and they'll be as good as new.'

She wasn't to be denied. 'But you've had those shoes since before I met you. The heels are down and you can see the scuff marks from here. Jamie, you must look respectable for the trial.'

'I will. I will.' He gazed at her in mild exasperation. 'Do you think anyone will notice my shoes at the trial? They're hardly likely to see them: I'll be in the dock . . .' He broke off, suddenly conscious both of what he had said and the tear slowly escaping down Ellen's cheek. He moved to put his arms round her again, but, aware of the pricking in his own eyes, he decided against it.

Ellen brushed her sleeve across her face. 'Two hundred and fifty pounds that barrister said. If we only had one of those five pound notes you could have a decent pair of shoes.' She sounded bitter.

'Forget the shoes, Ellen. I don't need them. What I do need is a good defence, and I've changed my mind about Gregory. He may be young but he knows his stuff.' Jim thought again of the meeting. 'He thought I might know who posted that letter with the money.' His laugh was hollow. 'We hardly know anyone who could scrape together fifty pounds, let alone two hundred and fifty.'

'There's something funny going on, isn't there?' Ellen looked at Jim as if he held the answer. 'Somebody posts a letter from Knightsbridge with two hundred and fifty pounds in it. That's well over a year's wages for a lot of folk round here.' He didn't reply. 'Then there's that inspector from Bristol who came all the way up here, just to talk about those unidentified children.'

There was a long silence. She knew her husband: he was wrestling with some problem; a problem that he desperately wanted to put into words but was fearful of expressing. Eventually Jim spoke. 'Yes,

I do think it's funny.' Once the silence was broken he found it easier. 'I suppose the money might be from someone who feels sorry for me. That sort of thing does happen; I read something like it in the *Empire News* last weekend.' He gave Ellen a wan smile. 'But we both know that sort of thing doesn't happen to people like us – especially now. It's the other business with Maguire I find more worrying. The desk sergeant at Millgarth police station was on it straight away. A senior copper doesn't spend three days away from his job to conduct a routine interview that any police constable could do.'

'So what's behind it all?' Ellen was anxious.

'I don't know.' Jim was thinking as he spoke. 'I suppose only he knew . . . or could be trusted . . . to put the questions and . . .'

Ellen finished it off for him. 'And hear the answers . . .'

They both started to speak, but thought better of it. Distractedly Jim tidied away a newspaper before turning to challenge his wife. 'So you think my answers were just as important as the questions?'

'Don't you?'

'I suppose so, but as you said before the whole interview had nothing to do with the accident. It was all about those children.'

Ellen was uncompromising. 'If that's the case, then the identity of those children is what this is all about. Somebody, somewhere, wants to find out exactly what you know.'

'This is crazy. You're just . . . what's the word . . . surmising all this. I don't know anything.'

Ellen was beginning to realise where her logic was leading her. 'But Jamie, maybe they think you do.'

'Come on, Ellen. Come on. Who are "they"?'

'I don't know.' The answer was snapped rather than spoken. 'But they've got to be the same people who can send you two hundred and fifty pounds through the post. And the same people who can make sure that only somebody they trust hears what you've got to say about those children.'

CHAPTER SIX

THIS TIME! COME ON, THIS TIME! Ron gritted his teeth, drew in a deep breath and swung the starting handle with every ounce of his strength. It fired. He straightened up, a fixed smile on his face and tried to sound nonchalant. 'That happens once in a while.' Rose smiled sympathetically through the windscreen, but he couldn't help noticing how her eyes were drawn to the surrounding hills. She didn't need to say anything: the middle of the Quantocks in late January was neither the best place or time to break down. He clambered back into the driving seat, vowing to have words with his friend back in Bristol from whom he'd borrowed the car. 'Don't worry, it'll be fine now.' She still seemed anxious. He glanced over. 'We should be in Dorrington in about twenty minutes.' He tried to cheer her up. 'I bet you there's a café open.'

She looked anxiously at her watch. 'I don't know. It's nearly half past two. Do you think this vicar will want to see us?'

'I don't see why not. But we'll find a café first and have a late lunch. I bet you're starving.' She didn't demur. As a matter of fact he was not at all certain that the vicar would agree to see them without an appointment, but this concern had progressively taken second place to a determination to find out a lot more about Rose Metcalfe. A relaxed lunch was just the setting for that.

'There. Over there.' Rose's pointing finger indicated a sign above one of the premises: 'Quantock View Café'. Obviously she was just as hungry as he was.

The menu was limited but substantial, and the shepherd's pie seemed to fit the bill for both of them. He decided to take the initiative. 'So, we seem to have quite a lot in common.'

Rose tried to keep the smile off her face, but didn't quite succeed. 'Now why do you say that?'

'Well, we both like shepherd's pie and . . . Somerset Maugham.'

She looked dumbfounded and then the penny dropped. 'You reporters. You were looking at our bookshelves last week.'

Ron held up his hands in mock-surrender. 'Guilty, I'm afraid. I can't help wanting to know the background of the people I talk to.'

'Well, that goes for me too. Now what else do you like, besides, that is, shepherd's pie and Somerset Maugham?' The rest of the lunch passed all too quickly. Ron learned that she had lived with her mother since leaving school, but hoped to move out soon and get a job. It would have to be in a city, though, as the sorts of job a woman could get in a place like Taunton weren't for her. It soon became apparent that, although she volunteered a great deal of information, there were areas of her life on which she refused to be drawn. When he pushed a little too hard on the subject of friends and friendship Rose moved the conversation on in no uncertain fashion. He thought of Dorothy, and guessed that she too had had an unhappy love affair.

For his part Ron was open about his likes, dislikes, hopes and aspirations, in particular his determination to move up the ladder in the newspaper business. He confessed, 'Of course sooner or later that'll mean moving to London.'

The smile faded just a touch. 'I hope that's not too soon.' Then Rose realised what she had said. 'What I mean is . . .'

He cut her short. 'So do I, Rose. So do I.' To his surprise Ron found he really meant it.

The bill arrived at the table without being requested. The lady was apologetic. 'Sorry, but we close at half past three.'

The vicarage was situated in a cul-de-sac, overhung with massive chestnut trees. No doubt in spring and summer it would present quite a spectacle: now it was January it was just gloomy. The vicarage itself was a rambling run-down Victorian affair shielded, to quite a degree, by overgrown shrubbery. The effect was far from welcoming. 'I don't think I should come in with you.' Rose was decisive. 'It would look odd, wouldn't it? I mean, are we on a Saturday trip out in the country or are you on a professional assignment?'

Her argument was unassailable: he had been worrying about this ever since they had left the café. 'Thanks. You're right. Do you mind staying in the car? I promise I'll try not to be longer than half an hour at the most.' He realised it sounded weak. 'Look, if all else fails I'll make up an appointment in Bristol that I've got to keep.'

Rose nudged him towards the car door in mock-exasperation. 'Lying to vicars. Is there anything that you journalists aren't capable of?'

On one of the pillars beside the gate was a modest brass plaque which stated that the vicar was the Reverend Malcolm Trevear. Ron was about to push open the gate when he noticed another plaque on the other side. He was forced to use his sleeve to remove the grime and see what was underneath. It read 'The Lord Eastermain Emigration Society: 'A charitable foundation dedicated to helping young people to begin new lives in the colonies.' He felt the adrenaline pumping through his veins. So 'pro bono publico', whoever he was, had been right. Then there was the Lord Eastermain bit as well: Ron didn't know who he was, but he would certainly find out as soon as he was back in the office on Monday. With a new sense of excitement he moved purposefully towards the front door.

The door was opened by a young girl. 'Yes, sir? What can I do for you?'

At first he thought she might be one of those youngsters headed for the colonies, but when she spoke her accent placed her as a local. She must be the maid. 'I wonder if I could speak to Mr Trevear. My name's Charteris, Ronald Charteris.' Experience had taught him it could be counterproductive to state exactly who he was right at the outset.

She gestured him into the hall. 'If you wouldn't mind waiting here, sir.'

Eventually a rather harassed middle-aged man appeared. 'Mr Charters, is it?'

'No, sir. My name's Charteris.' There was no response from the vicar. He was obviously waiting for his visitor to state his business. 'I'm from the *Bristol Echo*.'

'Are you indeed. Well, Mr . . . Charteris. Is your business urgent? I have two services to conduct tomorrow in two different churches, and that means two sermons to prepare.'

'It really won't take long, sir. I've been investigating the mystery of those two children who were killed in the Eastmead crash.' Ron paused quite deliberately, waiting to see if there was any reaction. There was none, so he continued. 'You're no doubt aware they were buried last week in an unmarked grave in the churchyard there.'

This time there was a certain testiness in the vicar's response. 'Of course I'm aware of it, Mr Charteris, and it's very tragic, but what has it to do with me?'

'Well you see, sir, I believe you're connected to some of these children's emigration societies . . .' This time there was a reaction, and the violence of it surprised him.

'Are you trying to impugn some malpractice on the part of the society?' A red flush spread up from the vicar's neck. 'Is this what you've disturbed me for?' He was almost shouting now.

'Sir, if you would just let me explain . . .'

'Mr Charteris, I don't need any explanation. You've tricked your way into this house using the dreadful business of that accident as an excuse. Apart from what I read in the newspapers I have absolutely no knowledge of those children. None whatsoever. Is that clear?'

It was a desperate throw but Ron felt he had nothing left to lose. 'And there is absolutely no possibility that they might have been orphans bound for the colonies?'

'How dare you! How dare you! Don't you think I would have contacted the police if that had been the case?' The vicar's face was now white with suppressed rage. 'I know how some sections of the press operate, and I would remind you that there is such a thing as libel. If you or your newspaper attempt even to hint at such a lie I'll make sure you pay for it. Now goodbye!'

As the door slammed behind him Ron gazed back at the house. For a second he saw the face of the girl who had let him in framed at one of the side windows, although now she looked as though she was dressed for outdoors. He thought she looked amused; perhaps she was used to the vicar's rages.

Ron made his way back to the car pondering the vicar's reaction. Something was not right. But what?

'You were quick.' Rose looked at him quizzically. 'Wasn't the vicar in?'

'Oh yes, he was in.' Again Ron looked back at the house, his mind churning with a range of possibilities. Then he realised she was waiting for something more. 'As soon as I mentioned what it was all about, I was shown the exit in short order.'

She was uncertain how to respond. 'Well, you're the reporter. Is that a normal response?'

'Sometimes. Sometimes . . .' He was still thinking about the vicar's reaction. 'Especially if people are caught off guard, but . . . well, I don't know.'

'So you thought there was something funny going on?'

'Or had gone on. Yes, I did. You see I'm no expert, but I happen to know there's been some disquiet in official quarters about the activities of some of these children's emigration people.' He saw Rose's look of bewilderment and explained. 'There have been suggestions about them being used as cheap labour in the colonies and dominions.'

'How do you know this?'

'Well, I'm in the newspaper business, and several Labour MPs have spoken up about it in the House of Commons. Maybe that's why the vicar was so touchy.' Ron leaned forward to switch on the ignition, then stopped. 'Rose, do you mind if we just stay here for a few minutes?'

No. Any particular reason?'

'A local girl let me in; she must be the maid. It's fairly late on a Saturday afternoon so there's a fair chance she'll be coming off duty soon. I glimpsed her through a window as I left, and I think she had her coat on.'

'So you want to waylay her . . . and then use me as a chaperone so she doesn't feel nervous about speaking to you?'

Ron grinned weakly. 'Something like that.'

Rose shook her head in disbelief. 'I think it's just as well that I'm finding out a whole lot more about reporters at this stage.' Ron was about to ask what stage that might be when she whispered in his ear. 'I think this must be her coming now.'

The maid gave a final wave as the garden gate clanked shut behind her, and was lost to view behind the hedge. Rose turned. 'So much for my acting as chaperone. I think she'd have taken the lift home even if you had been on your own.'

Ron turned his eyes from the gate. 'Probably my personal magnetism. Seriously, though, what she had to say was interesting,'

'Interesting, yes, but it knocks your theory on the head.'

'Not necessarily, and it was hardly my theory was it? '*Pro bono publico*', whoever he is, was the one who hinted at it.'

'Yes, but remember what she said. Children arrive from various orphanages. After a period here they are cleaned up and outfitted and then they go on to catch a ship.' Rose pursed her lips as she tried to get to grips with something which was puzzling her. 'But why would they go to a halfway house like that vicarage before going on to Australia or Canada or wherever?' Surely it would make more sense for them to go directly from the orphanage?'

'Oh I don't know, maybe a lot of them do. But you must admit it's a very handy way of muddying the waters if everything isn't as it should be – shortcuts in the paperwork, that sort of thing. After all, involvement by the clergy lends a veneer of respectability. It also cuts the link between the institution and the children's final destination.' Ron put his hands on the steering wheel, stretched and yawned. 'Sorry about that, but all this driving is tiring.'

For a while there was silence as they mulled over what the maid had said. Eventually Ron tried to sum it up. 'It's really all speculation, and couldn't be proved one way or the other, but as far as I'm concerned the important thing is that they were expecting a boy and a girl from an orphanage in Birmingham at the time of the crash. The girl confirmed that, and according to the letter the vicar and his wife were at Taunton station that night waiting for the train.'

'But Ron, remember the rest. She said those children were delayed and didn't arrive until the first weekend in November: that's nearly a week after the accident. In any event they only stayed a week and then went on to Southampton to catch a boat.'

'It could have been a different pair of kids.'

'I think you're clutching at straws.'

He sighed. 'We'll never know now. They're on their way to Australia.'

George dropped the piece of paper on Ron's desk in passing. 'The library asked me to pass this on. It's the stuff you wanted on emigration.'

'Thanks.' Ron dragged his mind from the article he was checking and started to read the note.

'How do you manage to get things back so quickly?' George's tone was petulant. 'Anything I ask for takes a couple of days, not lunchtime the same day.'

'I think it's because I request interesting information – not increases in rateable values and that sort of . . .' Ron's voice died away, as something he was reading seized his attention.

'Well, what's so interesting?'

'This.' Ron waved the piece of paper. 'You know the Lord Eastermain Society I was telling you about? Well, Arnold in the library has found out that Eastermain founded it a couple of years ago.' He checked the date. 'August 1926.' He read on. 'It had the aim of improving the lot of orphans and children from poorer families by enabling them to settle and train in Australia.'

George looked bored. 'So what? Titled do-gooders are always into one sort of charitable scheme or another.'

'But that's not the whole of it. In 1927 he was instrumental in setting up Carricktown Land Ltd with a handful of other people. And more to the point he's chairman now.'

'Ron, you've lost me. What's the connection?'

'Carricktown Land is a farming and cattle rearing company in Australia.' Ron emphasised the last word. 'Don't you see? I bet a pound to a brass farthing that these kids are bound for wherever the company is based.' He added triumphantly, 'You're always reading about how Australia is short of labour.'

'So he and his friends are using this society for their own benefit? Ron, grow up! It goes on all the time. Anyway, I hardly think it's a story the *Echo* would want to run. Have you checked it out with Gent?'

'Of course I haven't. At the moment it's just part of the investigations into those two unidentified kids.'

'Well, just be careful. Anything to do with titles is a very, very sensitive area. Just remember our proprietor has ambitions in that direction.'

The hotel wasn't in one of the better parts of town and, more to the point, it was off a bus route. Ron dug his hands into the pockets of his gabardine and plodded on. There weren't many people about, but then it was late. His thoughts turned to what he had discovered about the Eastermain Society. Arnold in the library had been helpful, but had made it plain that any further digging was up to him. So far he had only found out that Carricktown was a remote settlement in the north-west of Australia: exactly the sort of place that would need young labour capable of being trained. It fitted his theory, but would need further investigation.

A young girl passed with a nervous sidelong glance; he heard the receding clip-clop of her heels as she scurried nervously homewards. The sound brought Ron's thoughts back to Rose. She had been reluctant to settle on a firm date for him to see her again, and that puzzled him: they had both got on so well. He had suggested meeting the following weekend in Wells, as it was within easy reach for both of them and his parents lived there: it was a while since he'd seen them and they were due a visit. Perhaps that had been it: she had assumed he wanted her to meet his parents, and that had been jumping the gun. When Ron had telephoned her later he had had to be content with the promise that she would contact him at the office so they could fix something up. That had been last Friday; surely she would telephone by the end of the week?

The motor horn gave him a fright. Served him right for getting so lost in his thoughts that he had crossed the road without looking. Then another uneasy thought struck him. Suppose Thornton and his wife had been so exhausted by the trauma of the trial that they had decided to go to bed early: that would scupper his plans for a cosy interview. Ron checked his watch. It was just on half past eight. Surely they wouldn't be in bed yet.

The *Echo's* official legal correspondent had covered the day-to-day trial proceedings: Gent had been adamant on that point. Ron remembered the news editor's words: 'You write well enough, but we need somebody with legal experience for a court case.' That was fair, but he needed an interview so he had enough for an article. And it had to be tonight: now that Thornton had been found not guilty, it was more than likely he would be returning north the next day.

Ron turned a corner and there it was at last, the Mallandain Hotel. The front door was locked from the inside and it took several knocks before someone answered. The man who appeared looked at him with grave suspicion. 'Bristol Echo, you say. To see Mr Thornton.' His tone was almost accusing. 'All the newspaper people were here this afternoon.' It was evident that he hoped this would deter Ron. When it didn't work he fell back on the second line of defence. 'He's still in the dining room, but there's somebody with him.'

'I don't mind waiting.'

Then the ultimate threat was deployed: 'We lock the doors at half past nine.'

Ron was about to answer when the dining room door opened and a familiar figure made his way out. 'Why, Inspector Maguire. What brings you here?'

The question produced only a scowl. 'Police business, Charteris. Police business.' He headed towards the door only to turn back to reinforce his point, his vehemence surprising Ron. 'In other words, it's none of yours.' Ron's deliberate lack of response must have unsettled him because the next words carried a distinct menace. 'I hope that's clear, because if it isn't I think you'll find life as a reporter can become very difficult.'

'What on earth do you mean by th . . .' Ron's question tailed away as the front door slammed behind the inspector.

He turned to find the man behind the reception desk smirking. 'I suppose you want me to find out if Mr Thornton wants to see you now?'

'No thanks!' The words snapped out. Maguire's attitude had annoyed him. Who did he think he was, uttering threats like that without the slightest provocation? Gradually Ron's anger subsided. Perhaps, in Maguire's eyes, the very fact of a reporter not only being here but talking in private to a defendant just after he had been cleared was provocation enough – particularly if there was something to hide. Smiling now, Ron strode towards the dining room door.

CHAPTER SEVEN

'HOW DO YOU FEEL, Mr Thornton?'

'Do you have anything to say to the relatives of those who died?'

'Were you expecting an acquittal?'

Jim, aware of Ellen frantically hanging onto his arm, tried to field the questions volleyed at him from every direction, but it was Gregory who rescued him. 'Gentlemen, gentlemen, Mr Thornton has had a very trying few days. He needs a little time to come to terms with the verdict. I can assure you there will be a statement issued on his behalf this afternoon.' There was grumbling from the assembled reporters, but Gregory ignored it and hustled the couple to the waiting taxi.

'Congratulations, Jim.' The union branch secretary had made it to the taxi before them and shook his hand warmly.

Ellen kissed her husband's cheek. 'I told you it would be all right, didn't I?'

Gregory joined in. 'So there wasn't any fresh evidence. God alone knows why they chose to go ahead.' He shook his head at the folly of mounting the prosecution. 'But I must say the judge gave a fair summing up. He couldn't say so publicly, but I wouldn't mind betting there'll be a few words in higher legal circles about bringing this case.' He rubbed his hands together, unable to contain his elation, and beamed broadly at Ellen. 'I think, Mrs Thornton, we can safely say justice has been done.'

Sitting there, Ellen's hand in his, Jim didn't answer immediately. All that filled his mind was the frozen eternity between the judge's 'Have you reached a verdict?' and the foreman's 'We have. Not guilty, m'lord.'

'Still shaken up? That's hardly surprising.' Calvert, the union man, glanced across at Gregory. 'Are there any more legal procedures to go through, because if not I think we could all do with a nice meal. We can get one in the hotel.' He intercepted Ellen's worried look. 'Don't worry, Mrs Thornton. It's on the union.'

Gregory decided to concentrate on the practicalities. 'I'll sort out a statement for the press over lunch.' He added hastily, 'Of course I'll check it with you both before it's issued.'

Jim started to speak, then stopped as his voice choked up. He stared fixedly out of the taxi window until the blurring cleared. 'I'd like to thank you all for your help.' He had to stop again. Finally he managed to continue. 'This morning I thought I'd be on my way to gaol, not . . . not . . . going by taxi to eat in a hotel.' No one spoke, but he felt Ellen squeeze his hand.

'Do you mind if we leave you and Mrs Thornton to finish your tea?' Gregory asked. 'There's plenty in the pot. It's just that Mr Calvert and I need to sort out this statement. We'll only be a quarter of an hour or so.'

When they had gone Ellen busied herself pouring extra cups. Jim watched her. In profile she stood out against the light of the window. With her strong features and straight black hair pulled back she could almost be Spanish. Could there be any Spanish blood? Hardly: she came from generations of Yorkshire stock. He knew that some people considered her cold and standoffish, but he knew better. Anyway, he was lucky, luckier than he deserved, to have someone like her. It was a pity they hadn't met when they were younger – or at least when he was younger. He would be forty soon and she was thirty-three: if they were going to have kids they couldn't leave it too long.

She turned with the cups, cutting his ruminations short. 'Why on earth are you looking at me like that?'

'Like what?'

'As if you'd seen me for the first time.'

Jim reached out a hand and stroked her cheek. 'Maybe I have, Ellen. Maybe I have.'

Embarrassed, she glanced around at the few others in the dining room. He waited, half-expecting a mild rebuke, but instead he noticed a little smile. 'You must be feeling better. Will a cup of tea satisfy you?'

He smiled in his turn. 'For the moment.'

They shook hands. 'All the very best to you both, and try and put all this behind you.'

'Thanks for everything, Mr Gregory.' Jim waited until the barrister had disappeared through the doors before letting the forced smile slip and slumping back into his chair.

Ellen looked at him with concern. 'Jamie, you must be done in: I know I am. And we have to be up early tomorrow to catch our train.'

'But we need to talk about the future.' Jim was agitated. 'Calvert says the company might take me back, but not in any sort of technical capacity. I don't know if . . .'

Ellen stopped him. 'Tomorrow, Jamie, tomorrow. We can talk about all this then.'

Jim's shoulders drooped. 'You're right, love. We'd better make a move.' He was halfway out of his chair when he froze. 'Good God. What does he want?'

Ellen felt the draught from the door behind her and realised someone had entered the dining room. She leaned forward anxiously. 'What's wrong?'

'Sorry if I'm interrupting your meal.' The voice boomed out beside them, and she looked up to see a well-built middle-aged man. 'You must be Mrs Thornton.' Jim said nothing and the man continued as if this was perfectly normal. 'Let me introduce myself. I'm Detective Inspector Maguire. Your husband and I have met.' He caught Jim's eye and laughed slightly. 'Although not perhaps in the happiest of circumstances.'

'What do you want?' Jim's question was direct and a touch belligerent.

'Don't worry, it's not police business.' He seemed about to go on, but then changed tack. 'Sorry. I haven't congratulated you both on the acquittal. You might not believe it, but we don't always agree on the decision to prosecute: on occasion we have very little say in the matter.' He sat down on an empty chair. 'You don't mind me sitting, do you?' He seemed to take their agreement for granted. Thornton's mind went back to their previous meeting and a similar ploy; perhaps it was a standard police tactic. 'I need to have a chat, Jim.' He read the uncertainty in the other man's eyes. 'It'll be to your advantage to hear me out.' He glanced over to Ellen. 'Mrs Thornton, would you mind me borrowing your husband for a quarter of an hour or so?'

Jim broke in swiftly. 'I want my wife to hear whatever it is. We don't have any secrets.'

'I'm glad to hear it, but I'm sure you can discuss it with her after-wards.'

His tone was insistent and, embarrassed, Ellen got up. 'It's all right, Jamie, I'll see you up in the room.'

Jim's eyes were fixed on the picture on the wall, but his thoughts were ranging over what Maguire had just said, and in particular his final words. 'Remember, this is confidential. If you talk about it then everything could be jeopardised.' But nothing specific had been discussed, so how could anything be jeopardised? It could be a lot of old flannel. But why? For what reason? His mind was racing and nothing made sense any more. He desperately needed to talk it over with Ellen. Vaguely he heard raised voices by the reception desk, but his mind was still on other things.

Suddenly his reverie was interrupted. 'Mr Thornton?' A young man had burst through the doors and was making his way towards him. 'I realise it's late, but I wonder if you could spare a few minutes. My name's Charteris. I'm from the *Bristol Echo*.' He gabbled the last two sentences, obviously aware he was pushing his luck.

Drawing a deep breath, Jim kept his self control. For the first time that day he realised just how tired he was. 'Mr . . . Mr Charteris. If you're from the newspapers then my barrister gave a statement to the press this afternoon. I'm sorry, but I have nothing else to say.' He rose and headed towards the stairs, but hadn't reckoned on the persistence of the young reporter.

'I promise you this will only take a couple of minutes.'

'It'll take less than that, because I'm going to bed.'

'Can I ask why Detective Inspector Maguire was talking to you? Was it police business?'

'No, it was not.' Angry now, Jim faced the reporter. 'Did you hear what I said? I'm going to bed. Now will you leave me alone or do I have to call the management?'

Charteris decided on one final throw. 'Funny. I spoke to Maguire on his way out and he said it was police business.'

For three months Jim had kept an iron grip on his emotions. Throughout the accident, throughout the investigation, throughout the trial, during every waking moment he had held himself together. Now, like a boiler bursting, he erupted. Grasping the lapels on the other man's coat, he pinned him against the wall. His fury was such that he could only croak out the words. 'Mr Maguire and I were having a private conversation. A private conversation that has nothing to do with anyone except him and me. Do you understand? I said, do you understand?'

Charteris smiled disarmingly, then gently but firmly disengaged Jim's hands. 'Of course I understand, Mr Thornton. Thank you so much for your statement.'

The carriage jerked abruptly into motion and the newspaper on Jim's knee slid to the floor. As he picked it up he noticed Ellen's smile. He managed a wan imitation. 'You're looking cheerful.'

'It's you, Jim. You look so much better this morning. I was really worried last night when you came up to the room. You were in an awful state. Surely that journalist couldn't have been so bad?'

'Sorry, I must have been like a bear with a sore head. I probably didn't realise how down I was. It's marvellous how morning brings back a bit of perspective.' Some signals flashed by and for a moment he was distracted. 'Did you know that those signals are controlled by the Templeton box? They can be a bit tricky when the line's busy . . .' Jim stopped, conscious of the territory onto which he was venturing, and abruptly switched back to the previous subject. 'The reporter was just a pushy young devil chancing his arm. I expect he wanted something from me that he could claim was exclusive.'

'And what did that policeman want?'

'Maguire?' He stopped to collect his thoughts. 'You know, I find it difficult to say. He said quite a bit, but now you've put me on the spot it's difficult to pick out anything concrete.'

'Come on, Jamie. He must have said something.'

'Well, the usual sympathetic noises. Then he went on about not getting downhearted, keeping my head up, that sort of thing. I was getting quite fed up because the last thing I needed was a pep talk. Then he said something rather peculiar. He said something would turn up for me but I needed to be patient.'

'What was that supposed to mean?'

'I asked him, and he said . . . let me try and remember his exact words.' Jim screwed his face up in concentration. 'He said I would hear from someone after this had all died down. Naturally I asked who and when and about what. All he kept repeating was that I would have to take it on trust but that he gave me his word. Oh, and he also said not to mention it to anyone because if I did everything could be jeopardised.'

Ellen didn't reply straight away: she was as astonished as he had been the previous night. 'Why didn't you tell me all this yesterday?'

'Love, I was in a state. You know that. That damned reporter drove it all out of my mind.' Jim pre-empted her next question. 'I've been thinking about it and either it's a load of rubbish or it isn't. If it isn't, it seems to me he was giving me a message. If you think of that money that went to the solicitors, and the fact that Maguire travelled all the way up to Leeds just to question me about those kids, then . . .' He shrugged his shoulders. 'Well, there are wheels within wheels.'

'But why didn't he want me to stay? He knew you were going to tell me anyway.'

'That's easy. He didn't want any witnesses.'

'Do you believe him?'

'I don't know about that, but one thing I do know is that we can't plan our future on the basis that one day we just might hear something to our advantage. I know the company will take me back, but not in any job connected with engines.' Jim answered her unspoken question. 'That means a porter's job somewhere.' His voice took on a note of urgency and he grasped her hand. 'Ellen, I just couldn't do that. It's one thing joining the company as a youngster and working your way up, but I'd be stuck in a job like that for life. You see that, don't you?'

The answer was dragged out of her reluctantly. 'I suppose so, but how are we going to live?'

'I'll start looking as soon as we get back. There are plenty of engineering jobs outside the railways.' He made a deliberate attempt to sound cheerful. 'And if anything else turns up then that's a bonus.'

CHAPTER EIGHT

'YOU'VE BEEN WORKING on that copy for three-quarters of an hour now. It's not like you to get stuck.' George perched on the corner of the desk and tried to peer over Ron's shoulder to see what it was that was giving so much trouble.

The sheet was hastily turned over. 'Do you mind? It's personal.'

'Oh ho. Personal, is it? Now let me guess.' George put on an agonised expression. 'It's a job application.' There was no reaction. 'No, wait a minute, it's a plea to Jarvis for a rise.' Ron met his gaze stony-faced. 'Well, let's see. It's not office notepaper is it?' He answered his own question. 'No, it's not. So . . . you're writing to that girl in Taunton.' The ever so slight grimace was the give-away. 'I'm right, aren't I?' George was jubilant. 'You've fallen for her.'

'Shut up, George, please.' Ron glanced around anxiously. 'I don't want the whole office to know.'

'It's a bit long distance, isn't it? I mean, her in Taunton and you in Bristol. When do you get to see her?'

Ron lowered his voice. 'That's the problem: I don't. I mean, I haven't.'

'Haven't? You mean you haven't seen her? Not since that time you went out to the Quantocks?' George looked astonished. 'Well, as far as girls are concerned I must admit I'm sometimes backward at coming forward, but I don't think I'd let it go on that long. It must be – what – nearly a couple of months ago now.'

'All right, all right.' Ron was becoming increasingly tetchy. 'I've tried to telephone. She answered a couple of times and said she would ring back.'

'But she didn't?'

'No, and . . .' Ron seemed to be deciding whether or not to go on. George encouraged him. 'And what?'

'And now the number's unobtainable. The operator says it's been disconnected.'

For once George didn't have a ready riposte. He got up from the desk and started to whistle tunelessly. 'I suppose you've considered the possibility that, for whatever reason, she's thought better of it.' He shoved his hands in his pockets and stared around, trying to think of some plausible reason. 'Maybe she had somebody else on the go; was trying to make him jealous or something like that.'

'George. George. If the *Echo* ever decides to run an agony column then please feel free to apply for the job, but in the meantime don't practise on me.' Ron sat back and marshalled his arguments. 'First of all she contacted me. It was about those kids, remember. She thought there was something to that letter she got and I did too. She was interested in following it through and was only too happy to come out to the Quantocks with me. We picked up some interesting leads on the story, and besides that we got to know each other quite a bit better. And liked each other, I might add. She's a straightforward girl, I'd bet my life on it. So if she had second thoughts about either following up the story or seeing me again she'd have said so. We'd just met, for God's sake: there'd have been no great tragedy in either of us saying we didn't want to take it any further. But she didn't.' George was silent. 'Now if I'd met her in the ordinary course of events and this had happened I'd have let it go. But it's not in the ordinary course of events, is it? It's just one more funny thing to add to quite a lot of funny things.'

'And do you think there'll be a reply to the letter?'

'No idea, but it's worth a try. It's either that or go down to Taunton myself, and I've family commitments for the next couple of weekends.'

'I might be able to help you there.' George looked thoughtful. 'I'm off to Bridgwater myself on Saturday to see my sister. Taunton's just down the line . . .'

'George, I don't want you putting your size twelves into this. There might be a perfectly innocent explanation, and I wouldn't want to give the impression I was spying on her.'

'Don't worry, old son, don't worry. I'll be the soul of discretion. You give me Rosie's details and . . .'

'It's Rose, if you don't mind.'

'All right. Rose.' George smiled and held up his hands in mock-apology. 'You give me the details, and I'll find a local near at hand and get chatting to the landlord. If there's anything to find out that'll do the trick.'

Through the open door Gent looked morose, but that was normal. Ron decided that if he ever looked happy then that would be the time to worry. He knocked lightly. 'Have you got a minute, Mr Gent?'

'Oh, it's you.' For a moment the deputy editor looked uncertain whether he could spare the time. 'Come in, Ronald, but no more than five minutes, mark you.'

Gent had taken to calling him Ronald after the editor had taken a personal interest in the articles about the train crash and the unidentified children. Ron supposed it was as near to informality as the man ever got. 'It's your note about winding up the coverage of those unidentified children.'

'Oh yes, that. Well, you've written some good articles. First rate, in fact.' Gent paused, took off his spectacles and polished them. 'But . . . not to put too fine a point on it . . . both Mr Jarvis and I feel that unless something dramatic happens then the story has run its course.'

Ron had been expecting this, but he was still devastated. 'Mr Gent, there's a lot more to come out. I've strong suspicions that those children were on their way to the colonies, sponsored by a church-backed emigration society.'

Gent perked up. 'That's interesting: I haven't heard that theory before. Do you have chapter and verse?'

Ron's face fell. 'No, not exactly. But that inspector in charge of it all, Maguire, I'm positive he knows something. After the verdict he went to see the engine driver to talk to him privately. Maguire told me it was police business. Thornton, the driver, told me it wasn't.'

'Stop!' Gent slapped both palms down on the desk. 'Stop right there. You don't have an iota of proof for any of your theories, do you?' He took Ron's silence as an affirmative. 'Look, lad, I know what it's like to be a young, keen reporter. I was one myself a while ago.' Ron half-smiled at what he took to be a joke – but he was obviously mistaken as the smile wasn't reciprocated. 'Strangely enough, I also think there's something funny about this business, but where I differ from you is that I know you don't have anything we can dream of publishing now and you aren't likely to get anything we can publish in the near future either.'

'There is more, and I feel I'm getting close.'

'Ronald, one of the hardest things in this business is to know when to cut your losses, and both Mr Jarvis and I feel that's now.'

Ron got up to go; he felt drained. 'Well, thanks for hearing me out anyway.'

Gent came with him to the door. 'You know, I think the truth about this will come out one day.' Ron looked at him sharply. 'Don't worry, we aren't going to be scooped by one of our rivals. No, I think all will be revealed in fifty years' time when this year's public and political records are released.' For the very first time Ron heard Gent make a noise that approximated to a laugh. 'Don't look so downhearted, man. You've a fair chance of seeing them. I certainly won't.' But as he returned to his desk he was still muttering under his breath. 'Unless of course it's very secret, in which case it'll be a hundred years. Or if it's even more secret than that, they'll never see the light of day . . .'

'I wondered who in the office would be interested in this. And, like a flash, the answer came back: our Ron, of course. He's always wanting to get up to the Smoke and make a name for himself.' One of the senior reporters slapped a copy of a national on the desk and pointed to the minor news item. 'See, the *Daily Express* is getting a new editor. Now what's his name . . .' He peered more closely before rolling the name round his tongue. 'A. Beverly Baxter. Now, young Ronald, there's a name to conjure with.'

Ron tried to adopt a dispassionate demeanour. 'So why would it affect me?'

'Well, it's common gossip that Beaverbrook wants to take on the bigger boys and up the circulation.' He was referring to the *Express*'s proprietor, Lord Beaverbrook. 'If he's going to do that he'll need wider coverage, and that means more reporters. Of course a lot of them will be specialists on the nationals, and the word will already have been put out, but,' he paused for effect and glanced slyly at Ron, 'in times like this there's always a chance for a thrusting young fellow like yourself from the provinces.'

Ron felt himself getting more irritated. Underneath the genial banter he knew he was being patronised. 'I take it you're not pursuing it yourself?'

'Me?' The senior reporter adopted a bogus West Country burr. 'Why bless you no, lad. If they want anybody they'll want young, fresh faced go-getters like you, not broken-down old hacks like yours truly.'

'I see.' Ron knew his informant was only just forty, if that; he also knew that he had a reputation for deviousness. Of course, it could be just a matter of passing on information of interest with no ulterior motive, but on the other hand he could have spotted a potential challenger on his way up through the ranks – and one way or another wished to spike his guns. He decided that it didn't matter. This could be his break. 'Well, thanks for the information. I'll let you know if I decide to follow it up.' He turned again to the copy he was editing, while making a mental note to do no such thing.

'What did he want?' George flung his coat on top of a filing cabinet and eased himself into his chair.

It was the first time Ron had seen him that week. 'He reckons the *Daily Express* is hiring reporters.'

'In Fleet Street?' George whistled.

'Apparently; but a lot of it is inference.'

'Are you going to go after it, Ron?'

'Why not? It doesn't cost anything to send a *curriculum vitae* with copies of some recent articles.'

'Good for you. If you get anything it'll make a change from covering local council elections.' George sounded disgruntled. 'I've had enough of councillors to last me a lifetime. Gent will have to get somebody else next time.'

Ron was diplomatic. 'Well, it's nice to see you back in the office.'

'I never thought I'd say this but it's nice to be back . . .' George stopped abruptly as he remembered something. 'I know why I meant to get in here earlier. It's about your girl, Rosie . . . sorry, Rose.'

'What did you find out?' Ron found himself leaning over the desk, desperate, in equal measure, to find out what George had discovered and to prevent the information reaching colleagues at nearby desks.

George leaned over in his turn. 'They, that is her and her mother, don't live at the address you gave me any more. According to the landlord of that pub down the road, they moved three weeks ago.'

'Moved? Where to?'

'He didn't know, and I couldn't find out any more.'

On Ron's features incredulity and shock vied for supremacy. 'But she couldn't . . . she never mentioned . . .' His voice tailed off.

'Sorry to be the bearer of bad tidings.' George cast around for something to soften the blow. 'I popped along to see the house and there's a for sale sign outside. Some local firm called Graham and Son. I suppose they might know something.'

The train was due into Taunton at twenty to eleven. Ron checked his watch: it was ten to already and they had just left Bridgwater. He closed his eyes and cursed quietly. It had been bad enough wriggling out of the family celebration; now there seemed a fair chance he would find Graham and Son closed. After all, it was Saturday morning and almost certainly they would shut at midday. The train had barely halted when he leapt out and hurtled towards the station entrance. He caught a glimpse of the station clock: it was half past eleven.

'Graham and Son?' The porter thought for a moment. 'Oh, you mean the house agents. They're just across the road and down that street to the left.'

For a moment Ron thought he had missed it; then he saw the sign in the frosted glass of the door, A.L. Graham & Son, Auctioneers, Valuers and Estate Agents. Inside he was confronted by an imposing flight of stairs, but hardly had he set foot on it when a youngster popped out of a side door.

'Can I help you, sir?' He added helpfully and somewhat disingenuously that they were just about to close for the weekend. Briefly Ron explained his business. The youngster seemed uncertain. 'I think you need to talk to young Mr Graham. Can you come through to the office?'

'Come in, Mr . . . ?' The younger Graham didn't look very young, but Ron supposed everything was relative.

'It's Ron Charteris. Thanks for seeing me. I'll try not to take up too much of your time.'

Graham sat down and gestured to Ron to do likewise. 'Young Philip gave me a somewhat garbled account, but I gather you're trying to get in touch with one of our clients. If I can have the details then naturally we would be happy to forward any letters.'

'I'm afraid it's a matter of urgency. I need to see Miss Metcalfe today, or certainly this weekend.'

'Well, we're acting for a Mrs Gwendoline Metcalfe. Presumably the Miss Metcalfe you're referring to is her daughter?' Ron nodded and Graham looked distinctly unhappy. 'I really don't think that would be possible. You see, although we aren't lawyers or medical people we do have a certain duty of confidentiality to the people we act for.'

'Of course, of course, I understand that.' At this juncture Ron decided that the whole truth might be unhelpful. 'I think I'd better be frank with you. I'm a reporter on the *Bristol Echo*.' He passed over his card, which was studied with interest. 'Now Miss Metcalfe was extremely helpful with an article I was putting together. It's due to go out on Tuesday and the copy deadline is Monday. The problem is that

I need to check back on certain points. It's a legal matter. If I can't see Miss Metcalfe and clarify these points I'm left with two options: one is to go ahead and publish what I have and hope I'm correct; the other is to spike the whole article.' He could see that the tale he was weaving was having an effect. 'I don't need to add that I'd be very unhappy with either of those two courses of action.'

'I can see that. Of course we really shouldn't divulge this sort of thing without the client's express permission.' Graham was struggling with himself; then he reached a decision. 'We don't normally have reporters in here, but I like to think I'm a fair judge of character. Perhaps on this occasion it wouldn't be a breach of trust to give you the information you need.' He rummaged through some files in one of the drawers and, finding what he wanted, scribbled some details on a sheet of paper and passed it over to Ron. 'There you are, Mr Charteris. They can be reached at that address until the end of the month.'

Ron found the address without too much difficulty, albeit on the other side of town. The house itself was detached and had seen better days. Still if they were only here temporarily it presumably didn't matter too much. Walking up to the front door, he felt extremely diffident. After all, it could be just as George had implied: that she had simply decided not to take matters any further. Then his resolve stiffened. Of course it wasn't that: there were just too many things that didn't add up. He heard the echoes of the knocker reverberating along what he took to be the hall. There was no response. He was about to try again when he heard footsteps. His mood of diffidence returned and he retreated a couple of steps. What was he going to find?

The door opened to reveal a young woman. More than that, a very pleasant-looking young woman. Indeed, not to put too fine a point on it, a very pretty young woman. But one thing was certain: it was not Rose. 'Yes? Can I help you?'

Ron was confused and, for a moment, tongue tied. 'Sorry . . . sorry to disturb you, but I was hoping to find Rose here . . . Rose Metcalfe.'

'She's not here at the moment. Are you a friend?'

'Yes. My name's Ron Charteris. Rose and I met in January. I've been trying to get in touch with her.'

'I see.' The girl looked doubtful.

'I'm a reporter. Rose contacted me over something she . . . she thought would interest me. I met her and her mother here in Taunton.'

'You've met my mother?' Her look of surprise matched Ron's. Then she remembered that although she knew his name he didn't know hers. 'You must excuse me. I'm Rose's sister Christine. You'd better come in, Mr Charteris. Now I think of it, my mother did mention something about you.' He was shown into a rather down-at-heel drawing room and Christine gestured to an armchair. 'Have a seat and I'll go and find her. I'm sure she'll want to meet you again.'

Ron had barely sat down when Christine's mother arrived. Hurriedly he got up and shook her hand. 'Nice to see you again, Mrs Metcalf.'

'And you, Mr Charteris. Please sit down.' She looked towards Christine. 'Do you think you could make us all some tea, dear?' Once her daughter had gone she leaned towards him and when she spoke her tone betrayed some anxiety. 'Rose thought you might try to contact her.'

Ron thought he might as well be straightforward. 'Yes. I hoped to get to know her better. And besides that, she was helping me with an investigation.'

'Yes, I know.' He was certain she was about to say more, but she seemed to think better of it.

'Can I ask where she's moved to?'

'She's in London, or rather Purley in Surrey.'

'London?' His astonishment was plain to see.

'Yes. She's always felt Taunton was too small a town, and when the house was sold so quickly it seemed the ideal opportunity to make the break.'

'You've sold your house?'

Mrs Metcalfe glanced towards the kitchen, where a kettle whistled and there was the chink of teacups. 'The point is I wanted to sell and move elsewhere when Rose and Christine's father died.' She was speaking hurriedly now, anxious to say whatever it was before Christine arrived. 'Obviously I talked it over with the family and one or two close friends, but I hadn't seen any auctioneers or valuers.'

Christine's voice drifted through from the kitchen. 'I'll just be a couple of minutes.'

'All right, dear.' She resumed with just a touch of querulousness. 'Then that fellow arrived – unannounced, I might add.' She pre-empted his question. 'He was one of my husband's old contacts: I recognised the face but not the name. It was Rose he wanted to speak to and they had a long discussion. I didn't think any more about it, but it could only have been two days later that I had a letter from Graham's, the valuers. Someone had made an offer for the house.' Her eyebrows arched visibly and she added, not very convincingly, 'I suppose it could have been a coincidence. Still, it was a reasonable offer and you know that old saying about gift horses and looking in mouths. So we – of course I consulted the girls – decided to accept it. The only problem was that whoever was buying needed vacant possession very quickly. So . . . here we are.'

'Here we are where?' Christine had come through with the tea.

'I was telling Mr Charteris about the sale of the house.'

'Yes, you were very lucky.'

Like her mother, Christine didn't sound convinced. Ron decided he had better try to move the conversation on. 'And Rose decided it was an opportunity to branch out, so to speak.'

'Yes. She has an aunt in Purley.'

'We seem to be out of milk; I won't be a moment.' Christine made her way back to the kitchen.

Rose's mother seized the opportunity. 'Everything was done in such a hurry. I'm sure Rose will contact you once she's settled down.'

'Could I have her address?'

Mrs Metcalfe hesitated. 'It might be better if I passed on any message.'

'Well, if you feel that would be best. But if it's just that she feels it better that we don't see each other any more, then all it takes is a brief note. I'd accept whatever she said. I find it rather strange that she hasn't done that.' Ron decided to grasp the bull by the horns. 'Is there any other reason why I can't contact her directly?

'I really can't answer that.' The elderly lady shuffled awkwardly in her chair, as if searching for a way to end a conversation that was becoming embarrassing. When she did speak it was with an air of finality. 'Mr Charteris, all I can say is that I'll tell her that you have called when I next write, and if you care to let me have a letter I'll see that it's enclosed.'

CHAPTER NINE

MAGUIRE'S LETTER HAD been quite specific: Jim was to meet him outside Woolworths in York. Of course he had written back immediately. Why not at home in Leeds? Besides, it cost money to get to York and Maguire must know how hard up they were. The reply had been insistent: it must be York, and he would understand once they met. Any expenses would be refunded. The mantra of the first letter had been repeated above all: 'Tell no one!'

Jim was early and decided to kill some time at the station news kiosk. The headlines stared out at him from the news boards. 'Ramsay Macdonald to form government.' He didn't bother to read any of the details scrawled underneath. Bloody politicians. Nothing would change.

The city centre was not particularly busy, so he paused some way before the shop and scanned the entrance. Even now he was uncertain whether it was all some sort of elaborate hoax. But how could it be? Not from someone in Maguire's position – and all the way up here. At first Jim didn't see the figure behind the tram stop and partially hidden in the recess of the doorway. Then it registered: it was him; perhaps a little fatter than when he'd seen him last, but unmistakably him. Jim hurried across the road.

'Glad you could make it.' Maguire's words were friendly enough, but his eyes were still flicking up and down the street. 'There's a nice corner table in the café here – quite private really – we can have a chat.' As was his way, he took assent for granted and led the way inside.

The table was private and the alcove walls were solid. Maguire seemed to read Jim's thoughts. 'No chance of being overheard here. Anyway, how are things with you?'

'Not good. I still haven't got a job.' Jim looked bitterly at the other man. 'Nor likely to, given the circumstances.'

'You could always have gone back to the railways. As you've been found not guilty there's no reason for them not to take you back on.'

'As a porter?'

'Ah. I can see that would be difficult. Have you got anything else in mind?'

The downcast face opposite gave the answer as it reddened with a little flash of anger. 'You didn't come all the way up here to check my job prospects.'

'No, no, of course not. But you remember what we talked about before, about being patient? I can see you do. Well, there have been – how can I put it – developments.'

'Developments? What does that mean?'

'All in good time now. All in good time.'

Jim's patience finally snapped. 'This has something to do with those children, hasn't it? You've been able to identify . . .' He was halted by the finger held to the other man's lips.

Maguire lowered his voice. 'All I can tell you is that it is certain that no crime has been committed. The appropriate authorities are quite satisfied about that. But . . .' There was a long pause. 'It would be difficult, extremely difficult, should any of this become more widely known.' He looked across at the uncomprehending expression of the other man. 'Jim, believe me some very important people have been unwittingly involved – so it's been decided, at the highest levels, that no more action will be taken.' Anticipating an interruption, he hurried on. 'I know it's sad, but there's absolutely nothing more that can be done.'

'Is that what I've come all the way to York to be told?'

Sensing Jim's anger, Maguire leaned across, patted him on the shoulder and explained patiently. 'No. You've come all the way here to learn about something that has turned up. Something that is very advantageous, but something that we didn't want to discuss in Leeds. You have friends, relatives, acquaintances in Leeds. Wherever we went we might have been seen, and then you might be asked to explain. It's much better like this.'

'You said "we". Who else is involved?'

'A little while ago I mentioned that some important people have been caught up in this. One of them is here today to talk to you.' Maguire seemed to read Jim's mind. 'Don't worry, you won't recognise him – but I still had to be certain you had brought no one with you.' He turned his head towards the café entrance and nodded.

Jim followed his gaze to see a youngish man coming across to them. He looked to be in his late thirties, and by his gait and general bearing seemed inoffensive enough. It was only when he came nearer that Jim saw his eyes. He shivered slightly, for he had seen eyes like those in the war: he knew with utter certainty what lay behind them.

As the man joined them at the table Maguire introduced him. 'Jim, this is Anthony.'

He was about to ask 'Anthony who?', but thought better of it.

The voice, when it came, was pleasant enough, but the eyes didn't change. 'Nice to meet you, Jim. I take it our friend here has covered the general background? Good.' He seemed anxious to complete business, leaning over and speaking with some intensity. 'The information you gave our friend here was crucial – absolutely crucial. Given that, the way you have been treated is deplorable.' Anthony held up his hand, checking Jim's attempted interruption. 'Amends cannot be made publicly, but certain people are determined matters will not be left like this. They want to help you back on to your feet again.'

'How? I can't go back to the railways.'

'No, certainly not the railways. What you need now is a fresh start. A new career. You're still comparatively young; early forties, I would say.' He didn't wait for an answer. 'So these people have organised something for you. The details are in here.' He handed across an envelope.

'What's this? It's not some sort of a bribe, is it?' Jim felt panic rising. 'No, I don't want to have anything to do with this.' He thrust the envelope back to Anthony, only to have pushed firmly back again.

'Open it. It's nothing illegal.' Jim glanced across at Maguire, who quickly chimed in.

'It's totally straight, and I would know.'

Gingerly Jim opened the envelope, took out the sheaf of papers and looked questioningly at Anthony, who gestured towards the first sheet. Slowly Jim read it. 'I don't understand . . . a job in London, in the City.' He read on. 'They're offering me a job as a manager in . . .' He looked again at the heading. 'A stockbroking firm?' He could no longer keep the anger out of his voice. 'This is madness. I'm being made a fool of here. What the hell do I know about stocks and shares?'

Anthony was at his most reassuring. 'Don't worry, Jim. The manager bit is just the job title. Stockbrokers need clerical staff, just like everybody else, and that is essentially what you'll be doing.' For the first time a hint of impatience came into his tone. 'Just count on it, you will have very understanding superiors. Now concentrate on the salary.'

'But it's twice as much as I was getting as a driver. It can't be right, can it?' Anthony's nod confirmed that it was. 'And what about these other papers?'

Anthony pointed out an official-looking sheet headed 'Martins Bank'. 'An account has been opened in your name at this branch. Once you've settled down this amount will be paid in.' He took out a fountain pen, turned over the sheet and wrote down a figure, underlining it when he had finished. 'This should be enough to get you on your feet again.'

Jim stared at the figure: one thousand pounds. He opened his mouth to speak and eventually the words came. 'There must be something wrong. This can't be legal.'

'There's nothing wrong. We're dealing with very important people. And, as our friend said before, if it was illegal would either of us be having anything to do with it?'

There was no answer as Jim shuffled through the papers once more, desperately seeking some way of making sense of it all. There just had to be a catch. 'So what do I have to do in return?'

'Nothing. Absolutely nothing. Apart, that is, for your absolute discretion about the matters leading up to this.' It appeared Anthony wasn't sure if this had registered. 'Jim. You must forget everything you told our friend here. That is why it's best you go to London. Well away from all the people in Leeds who know about you and your background. Make a fresh start. After all, it's where you grew up. It shouldn't be hard.'

'When do I have to make a decision?'

'Now.'

'But I need to tell my wife. She might not like the idea.'

'She will. I'm sure she doesn't like living on the dole any more than you do.' The gaze was unrelenting.

'How long do I have?'

'Good man. You'll get a letter in the next day or two. Someone will want to see you – in London – within the week. He doesn't have anything to do with this directly – more of an organiser. After that . . . it can be as quick as you like.'

Abruptly Anthony stood up; it was obvious he was anxious to get away. 'I really must go now. Very best of luck. Enjoy your new life.' He shook hands. 'Our friend here will give you all other information that is necessary.' Just for a fleeting moment Jim was conscious of those eyes again; then Anthony was gone.

Jim suddenly realised that throughout the whole of this extraordinary interview Maguire had hardly said a word. He decided to try to find out more. 'How well do you know Anthony?'

'Not well at all.' Maguire released a sigh, as if he had been holding his breath for the last few minutes. 'But just well enough to know he isn't someone you cross. What you've agreed to you stick to.'

He spoke with such seriousness that Jim felt a compulsion to lighten the conversation. 'I suppose you'll be going back down to . . .' He wasn't allowed to finish his question.

'No. I'm starting a new life as well.'

'But surely not. To give up everything?' Jim looked bewildered.

His companion pulled out his wallet and picked up the bill. 'Yes, a bit of a wrench, but there are compensations. Oh, by the way, I nearly forgot the expenses.' He passed over a fiver and looked up enquiringly. 'Any more questions?' Jim shook his head. 'Then it's goodbye. I don't imagine we'll see each other again. Take care of yourself.' They shook hands; then he too was gone.

Gradually Jim's thoughts settled down as he walked back to the station. God, it was a funny business. Someone, somewhere must have some pretty nasty skeletons in his cupboard. But then his spirits lightened. What did it matter? It couldn't be outside the law: Maguire's involvement proved that. And Ellen would accept it without demur. She was getting as fed up as he was at pinching and scraping and counting every penny. He turned into the station, already a different man from the one who had left it only an hour before. Stopping at the tobacco kiosk, he was about to ask for five Woodbines but changed his mind. Bugger that, he thought, this time it's ten Craven A.

On the train Jim's mood became even more buoyant. There would be no excuse now for Ellen not to agree to start a family. He watched the suburbs of Leeds come into view as his thoughts turned to Anthony and how he had been described: a very important person, but not someone you'll recognise. He smiled at the melodrama of it all. But there was something nagging at the back of his mind for, strangely enough, the face was familiar. Was it just a facial type? No, he was positive: he had seen Anthony before. His smile vanished as he remembered exactly where and when.

CHAPTER TEN

CHEST HEAVING, RON eased to a walk at the sight of the tail-lights of the guard's van receding down the line. Bugger it! Now he had three-quarters of an hour to kill. 'Starnewshtandaard!' To one side the raucous incantation of the newspaper seller rose above the hubbub of Paddington station, and Ron dug in his pocket for some change. 'What'll it be, mate?'

His normal preference would have been the *Evening News*, by far the most substantial paper, but thoughts of the interview he had just completed made him hesitate, and he opted for the *Evening Standard*, one of the Beaverbrook papers. As he opened it the thought occurred to him that this was probably the nearest he was likely to get to the Beaverbrook organisation. That he had got an interview in the first place was wonder enough: out of the dozen or so hopefuls there today, he was the only one from the regional press. But there was no point in kidding himself: he had made a pig's ear of it all. His face screwed up in embarrassment at the recollection of his answer to how he would approach politicians in the national news. He must have confirmed all the stereotypes of a parish pump provincial.

Hurriedly Ron tried to concentrate on the paper. There was some national news but, not unexpectedly, most concerned London and the home counties. Flicking through, Purley caught his eye. The story was routine, but automatically his thoughts switched to Rose and the envelope that had come through his door the previous week. Even before he had opened the letter the scent had forewarned him. So she had received the letter he had sent via her mother; and she had replied to him directly. Not only that, it had been written from Surrey and he now had her new address. The letter was still in his inside pocket, its contents – though warm in tone – hardly clearing up why it was she hadn't contacted him before. 'I'm sorry for not being in touch . . . events have overtaken everything else . . . I do want to see you again . . . perhaps it's best to leave explanations until we can meet . . .' Ron nurtured the hope that somehow he could combine his interview with meeting her, but it was not to be: although the interview was at eleven, it was made clear that the process would last as long as was needed. True, there was an understanding that reasonable time off for job interviews was acceptable, but Gent had made it clear that he expected him to be at his desk the next day.

Ron checked his watch to find there was still another twenty minutes to wait. He continued flicking through the paper . . . financial news . . . parliamentary reports. The sports news must be here somewhere. Then he stopped. It was something he had skimmed over and had only just registered . . . a word . . . a name . . . what was it?' He turned back to the parliamentary pages. Yes, there it was, the word 'Eastermain'. To be precise it was the Lord Eastermain. The same one who had founded an emigration society for children and whose plaque was on that vicarage gate. Apparently he had made a speech in the House of Lords. Ron read it:

> In public life it is seldom that the opportunity presents itself to drive forward a policy that is of paramount political importance, while at the same time improving opportunities for many of the poorest members of our society. What I suggest to your lordships is that the various child emigration schemes do precisely this. The dominions need to populate and they wish that population to come from the mother country. On our part we have many children whose lives would, by any objective assessment, be limited should they stay here.

Ron gazed up to where a pigeon was fluttering between the roof girders and carefully folded the paper. The hypocritical bastard! Ten to one there would be no mention of his own emigration scheme, still less of his Carricktown Land and Cattle Company set up in north-western Australia, to which a lot of those children would be bound. As for the two dead children now lying in Eastmead church-yard, they were just an embarrassment, something best covered up and forgotten. For a moment he was tempted to go over to another newspaper seller just by the entrance who was selling the *Daily Worker*. Then he simmered down: he was a journalist and it was pointless to indulge in empty gestures. No, his approach would have to be investigative, and the first step on that particular road led to Eastermain's company and everyone connected to it.

With a jolt reality set in. What was the point of pursuing it? East-ermain and his cronies might be some of the biggest villains unhanged, but they were fireproof. Their positions in society saw to that. Besides, public interest had died away: the newspapers were no longer interested; certainly the *Echo* had made that plain. Slowly indignation ebbed away to be replaced by gloom. He had a story, or with a bit more digging would have a story, but even even if he acquired proof positive who would publish it?

'Don't tell me you're still on the trail of those kids!' George could hardly keep the grin off his face as Ron surreptitiously slid the notes he had made in the library into a desk drawer. 'Gent's not going to be best pleased if he finds you're wasting time on a dead story.'

'And he won't find out unless somebody tells him.'

George ploughed on, ignoring the tart response. 'What do you hope to get out of it?'

Ron's shoulders sagged. 'I don't know really.' For a moment he seemed totally despondent, but then he brightened up. 'Yes, I do know. What I want is a file of information. Information that, as you so rightly point out, I can't use at the moment, but . . . one day might prove very useful. Besides, I'm not spending very much time on it and now's the time to collect it all, while it's still fresh in people's minds.'

'So what have you found out so far?'

'Well, I've been looking into that firm, Carricktown Land, that I was telling you about, and checking out the people who hold directorships.'

George pretended to yawn. 'Fascinating stuff . . . it gets right to the heart of it all, doesn't it?'

'All right, you can scoff, but I'm going to see if I can get in touch with Maguire again. A pound to a penny he knows a hell of a lot more than has come out so far.'

George looked concerned, and this time it wasn't feigned. He spoke with intensity. 'Ron, you're becoming obsessed with the whole thing. For God's sake, man, think it through. If Maguire turns nasty and contacts the paper you're in deep trouble, and it isn't as if you have another job lined up.'

Ron's despondency returned. 'Yes, you're right. I suppose Maguire and I didn't part on the best of terms.' He thought for a while. 'Of course I could always have a word with Gerald Thomas: he's a desk sergeant I know.'

'If you must, Ron, if you must. But be careful.' George looked serious. He leaned across the desk and lowered his voice. 'I heard this morning that lay-offs are being considered.'

'What? Where did you hear that?'

George was evasive. 'I overheard something. It adds up, doesn't it? The circulation's started to drop again. So,' his voice dropped to a whisper, 'it won't do you a lot of good to put yourself in the firing line by upsetting the local bobbies.' Having delivered the bad news, he moved on. 'Any news from the *Express* yet?'

Ron was still trying to take in what had been said. He had begun to reconcile himself to the fact that all he could reasonably expect from the *Express* was a rejection, but coming to terms with that was based on still having a job. Apparently this was now no longer a certainty. He struggled to give an answer. 'No. No news. I told you before, George. I blew the interview.'

'Gerald Thomas?' The copper behind the counter checked with a colleague. 'No, he's transferred. Anything I can do?

Ron was caught off balance. 'Er . . . no thanks. It's something I need to check with him.' He turned away, unsure what, if anything, he could do now. There seemed to have been a complete changeover

in personnel: so far he had seen no one he recognised. Then a familiar face came into view. He hastened to intercept the figure striding
out of the station. 'Hello. It's Bill Ferguson, isn't it?' Ferguson looked
nonplussed, obviously having forgotten their previous meeting. 'It's
Ron Charteris. Remember, we had a chat in that café over the road.'

Light dawned. 'What can I do for you, Ron?'

'I was hoping . . .' Then light dawned for Ron as well. 'You're
back in uniform and you've got your sergeant's stripes. Congratulations. When did this happen?'

Ferguson looked pleased. 'It must be a month ago. I passed my
sergeant's exam the year before last, but you know how it is in this job:
you have to wait until there's a vacancy. I must admit I miss being in
civvies, but promotions don't grow on trees and I jumped at it.'

'Do you know, you're the first person I've recognised in here. Has
there been a reorganisation or something?'

'Root and branch, Ron. Root and branch. Of course once the
crash investigation was wound up we lost a lot of people, and then
the powers that be took the opportunity to move people around at
the same time. Don't tell me, I suppose you're looking for Gerald.'

'As a matter of fact I am.'

'Then I'll have to disappoint you. He's transferred to the Somerset force. Mind you, he comes from that way so he's quite happy.'

Ferguson seemed in a chatty mood so Ron pressed on. 'What
about Maguire? Is he still here?'

'No, he's gone as well.'

'Back on detective duties somewhere else?'

'Not exactly.' Ferguson sounded equivocal. 'I'm not really sure
it's official yet, so I don't know if I'm at liberty to say.'

'Come on, Bill. You can't lead me on like that.'

Ferguson hesitated, then appeared to make up his mind. 'I don't
suppose it matters: it'll be announced soon anyway. He's taken
retirement.'

'Taken retirement? But he can't be a day over forty-five, if that.'

'Forty-three, actually.' Ferguson looked wistful, and Ron judged the
sergeant was only about seven or eight years short of that himself.

'So how's he managed that?' Ron's mind was working overtime. 'It isn't a device, is it? I mean, to get rid of him?'

Ferguson was now looking distinctly uneasy. 'Ron, I really shouldn't be talking to you about this.' He half-turned to break off the conversation, then changed his mind. 'Look, none of this had better appear in your paper. As far as I know it's a genuine retirement. Mind you, how he can afford it . . . ?' The sergeant spread his hands in bewilderment. 'I did hear his wife came into some money . . .' He took a moment or two to ponder on this turn of events before saying with a sigh, 'Lucky bugger. Mine only spends it!'

'So is he still around here?'

'No, or not for much longer anyway. He's moving to Salcombe in Devon.' Having gone this far the sergeant relaxed. 'Do you know it?'

Ron thought back to day trips to the seaside. 'Vaguely. I was there once when I was a nipper. Mind you, that was before the war.'

'Well, it hasn't changed much. Do you know that beautiful little bay to the south of the town?' He could see the reporter was uncertain. 'It's on the way to the cliffs and Starehole Bay.' Suddenly Ron was back there, trudging with bucket and spade behind his parents, hardly able to contain his impatience to reach the beach. 'Yes. Yes, I remember. There are some marvellous big houses there, aren't there? I can recall my mum and dad fantasising about what it would be like to live in them.'

'Well, Maguire has bought one of those.'

'Good God.'

Ferguson was gratified at the effect his news was having. 'Good God indeed. I'm told he won't get much change out of three thousand pounds for it.'

Ron paused at the pillar box and there was a moment's agonising before he slipped the letter in. Would she be satisfied with what he had said? She would have to be; there wasn't any way he could get up to London before the end of the month. His thoughts grew blacker. Even if he did, what future was there for them with him in Bristol and her in Purley? God, he desperately needed to think about it all. There was an empty seat on a bench and he still had a quarter of an hour before he was due back at the office. Sparrows clustered around his feet, hoping for crumbs, and his mind was drawn back to the time he had last seen Dorothy. It was a depressing thought. Perhaps all his relationships with women were doomed to failure.

He took a deep breath and straightened his shoulders, as if the physical effort alone might shake him out of this mood. This was stupid. It wasn't as if he wanted to see Rose just for herself, although the last month or so had made him realise how important she was to him. No, he also needed to find out what it was that had been said when she met 'pro bono publico'. Obviously an offer concerning the house sale had been made, and it was an offer that couldn't be refused. And this had to be taken in conjunction with Maguire's 'retirement'. For a moment Ron wished he was one of those simple souls who believed in coincidences – but he wasn't. Maguire had been paid off, but for what? Perhaps when he saw Rose things would be clearer. She wasn't – couldn't be – party to any of this, but in a sense she, or at least her family, had been bought off as well.

And who else was involved? The random thought, once insinuated into his consciousness, wouldn't be denied. What about that engine driver – what was his name – Thornton? Maguire had been having a heart to heart with him, and had become pretty shirty when he realised he'd been seen. Then there was Thornton himself: he had really lost his temper. Of course the man had just been on trial, facing a possible life sentence. In those circumstances it was understandable – or was it? An overwhelming sense of relief might be a more likely outcome. But if an offer was in the air – an offer that might be compromised if anything came out – that might account for his reaction. Even more so to a man who, although found not guilty, had effectively lost his livelihood. Ron checked the time and rose to go. One thing was sure, no one would attempt to pay him off. What would his reaction be if they did? He smiled to himself. How big-headed could you be? All he had was theories – vague, unformed, unpublishable theories. Who needed to fear what he had found out so far?

Then, like a thunderclap, something else steamrollered its way into the forefront of his mind, driving out everything else like chaff before a gale. The letter! The letter that had arrived in the morning; the one that bore the printed crest of Beaverbrook newspapers on its reverse; the one he had cravenly feared to open. God, what a coward he was, wanting to maintain the illusion that there was still some chance for just a few more hours. But it was no good: he must open it now. He couldn't do it in the office in front of others – certainly not in front of George. Trembling, Ron sat down again and pulled the envelope from his pocket. After a moment's hesitation, with fumbling fingers he tore it open. At first he could make no sense of it. The sentences shimmered and danced on the page. At long last his eyes began to focus and individual words started to take shape. But why would anyone write a letter of rejection like this? The words were positively nonsensical. 'We are happy to inform you . . . the position of junior reporter . . . with effect from Monday fifth of May . . . at a salary of . . . please confirm you wish . . .' His mind took in, then rejected, an infinity of possibilities until only one was left. This wasn't a letter of rejection: he had got the job! He really had got the job!

CHAPTER ELEVEN

'ARE YOU SURE we've done the right thing, Jamie?'

Jim paused halfway through getting their luggage down from the rack and looked down at his wife. 'For God's sake, Ellen! What a funny time to ask a question like that.' He gestured at the window. 'We're nearly into King's Cross.'

'It was all so sudden. We didn't have time to think it through properly.'

He sighed. 'What was there to think through? Stay in Leeds with nothing to look forward to but the dole, or come down here to a secure job and a thousand pounds to get us started.' The last suitcase hit the floor with a thump. 'You don't need to be an Oxford professor to work that one out.'

'But that's it exactly. People like us don't have that sort of luck. There's got to be something funny about it.'

The train eased to a halt to the sound of steam being released. Jim recognised the signal and knew there would be another two or three minutes before they reached the platform. For a moment he was tempted to move the conversation on to other things, but his wife's anxious expression changed his mind. There was no one else in the carriage so he sat down and took her face in his hands. 'Stop worrying. Of course there's something funny involved. It's what I told you before – if the whole story ever gets out there'll be some red faces in very high-up places – but there's nothing criminal about it.' He gave her a kiss. 'Ellen, we have a new life ahead of us. Just remember that.'

'Three bedrooms! Jamie, there are three bedrooms upstairs!' Her excited shouts echoed down from the landing. 'And you should see the size of the airing cupboard.'

Jim climbed the stairs, a broad smile on his face, and this time it was Ellen who kissed him. 'How long is this rented for?'

'Two months, and then it's up to us whether we keep it or buy somewhere.'

'Buy somewhere?' Her doubtful look returned. 'Could we afford it?'

Jim sat down on the edge of the bed. 'Yes, we could. And we could buy it outright when that money comes into our account.'

'Are you sure we're going to get it?'

'Ellen. Ellen.' He held her hands. 'I've never known anyone like you. Every silver lining has to have a cloud. Now listen to me. That fellow who met us – Melvin – he gave me all the details while you were having that cuppa. I start work on Monday. It's Friday tomorrow so we have three days to get this place organised.' He remembered something else. 'Melvin gave me an advance on salary – over six months – just to get us started.' He produced an envelope with a flourish. 'See – fifty pounds. You'd better have some of this for housekeeping.' He began to peel off some fivers.

'Jamie.' There was a note of real alarm in her voice. 'There's nothing in the house, and the shops will have closed.'

He put his arms round her waist and danced her round the room. Then, putting his lips to her ear, he whispered, 'Let's celebrate the start of a new life. Let's go mad just for once.' She looked startled. 'Let's go out to a restaurant tonight.'

'Nice to meet you, Thornton.' Handshake completed, the man opposite eased his rather large frame into the chair. 'Sit down, man.' He indicated an upright chair on the other side of the desk. 'Now, as I was saying my name is Last and I'm the general manager. Having said that, this isn't a big firm so I've had to take charge of special issues.' He sighed deeply at the manifest unfairness of life. 'Now you'll see me in here most days, but your work will be in the main office.'

Jim decided the expression on his face – one of permanent irritability – was just an unfortunate mannerism. 'Yes. That was something I wanted to ask.' There was no easy way to express what he needed to, so he opted for the direct approach. 'All this work is new to me.' He added hastily, 'I'm sure I'll pick it up after a while.'

'I'm sure you will, Thornton.' Last appeared to be deep in thought, then recovered himself. 'I wouldn't worry about that. One of our senior clerks, Furniss, will show you the ropes: I've already had a word with him. But before we get onto that I think we need to have a chat.' He stretched his legs as if trying to ease his muscles but, apparently finding no relief, got up and started to pace the room. 'It's got be said, Thornton, that you come into the company by a . . . by a . . . rather . . . how shall we say . . . unorthodox route.' He relaxed a little, seemingly satisfied with his final choice of words.

'Are you worried that I won't fit in?' Jim knew intuitively that this first meeting provided an opportunity for plain speaking that was unlikely to occur again.

'No, I'm sure you'll be fine after a while. That's not the problem. It's just that people in the office will naturally wonder how you got the job.' Last paused and for a moment stared absentmindedly out of the window. 'Of course they'll assume it's because you know someone, so if I were you I would let them go on thinking that.' He ruminated on this last piece of advice. 'And while we're on the subject it would be politic not to go into too much detail about your background. Your immediate background, that is. If you mention the railways it might be best to hint at junior management or some sort of clerical post.' He checked some papers lying in front of him. 'It's good that you were in the war.' He must have noticed Jim's raised eyebrows. 'The point is, your appointment is likely to put some people's noses out of joint. If they know you were in the war they might think that played a part as well.' He glanced anxiously across to confirm that the point had been taken. Jim smiled and nodded. 'Good. We seem to understand each other.' Last checked his watch. 'I'll introduce you to Furniss now. He'll explain everything.'

'Of course, as soon as you find your feet, Jim, you'll report directly to Last.' Kenneth Furniss tried to sound reassuring. 'But in the meantime you can pick my brains whenever you need to.'

85

'Thanks. I rather think I'll be checking with you quite a bit.'

Kenneth didn't answer, his attention patently on Last as he left his office and went out of the main door. His tone was almost contemptuous. 'Half past three and most mornings he's not in until ten.' He turned back to Jim. 'God knows what we're supposed to do if there are any official documents that need signing. In fact if . . .' He stopped abruptly, suddenly realising that he knew very little about James Thornton and still less about the reasons behind his appointment.

Jim moved hastily to quash any worries. 'I'm grateful to have the unvarnished facts, Kenneth. I take you to mean that I needn't expect any practical help from that particular quarter?'

'Well . . . yes, I'm afraid so. He's not a patch on his brother.'

'Brother?'

'I know it's the way of the world to keep it in the family, but really . . . that man.' Kenneth shook his head. 'His brother Arthur used to be general manager, and John there was the junior in every sense. He was never brilliant, but while Arthur was around he more or less got on with things. But since he's been in sole charge . . .' Kenneth sighed. 'It wouldn't be so bad but De Villiers, the managing director, is semi-retired, so as long as Last doesn't make a major balls-up he never gets to hear of it.' He grinned a little wearily. 'And of course those of us who have the experience make sure that doesn't happen.'

It was all getting a bit political for Jim. He picked up on the original point. 'So what happened to Arthur?'

'He was killed. A tragic accident. You see . . .'

'Excuse me, Mr Furniss.' One of the junior clerks arrived with a sheaf of papers.

Kenneth broke off with an apologetic smile. 'If you're all right for the moment, Jim, I'd better get on with these.'

'So everything went all right?' Ellen watched him anxiously, ready to pounce on any hesitation.

'Fine. Absolutely fine.' Jim couldn't help but tease her a little. 'Mind you, once I've worked my way in I think part of my job will be to bury the bodies.'

'Jamie, be serious. Will you be able to do the job?'

'I suppose it'll take me a while to get on top of everything, but I can't see any problems. Most of it seems very routine.'

'And how did the others take to your coming in like this?' Her anxious look was back again.

'They seemed to accept it, but naturally they were a bit curious about where I'd arrived from. My boss, who's called Last, he's the manager and also a director, suggested I say as little as possible about my background.'

'Is that because they're worried?'

'No.' He responded with mock-exasperation at her continued anxiety. 'Look, I've leapfrogged over one or two people so there's bound to be some resentment. In the circumstances I agree with Last – best to say very little.'

His wife still seemed determined to look on the black side. 'Does that mean you've made some enemies before you're even properly started?'

Jim shook his head and continued sipping his tea. 'Ellen, at the moment I'm just feeling my feet, but I've learned enough to feel sure I'll be all right at this place. Mind you, the one interesting thing that did crop up was about Last's brother.'

'The one who's your boss?'

'Yes. Apparently his older brother was a director as well, and supposedly left this one in the shade.'

'You say "was".'

'Apparently he died in some accident.' Jim realised he was in danger of losing the thread of the conversation. 'Anyway, everyone seems to think that the sun shone out of his . . .'

'Jamie!'

'Sorry, love. But the serious point I'm making is that I may be seen as having been brought into the firm by the younger brother. In those circumstances I think it's best to let sleeping dogs lie, and make it plain that I don't want to know about the other one.'

CHAPTER TWELVE

'SO WHAT'S IT like working on a national newspaper? A bit different from Bristol, I shouldn't wonder.' Rose tried, but failed, to inject some interest into her questions.

'Not as different as you might think. I'm very much the new boy, so I get a lot of the unglamorous jobs.' Ron busied himself once more stirring his tea. This was awful. So far they'd spent ten minutes in formal, polite and pointless conversation, each waiting for the other to open up and neither being able to break out of the pattern they had made for themselves. 'Rose, we can't . . .'

'I've been worrying all . . .'

Both started speaking at the same time and both dissolved into giggles. 'Rose, I haven't seen you for three months and here we are talking as if we're at a vicarage tea party.'

Her giggles stopped. 'Perhaps we shouldn't mention vicarages – at least for the moment.'

'You're right.' He grasped her hand across the table. 'But you must know that there's more to seeing you than a newspaper story – or at least there is for me.'

She didn't answer directly, but neither did she try to take her hand away. 'I'm glad you got in touch now you're in London.'

Ron gave her hand a squeeze. 'Likewise.' It was an unanticipated moment of intimacy and briefly he was tempted to capitalise on it; but he hesitated and the moment was gone. 'Do you know central London at all?'

If she was disappointed she didn't show it. 'No, I don't often get up to town. But I expect journalists like you know it all.'

'Hardly, Rose. Remember I've only been here three weeks.' He beckoned the waitress over. 'Why don't we take a walk in the park? Kensington Gardens isn't too far away, and that's one place I have been to.'

For the best part of an hour they strolled. Not once was the subject of her moving to London touched on. Instead she talked about the secretarial course she had enrolled on and how much her typing and shorthand skills had improved. By the summer she would have taken her exams, and if she passed them she could start applying for secretarial jobs in the City or West End. When Ron asked if she had considered working in Purley she pulled a face: who wanted to work in Purley if you could come up to town each day? In his turn he told her of the people he had interviewed. Most were unknowns, but her eyes lit up at the mention of one minor celebrity. Then there were the characters in his office, men who had been in newspapers all their lives, and their stories . . . At this point he drew in his breath sharply, and she pretended to be all prim and proper.

Eventually Rose collapsed on a bench and gingerly slipped off her shoes. 'You don't mind, do you? But my feet . . .' She gave him a sidelong glance. 'It's all your fault anyway. If I'd known I would have come prepared for walking.'

The afternoon had been marvellous. Perhaps deep down he had had some doubts, but these were now banished. She was exactly as he had thought – a straightforward girl. Explanations could wait until later. 'What time do you have to be back in Purley?'

She raised her eyebrows. 'When I choose. I stay with my aunt, but she doesn't impose a curfew.'

'Let me rephrase that. When's the last train from Waterloo?' She told him. 'In that case you've plenty of time. We can go round some of the sights for a couple of hours and then have a meal.' Rose started to demur, but he persisted. 'Look, I won't take no for an answer. I know an Italian restaurant, Bertorelli's. It's reasonable and quiet with a nice atmosphere. One of my colleagues introduced me to it.'

'And I suppose knowing these sorts of places is one of the perks of your job?'

'Of course it is. I think you'll enjoy going out with a journalist.'

'This is the one problem I have with Italian food.' Rose looked annoyed as the pasta once more slid off the fork.

'I can see I'll have to give you private lessons.' Ron demonstrated by twirling his own fork.

She played along. 'And will I get a certificate at the end?'

'Of course you will.'

'I expect you give that to all the girls you go out with.'

Her tone was light-hearted, but he sensed a more serious purpose behind it. 'I've never given pasta-eating lessons before. I suppose until now no one's come along whom I felt deserved it.' She smiled, and he judged he had passed that particular test at least with flying colours. It presented an opportunity to become serious. 'Rose.' He searched for the right words. 'I need to ask. Why didn't you try to contact me?'

Her face coloured, and she looked confused. For a minute Ron thought he had badly misjudged the moment, then she took his hand. 'I meant to. Honestly I meant to.' This time it was she who searched for words. 'A few days after we went out to Dorrington that man came to see us.'

'I take it by "that man" you mean the fellow who wrote the letter, "*pro bono publico*"?'

'Yes. I recognised him from when Dad was alive. He used to come round from time to time.' She pre-empted the obvious question. 'His name isn't important and he asked me not to mention it.' There was a long pause; she was obviously finding it hard going. 'We had a long chat. It was me he wanted to speak to, not my mother.' She emphasised the next point. 'He knew that I'd contacted you. He seemed to know an awful lot. For instance that we'd visited that vicar and asked about those children. What he wanted was for me to forget about the letter.'

'That's ludicrous.' Ron was driven to intervene. 'Why did he send it in the first place if he didn't want it acted upon?'

'I asked him that but he was evasive. Said he hadn't checked . . . had been mistaken . . . he said it had been a big mistake. He said a lot more as well: innocent parties had been smeared, threats of legal action. It was all in that vein.' Rose realised she wasn't making a lot of sense. 'Sorry, I'm rambling. I just want you to know what he said.'

'But what did you think?'

Ron's question seemed to put her on the spot. 'At the time I didn't know what to think. His visit and everything . . . it was just so unexpected. Thinking about it afterwards, I felt that someone had . . . put pressure on him.'

'Did he threaten you?' There was a note of anger in Ron's voice.

'No.' Rose saw the doubt in his eyes. 'Not at all.' The doubt slowly ebbed away. 'What he did say was that I, and I suppose by implication you, had been caught up in all this inadvertently. As a consequence certain people had decided I should be compensated for all this fuss and bother.'

'Certain people? What did he mean by that?'

'I asked him who he was talking about, but he said he couldn't divulge their names.'

'"Their"? Are you sure he said "their"?'

Rose nodded. 'Is it important?'

'Well, it indicates it wasn't just one individual. Anyway, what sort of compensation had he in mind?'

'When he first arrived he chatted briefly to my mother, and she must have mentioned she was thinking of selling the house.' She put her knife and fork down. 'I'm sorry, Ron, this spaghetti is getting a bit much for me.'

He was impatient for her to continue. 'Don't worry; you can have a nice pudding to make up for it.'

'He mentioned about the house and said he might be able to help, but he couldn't promise and he would call back before the end of the week. In the meantime I had to agree not to get in touch with you. If I did it might ruin any chance of fixing something up.' By now she was looking thoroughly miserable. 'I know it sounds awful, but at the time it didn't seem so bad – after all it was only a few days.'

'So he came back?'

'Yes. Two days later. That same morning there was a letter from Graham's, the house agents, telling us there was a firm offer.' Her eyes pleaded with Ron. 'What could I do? Mother was over the moon. She'd wanted to sell ever since Dad died, but houses like our old one just aren't selling at the moment.'

He said as gently as he could, 'You didn't have to promise not to contact me.'

Rose coloured even more, but her tone took on a hint of asperity. 'But I did, Ron, I did. He said I should have nothing more to do with you. It shouldn't be hard since we had just met. If I did the house sale could be jeopardised.'

The waiter, who had been hovering with a dessert menu, took advantage of the momentary lull in the conversation. Both diners shook their heads. Rose waited until he was out of earshot before continuing. 'I decided to go to my aunt's in Purley because that would send a message to whoever was behind all this that I was going along with it. Just as soon as the house sale was through I was going to contact you as I promised.' Ron didn't respond, and it was then that she became angry. 'I don't know what sort of people you're used to, but I don't promise anything I don't intend to keep.'

In turn he became irritated. 'Rose, just because I didn't answer doesn't mean I don't believe you. I was just trying to work out any possible reasons for all this.' They both fell silent, reflecting on what had nearly turned into a quarrel. It was Ron who made the first conciliatory move. 'Of course I believe you. If the positions had been reversed I'd have done just the same.'

Her eyes glistened. 'I think you're just being kind.'

'No I'm not; I'm being realistic.' He could see the tears welling up and gently changed the subject. 'At least you've still got the original letter that chap sent you.'

Rose looked aghast. 'I'm sorry, Ron, but I don't. He asked for it back.'

Ron saw her off at Waterloo station. The goodnight kiss was more prolonged than he had anticipated, but perhaps she was feeling guilty. Then she broke away in panic. 'Ron, I must go: they've just announced my train.'

'Yes, they have – but it's been delayed by the fog for a quarter of an hour.'

Rose relaxed, and the conversation continued running along commonplace lines as it had ever since they left the restaurant. Every time Ron tried to change tack he was thwarted. Plainly she wanted to forget about the circumstances which had brought her to London. But certain things needed to be said. It looked as if he had to be direct. 'Rose. . .'

Once again she tried to steer the conversation into safer channels. 'Just look at that advertisement for Palethorpe's Sausages. I mean, whoever buys them . . .'

'Rose. Never mind about Palethorpe's Sausages. We didn't finish our conversation earlier.' This time he wouldn't allow her to interrupt. 'It's important that I tell you what I think happened.'

With no great initial enthusiasm she kept quiet, but as Ron spoke her interest was gradually aroused. 'So you think this policeman, Maguire, was bribed?'

'I'm certain of it; just as you and your family were.' She bridled, but Ron quickly placated her. 'I think I was bribed as well. I know, I just know that I ploughed that interview – so how did I get that job, a plum one as far as the Fleet Street ladder is concerned?' He anticipated her next question. 'As far as why is concerned I think it's obvious. You and I have got wind of that business of sending kids to Australia, while Maguire's probably found out a great deal more than we have. And who . . . it has to be Eastermain and some of his friends. It's not just the Emigration Society: the same names keep cropping up as directors and board members of quite a few companies here and abroad. I checked them in our library at work. Some of them are involved in a firm of stockbrokers just a couple of streets away from my office. I might have a wander round that way some lunchtime.'

'Is it wise? If someone pulled strings to get you that job, then those strings could just as easily be cut.'

'I'll be very discreet.' A cold night wind eddied round the cavernous spaces of the station and she huddled a little closer. 'I'm a journalist, Rose, and there's a story here. You never know, one day I might be able to use it.'

Something was puzzling her. 'If these people were just cutting corners when they were shipping children abroad I can see it might be embarrassing for it all to come out. She searched for words. 'But they're powerful people . . . Surely they could cope with any temporary embarrassment? They don't need to be involved in all this hole in the corner business . . .' She found it difficult to articulate the words. '. . . This bribing people to keep quiet.'

Rose didn't get an answer as at that moment the announcer heralded the departure of her train. Ron watched as she ran as fast as her high heels would allow, pausing only to turn at the barrier for a final wave. Deep in thought he turned towards the steps of the tube station. It was just as well she had gone when she did, for she had put her finger on something that had been niggling him as well. He just didn't know why these people had gone to so much trouble.

'It's not my area. Sorry, I can't help.' The sub-editor Ron had approached looked mildly irritated at being interrupted. 'And why are you interested in City stuff?' He answered his own question. 'Because anything to do with finance has to be checked out with Josh French.' He gestured towards the cluster of desks where the city staff worked, and turned back to the papers he was working on.

Ron looked over to the section that had been pointed out. He knew French, the City editor, a remote figure who was out of the office for much of the time. But his luck was in: French was lounging back in his chair. Even in that posture he looked smart, his well-cut suit contrasting with the shabby dress of most of his colleagues. For a moment Ron hesitated, wondering if French might take umbrage at being approached by a junior reporter, then he pressed on. He might be sent away with a flea in his ear, but it was worth a chance.

'So what can I do for you?' French was obviously in a good mood.

'I hope you don't mind, Mr French, but I wanted to pick your brains on some City matters.'

'It's Charteris, isn't it?' Ron nodded. 'Well, first things first, Charteris, we're quite informal in here. You can address me as Josh.' He gave a little smile. It had obviously been a very good lunch.

'Thanks, Josh.' He realised French was waiting for the question. 'Do you know a firm called De Villiers & Last in St Mary Axe?'

'They're stockbrokers, aren't they? I've heard of them but I can't say I know them. There must be a thousand or two stockbroking firms in the City.' He pulled out an expensive-looking cigarette case, opened it and passed it over.

Ron could see the cigarettes had been custom made. He smoked from time to time, but remembered that Rose had mentioned she detested the smell of tobacco. 'Very kind, but no thanks.'

French lit up. 'Suit yourself, but they're made by Rattray's of Perth and they're the best. I get five hundred sent down every month.' He inhaled deeply. 'Now, what was it you wanted to know about this lot?'

'It really isn't the firm; it's some of the people who work there.'

'Such as?'

He consulted his notebook and the names carefully copied that morning in the library. 'Well, there's the chairman, Lord Eastermain.'

'Eastermain, eh? Yes, I know him. Mind you, I didn't know he was chairman of De Villiers, but you can't keep up with everything.' French put his head back and blew a little smoke ring towards the ceiling. 'He's a war hero, you know – an MC and bar, no less. Won his bar at Messines Ridge in 1917, the same show that I was in.'

'You know him from the war?'

'Good God, no. He was in another outfit.' French was silent for a while, then decided to expand. 'There were a lot of top brass around at that end of the ridge, and that's why there were so many gongs handed out. At our end . . . well, the brass tended not to put in an appearance.' He guffawed. 'To be honest I didn't blame 'em.

95

If I'd had a choice I wouldn't have been there either.' He relapsed into silence again before resuming. 'Still, we were both lucky, I suppose. He got his medal and I . . .' he lifted his leg with both hands to demonstrate it didn't bend at the knee '. . . I got a Blighty packet . . .' Ron was silent; he couldn't think what to say. French rescued the conversation. 'The reason I know him is that I've met him at the odd City dinner. Now, who else have you got on that list of yours?'

Ron checked his notebook again. He had compiled the list after checking which names were common to the various companies that Eastermain was connected with. 'There's a Lattimer-Williams.'

'Ah yes, I know him as well. In fact I met him with Eastermain at . . . let's see . . . it was a drinks party at the *Financial Times* back before Christmas. I chatted to him and he was in the same show as well.' He stubbed his cigarette out in a rather ornate ashtray. 'I could be wrong, but I think they were in the same regiment, the Wessex Yeomanry.' He leaned towards Ron. 'Now come on, young Charteris. I've been answering all the questions. You've got a story there, haven't you? If there's a story with City ramifications then I want to know.'

Ron hesitated; he hadn't been prepared for a direct question. 'It's nothing really. Just something I've come across . . .' He tailed off, hoping that French wouldn't persist. It was a vain hope.

'Come on. Out with it!'

'I think he's been packing kids off to Australia to work in his companies there.'

French sighed a deep sigh of disappointment, then started to laugh. 'His Emigration society, you mean.' The expression on Ron's face must have given the City editor his answer. His tone became sympathetic. 'I don't like having to be the bearer of bad news, but I'm afraid you don't have a scoop. I wouldn't say it's widely known, but certain people are quite aware of what's going on.'

'But he's using his position in the House of Lords to push these schemes . . .'

French clasped both hands together in semblance of prayer and closed his eyes. His tone took on a note of supplication. 'Charteris!

Charteris! Listen to me. You need a crash lesson in City ethics. There are lots of little schemes going on: I come across them every day.' He made sure he had Ron's undivided attention. 'There aren't that many rules in the Square Mile, but one thing you never, ever do is breach the City code. Happily the City code is very simple: on matters of finance your word is your bond. Furthermore, you don't break the law – or, at least, British law.' French thought for a moment. 'Actually, I suppose that last bit is redundant, because if you use your imagination it's generally quite easy to bend the law to the particular shape you require.'

Despondently Ron made his way back to his desk, with the sound of French's laughter echoing round the room.

CHAPTER THIRTEEN

'ARE YOU OK, KENNETH?' Jim regarded Furniss with some alarm. The red face and thunderous expression indicated a recent and severe upset. 'Has Last been getting to you.'

'Last?' Jim was regarded as if he'd suggested the man in the moon. 'Last? Oh no, if it was him I'd know how to handle it. He's a prize idiot, but he also knows just how much he's carried and, more to the point, exactly who carries him.' Furniss jammed his pen into the inkwell with such force that the nib could clearly be heard to snap. 'God, look what I've done now.'

Jim liked Kenneth. Another man could have been resentful of the way that he, a comparative stranger, had been parachuted into the firm on a more or less equal status – which would have made it much harder to settle in. Instead Kenneth had gone out of his way to help. They had only known each other for only two months, but it seemed longer. 'You're upset. Do you want to talk about it?'

Kenneth did want to talk, but at the same time he was wary. Jim followed the battle as it played itself out on the other man's features, finally culminating in a decision to confide. 'I might as well. You're bound to find out sooner or later.' He glanced round the rest of the office with an expression of distaste. 'You've found out what this place is like – a hotbed of gossip.' He was finding it difficult to know where to start. 'You've just missed him.'

'Just missed who?' Jim looked genuinely bewildered.

'Lattimer-Williams, that's who.'

'I know the name. He's one of the directors, isn't he? I haven't come across him yet.'

Kenneth pulled out a packet of cigarettes and passed it over. Surprised, Jim accepted one: he had not seen his colleague smoke in the office before. 'If you're lucky there's a fair chance you won't. Come across him, that is.' Kenneth paused to inhale deeply. 'I used to see him regularly when they held board meetings here rather than in one of the big hotels, but now it's only on the very odd occasion that he or any of the others come in.'

'So I take it that one of the odd occasions was this lunchtime?'

'Yes, just my luck.' Kenneth hissed the next words. 'The man is an utter bloody pig!'

'Why? What happened?'

'He arrived just after you'd gone out, and of course half of the staff were at lunch. He started ranting and raving about the office being empty and demanded an explanation from me.' Kenneth stubbed out his cigarette with such venom that he burned his fingers. 'Shit!' He jumped up. 'Look, I can't talk about this here. Let's go for a walk down the corridor.' Once outside he seemed to calm down. 'Sorry, I was getting a bit carried away. You see, Jim, it wasn't that he was making something out of nothing, it was the way he did it.' Kenneth started to fumble for another cigarette. 'Called me useless and a disgrace. Asked what sort of senior clerk allowed half the office to be away from their desks. All this, mind you, in front of the juniors. Can you imagine that? In front of the juniors, the very people we're supposed to be in charge of!' He shook his head in disbelief.

'Wasn't Last around?'

'Oh, he was around all right but he kept his head down. The fact is, he's terrified of Lattimer-Williams – especially when he's in that sort of mood.' Kenneth sounded bitter. 'So we have a spineless nonentity for a manager and a dangerous maniac for a director.'

'Take it easy, Kenneth.' Jim was alarmed at the turn the conversation was taking. 'Those are pretty strong words.'

'They are, but they're considered. I came across one or two like him in the war. I expect you did as well.' Jim nodded. 'Then you know as well as I do you don't get on the wrong side of them.'

'So what was it all about? It sounds as if you were just a lightning rod for something that had happened elsewhere.'

'Very well put, Jim. Very well put. But . . . I don't know . . . I wish I knew.' Kenneth turned back towards the office. 'I heard him and Last having words afterwards. Truth to tell, I was still raging or I would have listened a lot more carefully. You know, you can hear a lot of what goes on in that office from where I sit – especially the way Last roars down the phone.' His sidelong glance smacked of defiance. 'You'll find it's the only way you learn anything round here.'

'And did you learn anything?'

'Not really; it seemed to be a private quarrel. But from what I heard he seemed to be doubting Last's judgement about people.' For the first time Kenneth smiled, although he patently didn't find the subject funny. 'It was probably about me.' He was silent for a moment or two. 'As I say, I was still fuming about being bawled out in front of everyone, so I didn't pay a lot of attention. Oh, I do remember Lattimer-Williams shouting about somebody called Gould.' Again Kenneth smiled, but this time with considerably more warmth. 'And he called Last a stupid bastard, I heard that all right. He kept repeating "remember Gould", "remember Gould", and then I think what he said was "I always had him tagged as a wrong un." He intercepted Jim's questioning glance. 'No, I don't know anybody called Gould. It must be someone outside the firm.'

For a couple of minutes Jim hovered outside Last's office. Did he really need to see him this afternoon? After all that Kenneth had recounted he might well be in a bad mood. Mentally he shook himself. Of course he had to see him; some of the documents required his signature. The work of the office needed to go on what-ever the manager was feeling like. Jim knocked on the door. The surface of Last's desk was completely clear but for what looked like a large photograph album. It was hurriedly shut as Jim came in. 'Some documents for your signature, Mr Last.'

The manager indicated a space by the album. 'Leave them there, Thornton.'

'There are one or two points I need to explain.'

Last listened as the various problems were outlined. Unusually he didn't query anything, but just went ahead and signed. Finally he put his fountain pen to one side, evidently wishing to chat. 'Which regiment were you in, Thornton?'

Jim was surprised; normally Last wasn't one for small talk. 'I was in the Leeds Pals battalion.'

Genuine shock showed on Last's features. 'Were you in . . . ?'

Jim didn't let him finish. 'I was. What was left of the battalion was broken up and I ended the war in the Yorkshire Light Infantry.'

A sombre silence descended, broken only when Last decided to pursue the subject. 'You were a sergeant, weren't you?' It was obviously a rhetorical question because he pushed straight on. 'Non-commissioned officers are the backbone of the British army, I always say.' Jim felt very uncomfortable. He didn't know which was worse, Last his usual pernickety self or trying to patronise him. Finally the manager patted the photograph album and it became clear where the conversation was leading. 'It's my regimental reunion this weekend. I may be leaving the office early this afternoon.' He opened the album and Jim could see photographs of what he took to be groups of officers. 'Surprising how you forget people as the years roll on. I've just been familiarising myself with some of the faces.' The chuckle was genuine. 'It wouldn't do to get the name wrong of someone you've shared a trench with.'

'I suppose not.' Jim felt some response was called for, but didn't really wish to prolong the conversation.

His manager didn't take the hint, but continued to talk as he turned over the pages. 'So I take it you haven't been to any reunions?'

Jim decided to be diplomatic. 'Not up to now.'

'Pity. You make friendships that last a lifetime.' Last focused on one particular photograph. Peering across, Jim found he could manage to read some of the names underneath it. There was a double-barrelled name that he was sure was Lattimer-Williams, and the Lord Eastermain also stood out. Beyond that it was difficult, but one shorter name attracted his attention. He followed the letters, trying to make it out. Was it Good or Gold? No, there were five letters. It had to be Gould.

'Mystery solved, Kenneth.' Jim adopted a stage whisper as he returned to the main office. 'Gould is one of Last's old army chums.'

'He told you that!' The astonishment showed on Kenneth's face.

'Of course not, but he's off to some army reunion dinner tonight. He had this album of photographs on his desk.' The other man's raised eyebrows made him a little testy. 'And before you ask, no, he didn't show me anything, but I was able to read some of the names from across the desk.'

'Upside down? Are you sure you got it right?'

'Yes, I'm sure. Look, do you want to hear what I've got to say or not?' Kenneth made a placatory gesture so Jim continued. 'It was a group of officers. I could make out Eastermain and Lattimer-Williams and this fellow Gould.'

Kenneth pushed away the papers on which he had been working and leaned back in his chair. He seemed to have recovered his humour. 'Well, it explains why L-W was in the office. It certainly wasn't for work.' Something was obviously amusing him. 'We can only hope they all have a pleasant evening, and that if Gould is murdered they have the decency to leave it until after the port is circulated.'

CHAPTER FOURTEEN

RON STARED ACROSS the street at the office opposite. Should he take a closer look? After all, what on earth could a stranger walking in off the street hope to find out about De Villiers & Last. Besides, Rose was right: he had better be cautious. If Eastermain and his friends really had used their influence to get him his job, then it was quite within their powers to have him sacked if they found him nosing about in their affairs.

He hovered on the edge of the pavement trying to make up his mind, then a gap in the traffic made the decision for him. Quickly he dodged across the street, but once at the other side he was disappointed to find the plaque outside the door contained nothing more than the firm's name. Just inside he could see a uniformed messenger. Plainly if he wanted more information he would have to venture in. But what pretext could he use? It was then that he thought of the war.

'Can I help you?' The messenger's tone was suspicious.

'Is Mr Lattimer-Williams in?' Ron was banking on the answer being 'no' and happily he was right. 'That's a pity. I was hoping to see him.' He intercepted the enquiring glance and for once hoped he didn't look too young. 'I knew him in the war.'

The suspicion evaporated. 'You were in the Wessex Yeomanry? Don't mind me asking, but are you after a job?'

Ron gave a non-committal smile. 'Well, I was hoping . . .'

The messenger was all sympathy now. 'Would you like me to see if our Mr Last is free? He was in the regiment as well.'

'Thanks, but it's really Mr Lattimer-Williams I need to talk to. He and I . . . well . . .' There was a nod of understanding from the other man. Ron made as if to leave, then appeared to think of something else. He hoped his acting wasn't too hammed up. 'Are there any other ex-officers in the firm. I might know the names.'

No, sorry, there's only those two and of course the chairman, Lord Eastermain.' The street door behind them opened and the messenger called over Ron's shoulder to greet the new arrival. 'Afternoon, Mr Thornton.'

Every instinct told Ron to turn, but he resisted it. It was only when the footsteps had progressed quite a way up the stairs that he slowly glanced round. It was just a glimpse, as the figure turned to climb the next flight. He had only seen the person once before, and then only for a few minutes, but it was enough. James Thornton, ex-engine driver, was now employed in a stockbrokers' office of all places.

He gathered enough of his wits together to ask a question. 'Was he in the Yeomanry as well?'

'Him? No, that's Mr Thornton. He started about three months ago in Special Issues. To be honest, I don't know his background,' he winked, 'but pound to a penny he's ex -army as well.'

'You did what?' True, she wasn't looking at him open-mouthed, but he knew that was exactly the way she was feeling. 'You just walked into that firm and started to question the messenger?'

'And see what I discovered. James Thornton, the driver of that train, now has a job with them. It proves that he was paid off as well. And not just paid off in any old way. For an engine driver to make a straight career swap into a stockbroker's office must be some sort of record. The only thing I can think of is that they need to have him where they can keep an eye on him. He must know an awful lot.' Ron looked mightily pleased with himself. 'I must say it's quite satisfying when your predictions work out.'

He was to meet Rose's aunt for the first time, and they had stopped halfway along the avenue where she lived. Eventually she found her voice. 'Have your predictions extended to what's likely to happen if any of them find out what you've been up to?'

'I told you before; I was very careful.'

'Careful?' The scorn in her voice was palpable. 'I thought we had an understanding.'

'We do. You know that. I meant every word the other night.'

'Well, you have a strange way of demonstrating it.'

Ron was starting to become irritated. 'I just don't see the connection between me following up something that might become a big story at some stage and our getting married . . .' He paused quite deliberately. '. . . At some stage.'

'So you feel like that. Don't worry: I'm certainly not going to hold someone to an arrangement they've had second thoughts about.' Flushed, she set off again down the road.

Ron was alarmed. 'Rose! Rose, please don't be like that. I've haven't had second thoughts.' By now he was hurrying to catch her up, and their raised voices were attracting curious looks from passers-by. He caught her arm, and eventually she allowed herself to be pacified. 'Just explain what you find so,' he searched for the appropriate word, 'so alarming about my doing a bit of detective work.'

Rose stopped again. 'We'd better settle this before we reach my aunt's. Ron, if we're to get married I might be able to work for a year or two before . . . or if . . . we have a family. And might is the operative word: you know as well as I do that a lot of organisations just won't have married women working for them. The point is, we're likely to be totally dependent on your income. I don't have any private means and neither do you.'

'My job's safe. I'm getting on well. As I get more experience there's always a chance of promotion or moving into a new area . . .'

She interrupted. 'Your job's safe at the moment, but how long is that going to last if you persist in taking chances by following up that story?'

'But I'm not taking . . .'

'Just listen to me, Ron. I haven't talked about this before, but all the time I was growing up my mother was worried sick about money. Dad didn't have a regular salary as a stringer.' Some of her anger was ebbing away, but he could see it was being replaced by a steely determination. 'Generally he earned enough, but . . . but she could never depend on it and she was always the one who had to manage the household finances. Year after year I saw what that did to her.' Her voice dropped as someone cycled past. 'Ron, that isn't going to happen to me.'

Several times he started to reply, eventually managing to blurt out, 'So what are you trying to say?'

'What I'm trying to say is that if we're serious about each other then digging into this mystery has got to stop.' She saw the hurt look in Ron's eyes and tried to soften the blow. 'You've collected a lot of information. That will still be there. One day it will make a good book, perhaps, but not now and not in the immediate future.'

He tried to reply, but all he could utter was a mumbled response. 'I didn't know you felt so strongly.'

'I do, Ron. If you ever start investigating this again then both of us must agree to it.' Her eyes held his and wouldn't leave them. 'Do you promise?'

'Rose, this is silly. We're grown-ups. All this promising business is for children.'

'Do you promise?'

He was beaten and he knew it. 'All right, I promise.' It was two o'clock in the afternoon, in a respectable suburban avenue and with a steady flow of people passing by, but this time it was she who kissed him.

CHAPTER FIFTEEN

HE WOULD RATHER have travelled down by train, but Ellen had been insistent. 'Why spend all that money on a car then go on the railway?' In the end Jim had given in, though in truth he didn't much like driving. In any event a Whit Monday bank holiday was hardly the ideal day to take a car down to Brighton. The numbers of cars must have doubled in the six years since they'd moved south. 'Idiot . . . !' He braked hard as an open roadster cut in front of him, forcing its way into the queue of cars waiting to turn right. 'Much good it'll do him.'

Ellen glanced over and frowned slightly. 'Are we going to have to wait long?'

'About ten minutes or so.' He surveyed the queue ahead. The country was supposed to be in depression yet half of south London seemed to be on the move. But it was a different world down here. All those years in Leeds, even on good pay as an engine driver, never provided complete insulation from the fear of poverty and hard times. Here – for most of the time – you could convince yourself of the unreality of that other world. All those semis going up in the new suburbs; factories being built all over the place; above all the City itself with its bustle and money-making. Yes, they had made a good decision. Then Jim's mind moved on to other things – something that had become second nature when the circumstances of their move came to the fore-front of his thoughts.

Maureen was becoming fretful, but it was a long drive for a four year old. Ellen leaned over to the back seat to calm her down. 'Why

on earth don't you get in the back with her? I can pull in along here.'
Jim's question was futile and he knew it.

'You know I like sitting in the front. Besides, she has more room
when I'm sitting here and she can play with her dolls.'

Ellen's tone effectively closed the subject and he didn't respond.
In matters relating to the child, the responsibility was hers alone.
This was not something that had been discussed: like most things in
their lives it was an unspoken agreement – just as he looked after
finances and she looked after the home. Still, he liked it that way
and so did she, or at least she had never complained. Not like some
of those young and not so young women secretaries in the office.
They described themselves as modern women, but heaven help their
husbands. The traffic lights were at red, and without thinking Jim
leaned over and gave his wife a peck on the cheek. She looked
amazed, for he was not given to shows of public affection. 'Just
thinking how lucky I am, love.' The words came out quickly to
cover his confusion.

The pace became slower as they approached the outskirts of
Brighton. 'I've packed some sandwiches for later, but I thought we
could eat in a café when we get there.' Ellen looked at him
anxiously, for even though he never kept her short of money she
could never entirely shake off the ingrained habit of frugality.

'Of course we will. We'll have a tip-top lunch.' He looked at her
affectionately, knowing full well what lay behind her comment.
Sometimes he felt she really ought to know more about their
finances. They were actually very well off – and some of their money
ought to be doing something useful rather than just lying round in
the bank account. Not that he would venture into the stock market:
a lot of very successful men had gone down in 1929. Two of them
were working in the office as clerks – and very grateful for the
chance at that.

Jim's mind went back to that fateful time six years ago, so bad for
so many, so good for him. Ellen had accepted what he had told her:
that he had helped the police with their investigations into the

unknown children, and that as a result of those investigations deep embarrassment had been caused to some very high-up people. The job had been his reward for being discreet. Of course he knew Ellen didn't really believe it was as simple as that, as she was no fool, but she didn't pursue the matter. He certainly knew there was more to it: he probably knew, or at least suspected, more than that copper Maguire. After all, he and he alone could remember what and who he had seen on that platform all those years ago. Sometimes he wished he couldn't.

'I'm hungry.' Maureen's little voice piped up from the back.

'We'll soon be there. What would you like?'

In her eagerness to make her choice heard, Maureen tried to clamber between the seats and into the front. Jim put out his hand and held her back, laughing at her eagerness. 'I want chips, Daddy. Lots of chips.'

Ellen's voice had a note of reproof, but she too was smiling. 'Girls who are good sit on the seat when they're told to, and then they might get chips.'

It was hot. Ellen put her head back on the deckchair, tempted to doze off. Instead she fixed her eyes on Maureen playing at the water's edge under her father's watchful gaze. He was really good with her. Even over the hubbub of the crowded beach she could make out Maureen's shrieks of dismay as a bigger wave washed up her legs. Things would have been so different if they had had to stay up north. She knew Jamie had been uneasy about the reasons behind their move – not that he had confided in her, but she had sensed it. A sudden shout roused her just in time to see Maureen skipping out of the way of another wave, and then the two of them making their way laughing and smiling back up the beach. Jamie really was much more relaxed nowadays. She pulled the towel out of her bag as he led a shivering Maureen back up the beach.

'Mummy, I was in the sea up to here.' She raised her hands to the top of her chest. 'I was really. Wasn't I, Daddy?' She turned to her father for confirmation.

'She was indeed. Be swimming sometime soon, I shouldn't wonder.' He gave his daughter a hug and looked at Ellen. 'Can you manage for ten minutes? I want to get a paper up on the prom.'

Ellen towelled Maureen vigorously. 'Don't be any longer. I'll be getting the sandwiches out once she's dry and dressed.'

The shop was doing good business, but it was mainly children buying sweets and somewhat to his annoyance he had to queue up behind them all. He really had come up on a whim as he didn't often buy papers. There were two on display, the *Evening Argus* and the *Southern Daily News*. The headlines in the *Argus* were political, and a long aversion to all things political made him choose the other paper. Leaning on the prom railings Jim saw that he had made a good choice: it was a very 'newsy' paper that took in a wide swathe of south Sussex. He flicked through, focusing especially on one or two of the juicier court cases, and was just about to close it when he glimpsed a picture. The quality wasn't good and it was hard to pick anyone out of the group. He looked at it intently: surely he must be mistaken. Then he noticed the individual photo beneath. There was no mistake. It was 'Anthony'. Then the real name registered, and his breath came out in a slow sigh. So that was who he really was. Jim sat down on a bench and tried to re-focus his eyes on the newspaper. It had been a memorial service. Certain phrases lodged in his consciousness. 'Unveiling of memorial plaque.' 'Comrades in arms.' 'Dreadful loss to the county.' 'Commemoration of tragic accident.' Then one line above all others leapt out: 'Eastmead railway disaster'. Eastmead! He must make sense of this. Who were they commemorating?

'Jamie?'

He turned to see Ellen and the small accusing head of Maureen staring at him through the railings.

'Daddy, we've been waiting for ages!'

Reluctantly he folded the paper. 'Sorry, love. I lost track of time.'

He ate the sandwiches mechanically and responded to his daughter's chatter, but in such a distant way that Ellen looked at him anxiously. 'Are you all right, Jamie?'

'Yes. Just something on my mind. I'll tell you about it later.'

Then Maureen tucked her head on her mother's lap, and gradually the questions gave way to murmurs and then to slow, regular breathing. Ellen stroked her hair and they exchanged glances.

'I have to finish reading this.' Ellen nodded, and he opened the paper again. He scanned the article and then he found who was being commemorated. He ought to have guessed: it was Last's brother. The pieces fell into place in a regular cascade. So that was how he had got the job. It wasn't a favour from friends; he was being employed by the family, so to speak. No wonder they felt safe even though he knew what he did: they were taking no risks as he was under constant surveillance. If his behaviour gave cause for alarm they would know instantly. Then his eye fell on the list of those contributing to the plaque and yet another familiar name jumped out. True, he didn't see him often – just a glimpse really when he came to board meetings. But if people at that political level were involved no wonder they were able to ignore the rules that governed little people like him. But who were 'they'? He now knew three of the names, but the purpose, the background . . . ? Ellen was gazing at him expectantly. 'Nearly finished, love. Just another couple of paragraphs.' Jim came to the end and slowly folded the paper, desperately trying to sort out the implications of what he had read. One thing was sure: whether she liked it or not his wife would have to be fully involved. But before he told her he needed to think it through. To decide what action they needed to take.

'Ellen, there's a lot to talk about.' He caught the look of alarm. 'Don't worry. It's just something I've found out about my job. We'll talk about it tonight after the little one is in bed.' Maureen started to stir. 'I think we ought to be heading home now.'

He tucked in the coverlet and bent down to kiss his daughter. She was already asleep. Tiptoeing towards the door, Jim carefully avoided the floorboard that creaked. Ellen was waiting on the landing, and she peeped in once more before quietly closing the door. 'Bless her heart, she's done in. Sorry I couldn't keep her awake in the car.'

'Not your fault, love. Besides, it's the seaside. All that sun and playing. Don't you remember what it was like?'

'We hardly ever got to the seaside when I was a girl. It was too far to Scarborough or Filey. I only remember going once on a Sunday school trip.' She glared at him in mock-exasperation. 'Not like you southerners. Always off to Margate or Broadstairs, I expect.'

Jim ruffled her hair affectionately. 'Broadstairs was much too posh for our family, and I never liked Margate much.' Then he remembered the revelation the day had brought. 'Look, we have things to talk about. Maybe you should put the kettle on.'

Ellen regarded him intently as he sipped his tea. She had always suspected there was far more to their move down south than Jamie had told her. Now it seemed she was about to find out more. At long last he finished his tea and took a deep breath. 'Ellen, what I told you before was true. About those children they couldn't identify, I mean.' There was a long pause, which she knew better than to interrupt. 'The only thing is I didn't tell you the whole truth.' He corrected himself. 'Or, at least, the bit of the truth I know about.'

The alarm showed on her face. 'Jamie, it's not criminal is it?'

'No, it's not criminal, or not as far as I'm aware. You remember me telling you that I saw the children get on the train at Birmingham, and there were some people around who might or might not have been with them. You remember Maguire came up to Leeds to see me? He was very interested in them; he was trying to find out if I recognised anyone.'

'And did you?'

'Not then, but I met one of them afterwards. He was that fellow Anthony who met me in York.'

'You didn't tell me that, Jamie.' There was a note of reproach in Ellen's voice.

'No, I didn't. Looking back, I suppose I should have, but that's water under the bridge. The important thing is I found out more today.' Wordlessly he handed over the copy of the *Southern Daily News* and indicated the headline.

She finished reading and looked up puzzled. 'The article's about somebody called Last. Do you think he's related to your boss?'

'Yes, he is. He's – or rather he was – his brother. More to the point, he's the one who was killed at Eastmead.' She still looked mystified. 'Don't you see? I don't recognise him and I can't prove it, but I bet he was one of the men I saw that night.'

'Aren't you jumping to conclusions, Jamie?'

'No, I'm not. Because the other man, the one I recognised as Anthony, is in this photograph.' Jim pointed to a figure. 'See, his real name is Captain Lattimer-Williams and he just happens to be a director of the company.' Ellen continued to look perplexed, driving him to new depths of exasperation. 'For heaven's sake, look at this other name: the Lord Eastermain of Penrick.'

The penny dropped. 'Isn't he in the company as well?'

'He is indeed. He's the chairman.'

'But I don't understand. What does it all mean, Jamie?'

'I'm not totally sure. But one thing's clear: I wasn't just fixed up with any old job. It was a job where this lot could keep an eye on me all the time.'

'But why?'

Ellen's question was one that Jim was desperately trying to answer himself. 'If I knew that, love, we wouldn't be sitting here trying to make sense of it all. But I'm beginning to have doubts that it just concerns those children.' He stood up and collected the cups. 'Still, we can go round in circles on that one. What we need to decide is what we're going to do.'

'Do? What do you mean? What can we do?' The clattering of crockery in the kitchen told her that she hadn't been heard. She was just about to shout a little louder when Jim re-appeared.

'It's all right, I did hear.' He walked over to the bookcase, glancing distractedly at it. Then he seemed to reach some sort of decision. 'Look, Ellen, I'm not happy about this. Not happy at all.' She tried to interrupt but he ploughed on regardless. 'We have a fair bit of money in the bank account and it's building up each month. What I want to do is put it in another account.' He seemed to be thinking as he spoke. 'In a different bank. In a different part of the country, even. Then if we ever need to move in a hurry we have somewhere to go to and a handy nest egg to live on.'

She looked doubtful. 'Well, if you're sure.'

'No, I'm not sure. Not sure at all. But I know one thing: I'd feel much happier.'

CHAPTER SIXTEEN

'JOHN! AMELIA! Stop that now or Daddy will get cross!' The three-year-old twins temporarily broke off their tug of war over a teddy bear, only to continue again with renewed vigour once their father's attention had returned to his newspaper.

'You two are going to bed for your afternoon nap.' Rose marched over to gather up her children.

'Do you want a hand?' Ron hoped his offer didn't sound too counterfeit.

'It's all right, Ron, I'll go up as well.' Christine put down her crochet pattern and followed her sister up the stairs.

Ron picked up the paper again, but his concentration had gone and he put it to one side. It had seemed such a good idea to have a family holiday down in Dorset. He liked the county, the bed and breakfast was fine and the town was just the right size: all the facilities you needed, but easy to get out into the countryside. The weather was good as well. So why did he feel so irritable? Probably it was Christine. Normally he got on well with her and it had seemed a good idea to invite her along, but things weren't working out. No one had talked about it openly, but both he and Rose had assumed that Christine would be prepared to babysit for the odd evening, leaving them free to go out together. It hadn't happened: not once had she offered to look after the children. Upstairs there was the sound of a rather petulant cry followed by some sharp words from Rose. John always resisted going to sleep. Ron shifted the armchair back to avoid an annoying shaft of sunlight. Such a lovely afternoon, but short of asking Christine directly there was no chance that he and Rose would be able to take a walk. Well, that was families: they would know better next time.

'Anything in the paper?' Rose slumped into a chair.

He passed it over. 'Have a read yourself. The Germans have invaded the Rhineland.'

'Is that serious?' Christine looked worried. 'It's only how many years . . .'

She started to do some calculations, but it was Ron who answered for her. 'It's eighteen years since the last lot ended and, yes, I think it's serious.'

'What, do you honestly think there'll be another war?' This time it was Rose's turn to be alarmed.

'Not immediately,' Ron was sombre. 'But the way things are going I reckon there's every chance a few years down the line.'

'But they won't let it happen, will they? I mean, the League of Nations will surely. . .' Rose faltered, not quite sure what the League of Nations was or was not doing.

Ron could see that they were both scared and adopted a more positive tone. 'Whatever happens it won't be for a long time, and you're right, Rose, there's too much at stake for politicians to let Europe go up in flames again.'

He was anxious to get off the subject but she wouldn't let go. 'If there's conscription as there was before, how old do you have to be not to do it?'

This was one question Ron would have preferred to remain unanswered, but Christine put her oar in. 'Don't you remember Mum going on about that cousin of hers? He got out of it because he was over forty-one.'

'Forty-one!' Rose looked stricken. 'Ron, you're only thirty-five.'

'Look, you two, this conversation is ridiculous. First, there's no war – nor likely to be one for quite a few years, if at all. As for the likelihood of my being conscripted . . .' His exasperation must have shown because the women went quiet. 'Anyway, we're on holiday, and it's a great afternoon. Don't you two want to take a walk somewhere?' He hoped Christine would take the hint and offer to stay behind, but as ever she didn't.

Instead it was Rose who answered. 'I'm a bit tired, Ron, but I don't mind if you want to go out by yourself.'

Ron decided to walk down towards the river. There were better views there and the route led away from the main road. His mind was still churning round thoughts of Christine and her selfishness, and only slowly did the shouted orders and the stamp of marching feet permeate his consciousness. He was abreast of a barracks of some sort. Mildly curious, he glanced at the sign beside the gate, which read 'Wessex Yeomanry Depot'. It took a while for the penny to drop. That was the regiment, the one those officers had been in. The ones whom he suspected of being involved in shipping those children to Australia. He stood for a while as the memories came flooding back. Of course he had kept his word to Rose. From the day she had given him the ultimatum he had dropped the investigation. She had been right: it was too risky; and given her stand there was no way he could have risked losing her. Everything he had discovered was still in a file in the attic. He hadn't looked at it for years, but it was surprising just how much he could still call to mind.

A corporal came out of the guard house, saw him standing there and marched over. 'The museum doesn't close until five, sir.'

'Sorry?'

'The regimental museum, sir. I assumed that was what you were looking for. It's about two hundred yards back down the road.' He pointed to a building outside the barracks complex.

'Thank you.' For all of thirty seconds Ron followed the directions without thinking of any consequences; then he stopped. He had promised Rose that they would both need to agree before he engaged in any more digging. But that was crazy. It had been six years ago. And besides he wasn't digging: he was on holiday and visiting an army museum out of interest.

It was a cavernous place with room after room filled with regimental memorabilia. Fascinating though the Peninsula War or the campaign in the Sudan might be to the military historian, Ron was anxious to find material relating to the Great War. At last he found it, but where to start? There were photographs on every wall and in every alcove, as well as volume after volume of regimental history. Despairingly he glanced at his watch. He needed to be back by five: Rose would expect him to be around to take the twins for a walk before their bath and tea. He had just over an hour.

'Looking for anything in particular, sir?' A greying man in sergeant's uniform emerged from behind a set of shelves.

He was stuck for words. 'Yes . . . just checking on relatives from the war.'

'Do you know which battalion?'

'No . . .' Ron had an inspiration. 'That is, I think the colonel's name was Eastermain.'

'Ah – the Lord Eastermain?' Ron nodded. 'Yes, I've met him. He comes in from time to time. It's the second battalion you want. If you'll just follow me.' The sergeant led the way to yet another alcove. 'We still have work to do, but there are quite a few photographs . . .' He squinted at one such fading photograph and spoke rather querulously. 'What a place to put it: it gets far too much light there. Anyway, that's Lord Eastermain.' His finger indicated a figure with a walking stick, in front of a group of men who all appeared to be drinking from a wide variety of containers. One was even brandishing a champagne bottle. In the background was an imposing château with a large and expensive looking car parked in front of it.

'They look very happy.' Ron tried to get the sergeant to open up a bit. 'Were they going on leave or something? That car doesn't look like an ordinary army staff car to me.'

'No. The picture was taken on Armistice Day, and they were out of the line at the time. You can see that by the château behind them. As for the car . . .' The sergeant peered more closely at the photograph. 'I think it's a Bentley, and not an ordinary one at that. The normal colour would be black but that looks grey to me. Probably some bigwig from rear echelon.' He stepped back and became quite conversational. 'You know, quite a lot of well-connected people had jobs – if you can call it that – carrying dispatches up to divisional headquarters. Some of them even had their own transport, like here. As to who he was . . .' He smiled and shrugged his shoulders. 'But whoever he was, he was obviously a friend. You can see he's left his own glass on top of the car.'

It was Ron's turn to study the picture more closely. 'So he has.' He decided to try a little flattery to see if any more information was forthcoming. 'That was very observant of you, sergeant. I don't think I'd have spotted it. And you have no idea who it might have been?"

There was a shake of the head. 'No, but a car like that . . . Let's just say he must have been someone very high up.'

'So I wonder why he isn't in the photograph?'

The sergeant was patience itself. 'Because, sir, he's probably the one taking the photograph.'

'Of course. How silly of me.'

'Now if you'll excuse me.' The sergeant pulled out some binders from under a desk. 'I can't recognise any of the other officers, but these are the scrapbooks for the second battalion. You're welcome to look through them. They're not complete yet – new material comes in all the time – so if you find stuff not stuck down please leave it in place.'

'Thanks. You've been most helpful.'

Ron studied the picture more closely. It would be interesting to know who the person was taking the photograph, but he dismissed it from his mind: it was a side issue. He returned to the figures in the photograph. As the sergeant had said, they were celebrating and using everything from tin mugs to mess tins. He counted the men: there were eight in all, but no names. Maybe they were on the back, but it was under glass: there was no way to check. He was about to turn to the scrapbooks when something struck him. The photograph had been doctored: the right side had a margin, but the left ended abruptly. It had been cut, fairly carefully it was true, but it was obvious nevertheless that someone or some people were missing from that side. Why? He tried to puzzle it out, but eventually gave up.

The scrapbooks were fascinating and poignant. As Ron flicked through the letters and diaries a flavour of the Great War came through strongly. Of course the war had coloured his youth. He had listened to the stories but, now he thought of it, hardly any of them had come directly from soldiers themselves. What he was reading now was the unvarnished truth. One corporal had even kept a record of all the birds he had recognised. There weren't many, and the journal stopped abruptly in July 1916. The Somme! Ron closed the book and replaced it under the desk. He really didn't want to go on.

Again he checked his watch. Another half-hour, then he must go. Reluctantly he opened some of the other books, closing them swiftly if they resembled the first. He was ashamed of his cowardice, but unwilling to allow the power of those raw emotions the opportunity to bridge the years. The last book was different. It contained photographs: individual portraits, group photographs, company photographs. Unlike the letters, he found them strangely comforting. They showed men smiling at the camera, men happy at being recorded for posterity, confident perhaps that they would be part of that posterity.

Then he saw it, the photograph that was on the wall. But this one was complete: there were ten men shown. The photograph was loose so, despite the sergeant's injunction, he picked it out and walked over to compare it. There could be no doubt. But would there be names? Ron turned it over. There were. The Lord Eastermain and Lattimer-Williams he knew, but he pulled out his notebook and recorded the others. Two of the men were called Last. Perhaps they were brothers. He remembered the firm in the City where he had seen Thornton: it was something Last . . . De Villiers & Last; that was it. So there must be connections. Hurriedly he noted the others, before concentrating his attention on the two who had been edited out of the original. One, squatting on one knee, was called Gould, Captain John Gould; the other, standing upright, was a Major James Frobisher. What could they have been guilty of to be cut out of such a momentous photograph?

Conscious of the time, Ron swiftly leafed through some of the other photographs. They were mainly post-war events, regimental reunions and the like. He recognised some people, even in dress uniforms, but there seemed to be no further clues. He sat back idly replacing everything in its correct order. They seemed to have used the same photographer for all their functions: James Frobisher Ltd of New Bond Street. James Frobisher! It had to be him: the officer who was pictured in the photograph. It would be too much of a coincidence not to be. And New Bond Street – he must be a society photographer.

'Don't see you in here often, Ron. What are you after?' Ellis Grindrod, the art editor, was a Lancastrian and made a virtue out of being direct.

'Do I have to be after anything, Ellis?'

'Course you do. Now come on, I'm busy.'

Ron decided to be equally direct. 'Do you know a photographer called James Frobisher?'

Ellis paused briefly in checking some advertising graphics before continuing. 'Ron, how old are you?'

'What's that got to do with it?'

'Never mind about that. How old are you?'

Sheer cussedness made him toy with the idea of adding ten years, but he decided against it. 'If you must know, I'm thirty-five.'

'And you joined the paper when?'

'It was 1929. Ellis, where on earth is this leading?'

Satisfied, the art editor put down the copy and finally gave Ron his full attention. 'That explains it. You're too young to know.'

'Know about what?'

'The scandal.' Irritated, he waved off yet another interruption. 'Yes, I do know about Frobisher.' Ellis's face was a study in concentration. 'He was a great photographer – as far as portraiture was concerned, that is. He was also quite a character. Came from a charmed background, of course. You know the sort of thing I mean, upper crust, a bit of a dilettante and well connected in all sorts of ways. I think he played cricket for Hampshire before the war – I need hardly add as an amateur. And he was a war hero as well. You can check in *Who Was Who*, but I think you'll find he got an MC and bar.'

'Who *was* who'? And you keep referring to him in the past tense. Do you mean . . . ?'

'That he's no longer with us. Now, how can I put this without seeming indelicate.' Ellis put his hands behind his head, swivelled the chair round, then went on, having found the phrase he was searching for. 'Frobisher had certain predilections. Not to put too fine a point on it, he was caught by the police in a gents' toilet some-where down the West End.'

'I see.' Ron's thoughts went back to the photograph.

'Yes. It was 1922. I remember the year because I'd just got this job. Now, normally someone with his connections would have skated away from it all, but . . . I seem to remember the idiot tried to deny it and instead of being dealt with by a magistrate it went to the crown court. Even then he should have been found not guilty . . . host of character witnesses . . . war record . . . all his army chums speaking up for him and so on.'

Ron became impatient; Ellis was dragging it out. 'So what went wrong?'

'One of his army mates went wrong, that's what. Gave evidence against him. He got two years and dropped out of public life. Then the poor devil committed suicide.'

'Can you remember when that was?'

'Not precisely, but it was 1927 or '28.' Ellis swivelled back to face his desk. 'Anyway, what's your interest in all this?'

Ron sounded deliberately vague. 'Oh, it's background for another story. But thanks for filling me in. If you can remember the month it happened I'll be able to check the reports in the library.'

'Oh no you won't.' Ellis grinned. 'His connections couldn't save him from going down, but they could put a stop to publicity. I think you'll find the trial wasn't covered in any of the dailies or the evenings.' His grin became even broader. 'As far as we were concerned, strict instructions came from the very top, and I mean the very top, that nothing was to be reported. So of course everybody immediately took a deep and abiding interest in every last detail. Why do you think I remember so much?'

'We're going down to the Grapes, Ron. Want to join us?'

The paper had just been put to bed and the usual suspects were heading for the pub. Ron waved them away with amused tolerance, thinking back to the days when, more often than not, he would have joined them. 'Drunken sots! Don't tempt me. I've a wife and kids at home.' The badinage continued until they drifted off down the stairs and he was left on his own.

Better be getting home now. He stretched to try and shake off the tiredness, then on impulse reached inside a desk drawer to pull out the old copy of *Country Life*. Although he had known Ellis would be right about news reports, he had asked one of the assistants in the library to check on anything he could come across about Frobisher. The result was interesting, if not particularly illuminating. He turned to the page he had folded back and looked at the photograph again. It was one of the photographer's formal portraits, the subjects a boy and a girl aged, he would guess, about ten and eight. The caption identified them as 'John and Letticia Lattimer-Williams, son and daughter of Captain James and Mrs Marie Lattimer-Williams of Burnhook, Hampshire'. He checked the issue date again: March 1922.

So what had he got so far? Only a lot of odd facts about this coterie of ex-officers. They operated as a sort of old comrades freemasonry, helping each other out in personal and financial fields. As far as the shipping of children to Australia was involved, there were probably only a few prime movers, led by Eastermain. But all would have been aware of it and would no doubt have helped out as and when needed. In one way or another the likelihood was that most of them were also involved in covering up the deaths of those children. As for that photograph in the museum, it was clear why Frobisher had been cut out. And Gould, the other man, must have been the one who gave evidence against him.

Reality started elbowing its way to the forefront of Ron's mind. He had to face it: there wasn't a story – at least not yet. Nothing that would stand up to the cold light of day. And there was one other thing he had better not forget: they had influence, a lot of influence. The last fact depressed him. After all, he had a wife and family to consider now. Rose's words came back to him: words to the effect that if they could pull strings they could also cut them.

If he was ever to get anywhere he would need to delve a whole lot more deeply. So what, if anything, was he going to do about it? And, after all, what was the point of doing anything if that same influence prevented his findings being published? It would be ten years in a couple of years' time . . . Ten years! Ron's heart leapt. That was it! There was bound to be renewed speculation on the anniversary; it was that sort of story. And if there was general interest that surfaced naturally it would be much more difficult to bury the whole thing. But he needed to put something together . . . After all, any promotion was blocked here . . . it was a question of connections . . . if he really wanted to get on . . .

Then thoughts of his wife came up and Ron was back in the depths again. Rose would still be totally against it. Since the birth of their children she had become much more worried about everything. Then he found his emotions see-sawing upwards again. Nothing needed to be done immediately. The anniversary was still two years away – more like two and a half. He would work on the story as time permitted and see where it got him. At an opportune moment he was sure he could talk Rose round. After all, she was ambitious for him as well.

CHAPTER SEVENTEEN

'THORNTON. COULD YOU step into the office a minute?' Jim looked up to see a figure silhouetted in the open door of one of the offices opposite. A door that bore the ornate and, to Jim's mind, over-elaborate lettering: 'J.L.D. Last. General Manager'. He made his way over, puzzling a little at the peremptory nature of the summons; normally Last would have asked his secretary to deliver a message.

'Come in, Thornton. Oh, and close the door behind you.' The office's large plate glass windows faced the street, the amount of light contrasting markedly with the much darker main office. It took a moment or two to adjust his vision, and it was only then that he realised there was another figure in the room; a figure slumped in a swivel chair with his back towards him. 'Thornton, I'd like to formally introduce you to one of our directors, Captain Lattimer-Williams, although I gather you've met before – informally that is.'

Jim felt his throat tighten as the swivel chair turned towards him. 'Nice to see you again.' The figure rose and a hand stretched out, the posture a welcoming one but the face neutral. The face was a little more lined than all those years ago in York and the hair was a little more grey, but the eyes were the same. The eyes that he hadn't been able to take in under the night lights of that platform in Birmingham. Of course, ever since his chance sighting of the newspaper photograph in Brighton he had known who Lattimer-Williams really was, but despite this he found he was ill prepared for this meeting in the flesh. Suddenly he was aware that the expression on

125

'Anthony's' face had changed, the neutrality replaced by suspicion. 'I thought you might have been surprised to see me, Jim?'

'It's you . . . Anthony . . . sorry, Captain Lattimer-Williams.' Jim's words sounded inane and he knew it, but nevertheless they came tumbling out thick and fast.

If Anthony detected fear amid the babble he did not show it, and slowly the look of suspicion started to fade. 'Sorry, Jim. I've been in for the odd meeting from time to time and I really ought to have had a word before . . . but time . . . well, you know how it goes.'

Last's expression indicated that he disapproved of the use of first names. 'Sit down, Thornton.' He indicated the only other chair, which was stiff and upright. 'Now, the reason we wanted a word is that we've been rather anxious about you lately.' He looked at the other figure, who nodded his agreement.

'Yes, Jim. What Mr Last tells me is that lately he feels you've been worried, not to say pre-occupied.' Anthony leaned forward, those eyes boring into his.

'Worried?' Jamie turned to Last. 'Is there a problem with my work?'

It was Lattimer-Williams who answered. 'No, Jim. That's the least of our worries.' Those last words burned into Jim's mind, 'the least of our worries'. Did this mean what he thought it meant? 'You see, we brought you down here. We helped you back on your feet. If there are problems we want to know about them.' His face broke into what would have been a reassuring smile were it not for those eyes.

'No, I don't have any problems – or at least nothing worse than most families have.' Jim decided he had to try and take the offensive. 'Captain Lattimer-Williams, as you recollect I gave certain under-takings before I took the job.' There was an exchange of glances between the two men opposite. 'All I can say is that I have stuck absolutely to those undertakings and intend to continue to do so.' He waited for a response but none came. 'After all, I take it that's the reason for this conversation.'

Again there was a long silence, so long that Jim felt they were waiting for him to continue. Eventually Last spoke. 'Something rather disturbing has come to my notice . . . that is to say, to our notice.' He licked his lips, obviously unsure how to continue. It was Lattimer-Williams who rescued him.

'I think it's cards on the table time, Jim. Don't you?' Once again he leaned forward. 'We're both old soldiers and I'm sure we appreciate plain speaking.' Jim looked uncomprehending. 'We know you're transferring money to a bank account in Yorkshire – a bank that is not the one you currently use. You've been doing it for over two years now.'

Jim was devastated. All his plans, so carefully made, were unravelling. It must be someone in the bank, in Martins. Of course, that was it. They had set up the account. They would have made sure they were in a position to know about something like this from the very start. What a bloody fool he'd been. He was reduced to bluster. 'That's my own affair. What I do with my money is up to me.'

The way he was interrupted was brutal. 'No it isn't, Jim. Not something like this. Don't forget it is, and always has been, a two-way process. We took you in here. Gave you a career. Helped with your defence.' His voice rose and a small fleck of saliva trickled down his chin. 'Yet you talk about an undertaking being given. In fact you've have just assured us that those undertakings will continue to be honoured. And what do we find?' Anthony slapped his hand on the table with a force that made the others start. 'You're making preparations to start a new life. Without telling us. Covering your tracks.' He stood, and started to pace the room – a manoeuvre that only added to the growing sense of menace. 'Now look at it from our point of view. Do you think we should still be happy with your assurances?'

'Just because I choose to make alternative financial arrangements doesn't mean I would go back on my word.' Jim started to feel angry. To be put in this position; made to feel like a criminal – all because of what he chose to do with his own money. Somehow it burst out. 'Those two kids must have very important connections if it leads to this sort of interrogation and you start to question my motives.' He regretted it almost as soon as the words were out of his mouth.

127

He was expecting an outburst, but the question was almost silken. 'I take it you haven't been carrying out any further investigations of your own, Jim?'

He shook his head. 'No, I haven't. But can you blame me for wanting to take steps to secure my family's future? All of this.' He waved his hand round the office. 'The way I got the job. The way you all seem so concerned that one day I might decide to leave the firm. I have to ask myself . . .' He started to falter, then screwed up his courage. 'I have to ask myself if seeing those two kids on the platform that night was the whole of it.'

The response was quiet. Quiet but deadly. 'And what answer did you get to this question you set yourself?'

This time two sets of eyes were on his and he knew his answer would be crucial. 'It has to be that. There was nothing else, was there? But it must be quite a scandal, involving God knows who.'

There wasn't an audible sigh of relief, but Jamie could feel the tension ebbing. Last glanced at Lattimer-Williams, apparently uncertain who should take the lead. Finally it was 'Anthony' who spoke. 'Jim, I'm sorry if this seemed like a major interrogation. I suppose in a way it was.' This was said with what passed for a smile. 'Of course you're right: the background of those children is the key to it all. The key to why we have to take it so seriously. The key to why no one must know anything more. You do understand that, don't you?'

The eyes caught and held his own. There was no smile now, and the pause that followed indicated that a response was expected. Jim nodded. Lattimer-Williams relaxed and the atmosphere lightened. 'You see, I had to assure myself that you hadn't been doing any delving into the subject. That we could still rely on you.' He stretched backward in his chair. 'Speaking for myself, I'm happy to say that I feel we can.'

The whole episode had shown who was in charge, but Last, very much the junior partner, felt it appropriate to chime in. 'Yes, Thornton, bearing in mind the circumstances, what you did was unwise – most unwise – but I think we can put it down', he glanced across at

Lattimer-Williams, 'to an error of judgement. Mind you, there would be a very much better rate of interest in one of Martin's special accounts. Still, what you do with your money is up to you . . .' He tailed off, aware that the other man wanted the last word.

Once again Jim felt those eyes boring into his. 'We'll say no more about any of this. But if, in the future, you choose to do something that you think might give us cause to doubt your assurances, then please have a quiet word with Mr Last. He'll respect any confidences, and it'll avoid any unpleasantness like this in future.' He laughed. It was the first time that Jim had heard him do this. He thought he preferred the stare.

'What now, Jamie?' Ellen had heard him out in total silence, and this was her first question.

'I'll need to think it through.'

'But shouldn't we close that account? Transfer the money back? That way they'll know you've taken heed of what's been said.'

'No. We just keep things the same as at present.' He pre-empted her objections. 'They know what I'm doing, and as long as everything continues as before they won't be suspicious. Besides, surely it's wrong to think that these people know everything. That money's been going out for two years, yet they've only just discovered it. So there can't be a regular informant at the bank. More than likely something or someone has alarmed them, and as a consequence they're checking up on me and, just as likely, Maguire as well.'

'Could it be Maguire?'

'Maybe. But he's got more to lose than me. I'm positive he got a bigger payoff.'

Ellen's calm began to desert her and her voice rose. 'This is stupid. Didn't you get any idea of what it was all about?'

Jim put his arms round her, held her tightly and kissed her. Normally she wasn't demonstrative – kisses were for bed, not for the living room at seven o'clock in the evening – but this time she accepted, even responded a little. It was so out of the ordinary that for a moment he was tempted to put off what he was about to say, which would certainly kill off any embryonic passion. But he knew it had to be said and now was the time to say it. 'Today confirmed one thing. Lattimer-Williams let slip that they helped in my defence. So that anonymous two hundred and fifty pounds my barrister got was from them. And I learned something else. Something they didn't intend me to learn.' Ellen pulled away, his tone serving as a warning. 'They wanted me to focus on those children as being the only reason for all this secrecy, all this hole-in-corner nonsense, and they could hardly hide their relief when I went along with it.' Jim put his arms round her again. 'Before today I only suspected there was more to it than these children. Now I know there is.'

CHAPTER EIGHTEEN

'THEY CAN'T LET it happen again.' Rose's mother looked up in panic from her newspaper.

Ron tried to soothe her. 'Nothing has happened yet – at least not to us. All the politicians are working for peace. I really don't think that 1939 will be the year we go to war again.' He hoped he sounded more confident than he felt.

'But it says here that Germany and Italy have formed an alliance.' She glared at Ron as though he was personally responsible. 'Now why would they do that if they were after peace?'

'Look, there's a lot of bluffing going on. They want everybody else to think they're preparing for war. And we want them to think we'll be ready for them. I mean, look at the way we announced conscription at the end of April.'

'Well, it's June now, so it doesn't seem to have fooled them.' Rose received an icy stare from her husband for her unhelpful interjection.

The French windows suddenly burst open and young John appeared, clutching a cricket bat. 'Dad. Dad. You promised to play with me this afternoon.'

A reproachful wail from his sister Amelia indicated that she was following close behind. 'No, he was going to mend my doll.' She put her tongue out at her brother and produced her trump card. 'The one that you dropped.'

The judgement of Solomon was called for. 'We're not going to do either. Instead,' Ron had to shout to make himself heard, 'instead . . . we're going down to the common for a walk.' He caught Rose's eye. 'Coming?'

Cricket and dolls forgotten, the children were soon scampering on ahead. Rose took the opportunity to quiz him. 'Do you really think there's any chance of avoiding war?'

'No, as a matter of fact I don't. And you might have kept quiet while I was trying to reassure your mother.'

'Sorry.'

This subdued contrition was, to say the least, untypical. He wondered if she was feeling all right. 'More to the point, Rose, we need to have a heart to heart about this.' She was busy watching the children and didn't answer immediately. 'The kids are fine over there watching the model boats. Come on, the grass is dry: we can sit here.'

His wife's face was drawn. 'You're making it all sound very bad.'

'It's not that, Rose, but we need to take sensible precautions.' He started to speak several times, then finally blurted it out. 'If the war starts – and the people who count think it will – London and most of the other big cities will be bombed.'

'How can you be sure? Her face betrayed her shock. 'I know the newspapers are full of it, but surely a lot is speculation?'

'No. Quite a lot of the great and the good are skipping to America.'

'Ron, how can you say that?'

'Because it's true, that's why. I hear that most of the transatlantic liners are booked up for months in advance.' He laughed without mirth. 'I dare say if we're all proved wrong they'll be back just as quickly.'

'So what can we do? I take it you're not suggesting we go to America?'

'No, but . . .' He steeled himself to say it, knowing the reaction it would provoke. 'You could go to your mother's with the children.'

Rose looked stunned. 'Are you serious? . . . No. That's definitely not going to happen. Leave you here on your own? What do you take me for?'

'Please listen to me. Whatever you feel, please listen to me.' Her protests died down – along with her colour – as he explained. That the government was already making contingency plans to deal with the massive civilian casualties that were expected. That schemes were afoot to organise mass evacuations of children from the cities to safety in the countryside. That if this were to happen children would be evacuated on their own to God knows where. Did she want that to happen? Wouldn't it be better to move to Taunton in advance to get the kids settled in?

Eventually Rose put her hands over her ears. 'Stop. Please stop.' She fixed her eyes on the children and for a long time didn't speak. 'How do you know all this, Ron? You're not a member of the government, and if it's true why didn't you say something before?'

'I'm in the newspaper business. We don't get all the information but we pick up a lot. Most of it we can't print because of D Notices.'

'D Notices?'

'That's the censorship system.' Absentmindedly he chewed a blade of grass. 'The reason I didn't say anything before was because I didn't want to worry you. Up to now there was always a chance it wouldn't come to this.'

'But not now?' Ron shook his head and, musing, she turned back to the activity by the boating lake. 'I suppose it would be for the best. After all, if things turn out not to be too bad we could always come back here. And they like going to Grandma's. She always does the sorts of things we don't have time for.' Rose was rationalising the situation even as she spoke. 'Mum's going back down there at the end of the week.' Then she reached a decision. 'I'll speak to her about it tomorrow.'

Ron put his arm round his wife and leaned over to try and give her a kiss. 'We must have tired them out today. They haven't woken up once.'

'So far.'

'All right, so far. But you don't have to sit there all tense, waiting for someone to cry.' This time he did manage to kiss her, only to have her turn her head away. Exasperated, he slumped back on the pillow. 'Aren't you the great romantic?'

'Romance can wait for a while. We need to talk.'

'About what? Didn't we sort it all out this afternoon?'

'Yes, but before I talk to Mum we need to agree when the best time is to go. If possible I'd like the children to finish here at the end of the summer term, then go down during August.'

'That sounds fine to me.'

'But do we have that sort of time?'

'I don't know, Rose.' Then he realised how grumpy he sounded. 'I suppose so. We might as well work on that assumption. Any more questions?'

'Just one. Could we get away somewhere together for a few days after we go to Taunton?'

'You mean just us? Leave the children with your mother?' It took Ron a little while to come to terms with the idea. 'Would she cope?'

'Of course she would, and Christine's there to help.' She swept aside the objections. 'She's fine as long as she doesn't have the primary responsibility.'

He lay there for a while thinking about the implications. 'I don't think there'll be any problem with me taking some leave. That just leaves the problem of where we go.'

'Oh, you choose. I really don't mind as long as it's a complete change.' Rose yawned. 'And that we can afford it, of course.'

The possibilities ebbed through Ron's mind until he suddenly thought of Salcombe. Memories came back of his visit to the regimental museum in Dorset, and his determination to produce something by the tenth anniversary of the accident. Much to his surprise it had taken very little effort to overcome Rose's objections: the passage of time seemed to have lessened her fears. In the event it had all been in vain, for without the children's names there just wasn't a story, and in London at any rate there were no more leads to be followed. He had considered and rejected the idea of trying to contact Thornton: despite the fact that it had been ten years, those ex-officers might still be able to make things awkward for him. But Salcombe, now that was something else. Ron had no idea if Maguire was still living there, or his address or, for that matter, if he would have any useful information. But if he was still around then a trawl through the telephone book should find him. And the way the world was going, who knows where all the players in this drama might be in a year or two? If he was going to do something it had to be now.

'Rose?'

The answer was a drowsy mumble. 'Have you thought of some-where?'

'Yes. Salcombe. I went there when I was a youngster. There are great walks, nice little pubs, you'll like it.' He turned to his wife. 'Rose. Rose?' Ron shook her gently. 'Did you hear what I said?' But she was asleep.

The number was almost obscured by the hedge, but this must be the house. He wiped away some sweat and flexed his toes inside his shoes. It was a warm morning and the walk had been longer than expected. Of course the penny had soon dropped for Rose. Her reaction had been to swiftly extract a promise that their holiday came first and any chasing after Maguire a very distant second. They were due back in Taunton tomorrow and this was the first time Ron had been able to get away.

There was no sign of any bell or, for that matter, warnings about dogs, so he pushed open the gate and walked up the short drive. The garden was overgrown and there was a deserted feel to the whole place. Don't say it was going to be empty. The oversize brass knocker was stiff, but he could hear the sound echoing throughout the house. If anyone was in that should rouse them. He stood back from the front door, only to be surprised when a figure – a rather unkempt and shambling figure – appeared from round the side of the house. 'Who the hell are you?'

Ron didn't recognise him, but it was over ten years since their last meeting. 'Mr Maguire?'

'Yes. Do I know you?'

'I'm Ron Charteris. We met some time ago in Bristol.'

'Bristol. I haven't been to Bristol in years.' He leaned forward to peer into Ron's face and in doing so nearly toppled over. Then things began to slot into place: it was half past ten in the morning, yet the man was drunk.

'We met when you were still a detective inspector.'

'Ahh . . .' Maguire managed to invest the slurred sound with the wisdom of the ages. 'Come on round the side. I'm sitting out in the garden.' Dutifully he followed him along a path that led to a terrace at the back. On it were several chairs and a table with a selection of bottles. 'You'll take a drink?'

Ron was about to say no, when it occurred to him that joining Maguire might possibly ease any conversation along. He affected a show of hesitation, before giving in. 'Oh, why not. I'm on holiday. A whisky, if that's all right.'

'No problem.' Maguire picked up the bottle before he realised there were no more glasses. 'Won't be a minute. I'll just get you something to drink out of.' Unsteadily he made his way through some French windows. Ron wondered if there was still a Mrs Maguire in the picture. From the state of the terrace and what he could see through the French windows it certainly didn't look like it. The ex-detective inspector reappeared with a cup in his hand and answered this very question. 'Can't seem to find any glasses. My wife's staying with her sister for the moment.' He poured a very generous amount into the cup. 'You married . . . Tom?'

'It's Ron and yes, I am married.'

Maguire raised his glass. 'Well, here's to married life and our good ladies. Where would we be without them?'

'Where indeed?' Ron raised the cup and took a small sip. 'Very good whisky, Mr Maguire.'

'It's Vernon.'

'Yes. Excellent whisky, Vernon.' Given Maguire's state, he decided that nothing was lost by directness. 'I'm a reporter, and I met you when you were in charge of investigating the case of those unidentified children in the Eastmead crash.'

'Reporter?' He could almost hear the wheels churning in Maguire's brain before recognition dawned. 'I remember you. You were the bugger who kept poking his nose where it wasn't wanted.'

''Fraid I was, Of course I realise now it was far too sensitive in 1929, but . . . there's been a lot of water under the bridge since then. It's over ten years isn't it?'

'So you're still at it.' The whisky bottle was again upended into Maguire's glass. Ron shook his head as it was waved in his direction. 'And what do you expect me to tell you?'

The tone wasn't as antagonistic as Ron had half-prepared himself for. He took another sip. Perhaps if he threw out a few questions at random he could gauge something from the sort of response they generated. 'Well, you told me yourself you were checking out if those kids came from Ireland.'

Maguire sighed. 'All this speculation was done to death at the time. We couldn't find any evidence one way or another.'

'What about the orphanage in Birmingham?'

The reaction was immediate. 'What orphanage? Who told you about that?'

'One of your enquiry team – I've forgotten the name.'

For the first time Maguire seemed worried. He raised the glass halfway to his lips then put it down. 'You're getting into deep waters here, lad.'

A raw nerve had certainly been touched. Ron hoped he had managed to conceal his jubilation. 'Then there was that bunch of ex-officers. The Wessex Yeomanry, wasn't it?'

'What the hell do you know about them?'

Maguire was angry now. No, more than angry, he was apprehensive. Ron went on the offensive. 'I've found out quite a bit about them. I think they were mixed up in some scheme to ship kids to Australia, and it was two of those children who died.'

The reaction was totally unexpected. Maguire burst out laughing, which seemed to stem from relief more than anything else. 'You've got it all wrong there. I know they weren't kids from an orphanage.'

'You know that?'

'Of course I do. You might or might not choose to believe it, but I was one of the best detectives in the south-west.' He seemed to be wrestling with himself about whether or not to divulge something. 'They were kids from the top drawer. Of course everybody suspected it at the time, but nobody could prove it. Except me, that is.'

'You could prove it?' The tone of voice needled Maguire.

'Typical, isn't it? For you civilians all that counts is proof that stands up in court. Let me tell you, lad, that the police often know far more than they can go to court with. I had information from . . .' He stopped, some sort of warning signal having reached his whisky-befuddled brain. Knowingly he tapped the side of his nose with his finger. 'From, let's say, the sort of source you don't argue with.' The continued expression of doubt on his visitor's features led him on. 'Oh, I never found out their names but they were from the wrong side of the blanket.' He thumped his glass down on the table. 'So inheritance would be at the bottom of it all.'

'But if you didn't know their names how could you be certain?'

Maguire suddenly became belligerent. 'Because I was a detective, of course. I dealt in facts, not fiction, like some reporters I could mention.' He was enjoying Ron's apparent discomfiture. 'And I have proof.'

'You keep talking about proof. What proof?' The disbelief in Ron's tone had exactly the effect he hoped for.

Maguire glowered. 'Photographs.' He got to his feet unsteadily. 'Don't go away.' Once more he lurched through the French windows, only to reappear after some time with a dusty folder. He sat down heavily and began to leaf through it. Ron didn't interrupt. Intuitively he realised that any interjection on his part might puncture this latest alcohol-fuelled fit of bravado. At last there was a grunt of satisfaction. 'Here they are.' He placed a series of photographs face up on the table in front of him. From where he was sitting Ron could see the same children in all of them. He moved round the table to view them more closely. 'See, they're society kids. You can tell that from the clothes and the pose.'

Ron gazed at the young faces staring up at him. Perhaps it was the whisky he had drunk. Perhaps it was because of his growing irritation with this pathetic drunk who was attempting to patronise him. Whatever it was, he said something he was to regret for a long, long time. 'I suppose you got these from Lattimer-Williams.' He had the gratification of seeing Maguire's expression turn to one of absolute astonishment. 'Because for your benefit these are his children, John and Letticia Lattimer-Williams.'

'What do you mean, his children? I know they weren't . . . I mean they can't be . . .' The bluster slowly petered out as Maguire's thought processes laboriously caught up with the implications of what had been said.

Ron couldn't keep the contempt out of his voice. 'I'm sorry to puncture your grand theory, but both are legitimate and, as far as I know, both are alive and well!'

CHAPTER NINETEEN

ELLEN BRUSHED AWAY an insect. That was the trouble with sitting out in the garden, but this Saturday in late June was far too hot for afternoon tea indoors. She glanced across at her husband, who was busy reading the mail. 'How was the office this morning?'

He seemed engrossed. 'So so.'

She returned to her magazine just as Jim put the letter down. He was still mulling over what he had just read, but couldn't help noticing that she was skimming through the *Red Star Weekly*. His rebuke was mild and half-hearted. 'Do you really enjoy those lurid romances?'

She was dismissive. 'We can't all read serious newspapers every day. Anyway, it's a relief to escape from news about the war.' The words reminded her of something and she looked across the table. 'Jamie, do you think the Germans will invade?' There was no response. 'Jamie!'

With an effort he switched his thoughts away from the letter. 'Yes, love?'

'I said, do you think the Germans will invade?'

'What makes you say that?'

'Something I read about in your ever so serious newspaper, that's what.'

He briefly considered the question. 'My guess is no. Not this year anyway.'

'Not this year?' She picked up the newspaper and found the article. 'It says that they might, but that we'll be ready for them.'

Jim glanced over the article. His answer was swift and dismissive. 'Most of that is rubbish, and what isn't is propaganda.'

'How can you know that?'

Jim could tell from his wife's tone that she was hurt, and his voice softened. 'Every country tries to put the best possible interpretation on defeats – and we were defeated at Dunkirk this month.' He anticipated her objections. 'Granted, we saved the army, or the bulk of it at any rate, but it was still a defeat. At least we still have a navy, thank God. Anyway, that's why Hitler won't invade yet: he'll need time to prepare. And since he can't invade in winter that means next summer at the earliest.'

There was a silence while Ellen digested this. 'So what you're saying is we shouldn't be planning next year's summer holiday yet awhile.'

Normally she wasn't given to making jokes, but this time there was a barely concealed smile on her face. 'Something like that.' He grinned absentmindedly before his serious expression returned and his eyes swung back to the letter.

'You've been engrossed in that since you opened it. Who on earth is it from?'

'It's from Maguire. Vernon Maguire.'

The colour drained from her face. 'The policeman? The one you met in York? The one who retired to the West Country?'

'The same.'

'But you haven't heard from him since . . .'

He finished it for her. 'It was eleven years ago: 1929.'

She swallowed hard before nerving herself to ask, 'Then why on earth has he written to you now?'

'Read it for yourself.' He passed the letter over.

She scanned it rapidly, her face white. 'He says he knows that the photograph he has isn't of the children who died.' She appealed to her husband. 'What photograph? What's he on about?'

'Ellen, I know as much as you. But, reading between the lines, I think he somehow got hold of a photograph when he was in charge of that investigation. A photograph he thought was genuine. Now he finds it isn't.'

She paused and turned over the page. 'He says he found out from that . . . bloody reporter. There was a look of bewilderment on her face. 'Jamie, this doesn't make sense.'

'The only reporter I know about was that one who buttonholed me in Bristol. You must remember him? But after all this time . . .' Jim shook his head.

She returned to the letter. 'He thinks Lattimer-Williams fooled him to . . . to cover up something else.' She stopped reading. 'What does he mean by that?' An agonising thought struck her. 'You haven't been keeping things from me, have you?'

'No. No, I haven't.' He put his arms round her. 'This is a bolt from the blue for me as well.'

'Then why are you so calm?' There were tears in Ellen's eyes now. 'Just when I've managed to put all this to the back of my mind, up it comes again. And I . . . and I . . .' This time the tears welled over and it was some time before she was able to grind out the final words. 'I don't have any control over any of it.'

'I might seem calm, but I'm not. I'm still trying to make sense of it.' Jim held her tight until her shoulders stopped shaking. 'Everything in that letter is new to me. I didn't know he had any photographs, but then it doesn't surprise me if Lattimer-Williams fooled him. Remember me saying that I was certain there was more to the whole business than these children never being identified.'

'Yes, but what?'

'You didn't finish the letter, did you? He goes on to say that he thinks there's some very dirty business involved, and he's determined to get to the bottom of it. He's probably right, but whatever it is he's a bloody fool to go rooting around in that particular cesspit.' Jim slumped back in the chair, a picture of despondency. 'Why can't he just leave well alone?'

'Come on, Jamie. There must be a reason. Why do you think he's doing it?'

'Oh, I don't know. Professional pride, maybe. He is an ex-copper.' He was conscious that Ellen was hanging on his every word, waiting for the revelation that would explain everything. He shrugged his shoulders helplessly. 'I bet he thinks his contacts in the police make him fireproof.'

'But you don't?'

'No.'

There was a note of anger in her voice now, as if Jim knew more but was refusing to release it. 'But why contact you after all this time?'

'How the hell do you think I know? He reacted to her anger then felt ashamed. He put his hands on her knees and fixed his eyes on hers. 'I truly don't know. If I had to guess then I think it's because he hopes I have some information he hasn't.' Her look of alarm registered immediately. 'Don't worry, I haven't and even if I did I wouldn't reply. I've absolutely no intention of answering this.' There was still an element of doubt in Ellen's expression and he grew impatient. 'Come into the house with me.' He grasped her hand and pulled her up from the chair. Then, still holding her hand, he marched her into the sitting room and stopped in front of the fire-place. He brandished the pages in front of her, before tearing them to pieces and throwing them into the hearth. Then he bent down to strike a match. Together they watched the flames flicker up the chimney. He tried to sound confident. 'I trust that's the last we'll hear from Vernon Maguire.' What he didn't mention was the end of the letter, which she hadn't read. The bit that contained Maguire's injunction to look out for himself.

'Is that the post?' Ellen's voice echoed down to the hall.

He picked up the two letters; both were bills. 'Yes. Nothing exciting – just the electricity bill and . . .' He stopped in mid-sentence for there, under the lower letter, was a postcard. The picture was of some seaside scene. He turned it over and all that registered was 'Best wishes, Vernon.'

He heard Ellen's footsteps on the stairs. 'And . . . what was the other one?'

Jim made an instant decision and guiltily shoved the card in his jacket pocket. 'Oh.' He picked up the other one. 'I think it's the bill for those plumbing repairs.'

He gave her a quick kiss and glanced at his watch. From upstairs there were faint sounds of movement. They both smiled at each other, then Ellen turned and shouted up the stairwell, her voice rising with each instruction. 'Maureen Thornton. Get up this minute. You'll be late for school!'

The tube was crowded and Jim couldn't get a seat. Nevertheless he carefully extracted the card from his pocket and started to read. 'Hope you received my letter . . . No further sign of that reporter but thought I saw our friend the other day . . . he was in uniform so might just be down here on duty . . . felt you ought to know.' He stared at the tube map. By 'our friend' he must mean Lattimer-Williams. What the hell was Maguire up to? Surely the fact that he hadn't had a reply to his first letter must have conveyed the appropriate message? Jim scanned the postcard again, but there was no more information. The tube lurched, and he muttered an apology as he bumped into a neighbouring straphanger. He didn't feel good about not telling Ellen, particularly after what they had agreed, but on reflection he'd done the right thing to stuff the postcard in his pocket. She would just have worried unnecessarily.

'Wouldn't mind being there myself.'

He switched his eyes from the message to find the neighbour he'd just bumped nodding towards the seaside scene on the front of the card. 'Oh yes.' There was a flustered pause. 'Yes, very pleasant . . .' He managed a weak grin. 'Better than the Northern Line, anyway.' He put the card back in his pocket and spent the remainder of the journey trying to work out the implications of it all.

It was mid-morning before Jim could bring himself to broach the subject with Kenneth Furniss. 'Haven't seen L-W around much lately, Kenneth.' He hoped he had injected the right degree of casualness.

Kenneth looked a little surprised. 'Well, he's hardly ever in as it is. Don't say you want to see him about something?'

'No, no, he's just one of the faces that seems to have disappeared lately.'

'All I know is he's in the services now. The army of course.' Kenneth anticipated the next question. 'Don't ask me what outfit: my guess would be something connected to the war office. He must be in his late forties now – too old for active service.'

'I don't think so, Mr Furniss.' Kenneth swung round, annoyed at being interrupted, to find one of the young clerks hovering at his elbow. He sounded apologetic. 'I couldn't help overhearing as I was passing. Major Lattimer-Williams was in the other lunchtime so I took a chance and buttonholed him. You see, I've got my call-up papers for the navy.' He articulated the last word as if he were talking of banishment to Siberia.

'And got your head bitten off for your pains, I shouldn't wonder.' Kenneth was unsympathetic.

'No, he was quite civil. Especially when I said I wanted to go in the army: my dad was in the Rifle Brigade in the last war.'

'You want to go into the army!' Kenneth looked at Jim in disbelief and shook his head. 'Look, lad, both of us were in the army and I think we can safely say that you should stick with the navy.' Jim nodded his emphatic agreement.

The youngster looked pleased with himself. 'Well, I'm glad I talked to Major Lattimer-Williams because he said I can have my cake and eat it. He suggested I volunteer for the Marines and he would put in a word for me. He said he'd been to see some Marines training and was very impressed with them. So he must be involved in active service.'

Jim hardly dared ask. 'Did he say where?'

'He was going to, but he stopped. I suppose it's security and everything. Then he just said it was somewhere down in the West Country.'

CHAPTER TWENTY

'HOW ARE THINGS at the *Echo*? Any of the old crowd still there?' Ron shook George's hand warmly. It must have been two years at least since they had last met.

'Let me get you a pint before we delve into all that.' George disappeared in the direction of the bar while Ron sat back and revelled in the sound of Bristolian accents around him. It really took him back to his days on the *Echo* . . . let's see, it was 1940 now . . . Good God, eleven years ago.

George returned with two glasses. 'Here you are. Try a pint of my namesake, George's. It's better than some of the stuff you get in London, I'll be bound.' He took a long draught. 'Cheers. Anyway, how's Rose and the family?'

'They're fine. Rose seems to have settled down in Taunton again and the kids love their school.'

'Are you managing without them in London?'

'Just about. It's not ideal.' Ron couldn't quite contain a sigh. 'Not ideal at all.'

'And you wouldn't want them moving back?'

'Oh no. It's bad enough in London now and there's worse to come. At least they're reasonably safe in the west.'

George took his cue from the way the conversation was moving. 'What's the gossip in Fleet Street? Are we likely to be invaded?'

'Opinion seems to be divided. It'll be next year if it happens at all, but do they have to bother? I mean, all these air raids are playing havoc in London and, as I said, it's going to get worse. And not just London.' He realised the implications of what he was

146

saying. 'Look, let's get away from the war. What's been happening at the *Echo*?'

For the next twenty minutes George filled him in on events and people on the paper and in the locality before changing the subject. 'Ron, it's great to see you on your way back to London, but this isn't totally a social call, is it?'

Ron started to protest, then stopped. Even after all this time George knew him too well. 'Most of it is a social call. I really did want to see how you were getting on . . .'

'But . . .' George teased out the confession.

'Do you remember the mystery of those two children in the East-mead crash?'

'Bloody hell, Ron. Don't tell me you're still chasing that up.' The glass stopped halfway to George's lips. 'It's history now and, besides, there's a war on. Newspapers don't have time for that sort of thing.'

'It's not for the paper. It's for me. There's one hell of a story there. The more I find out, the more intriguing it all is.' Ron told George about his visit to Maguire almost a year before and what had transpired. 'So you see he'd most definitely been got at – by someone pretty high up.'

'From what you say it was probably this fellow Lattimer-Williams.'

'No, I'm not sure he would have had the clout to sort out a senior detective by himself. Anyway, that's as maybe. He was obviously worried when I mentioned the Birmingham orphanage, so I decided to concentrate on that. I say concentrate, but all of this had to take second place to work and we've been pretty busy.'

George finished his pint. 'Amen to that.'

'Can I get you another?'

'No thanks. I've got to pace myself these days. You were saying?'

'Well, that vicarage in the Quantocks was Church of England, so I assumed that ruled out Catholic orphanages. And with the help of someone I know on the *Church Times* I was able to get a list of four possible establishments. I wrote to them all saying that I was trying to trace a boy and girl who might have gone to Australia in late October 1928.'

George broke in. 'Look, I'll have another pint. I can see this might take some time.'

'Time, gentlemen, please!'

The landlord's shout drew a groan from George. 'What a sense of timing you have. It's just like the old days. Come on then, you'd better finish what you were saying.'

'Eventually I got replies from two of these places. One was the sort of dusty answer I half-expected, and the other referred me to a priest who's now retired but was in charge of the place at the time. He lives in Malvern, so I've written to him there.'

'And what did he say?' In spite of himself, George's interest was aroused.

'I don't know. I'm still waiting for him to reply.'

'You don't know!' George regarded Ron with disbelief. 'I've listened to all this rigmarole and it peters out like that!' He checked the clock on the wall. 'You might have forgotten, but this is Bristol. We can nip over to the Balaclava in Felton Street and they don't shut there for another half-hour.' He sounded determined. 'After all that you're certainly going to buy me a pint!'

The Balaclava didn't exactly look appealing, but given the state of Bristol's licensing laws beggars couldn't be choosers. Reluctantly Ron bought the drinks, but decided it was not a place to linger. 'George, when I went over that bit about orphanages I was just filling you in on the background, such as it is.'

'So we're coming to the nitty-gritty now, are we?'

'In a word – yes.' Ron hurried on before his friend could interrupt. 'Do you remember that police sergeant, Ferguson?'

'Ferguson? Oh yes, I know him, but he's not a sergeant now: he's a superintendent.'

Ron's face fell. What he had in mind might be difficult with someone of that rank. Do you know him at all well?'

'No – but I've asked questions at press interviews.'

'What I mean is, does he know you?'

'I suppose so. Ron, what are you getting at?'

'Do you think you could get me an interview? It only needs to be a short one.'

148

'Ron, be serious. He's a super. You want to talk to him about a case that, as far as he's concerned, has been dead for over ten years. It's wartime, so he's up to his ears in all sorts of other things. And to cap it all I take it that this has to be tomorrow morning, because you're due back in London tomorrow night.' George rolled his eyes. 'Is there anything else you need? Does the prime minister need to be there too?'

'Come on, he's met me before, and don't forget to tell him I'm in Fleet Street now. That might just impress him. And you can say I'm writing a book on – oh, I don't know – great police mysteries, or something like that, and as he was a key investigator into the case of those children I'd like to interview him for half an hour or so.'

George still looked doubtful. 'Somehow I don't think he'll buy that.'

Ron replied with some asperity. 'Yes he will. If there's one thing that Fleet Street's taught me, it's that although faith might conquer all, vanity comes a bloody close second!'

The central police station was busy, busier than it had ever been in his day. Ron noticed several military police. George was right: policing nowadays had more dimensions to it than before the war. One of the constables at the desk directed him to a line of chairs and, after what seemed an age, a corridor was pointed out and directions were given to Ferguson's office.

'Come in.' Ferguson had put on weight, but then so had his visitor. 'Nice to see you again, Ron.'

'And you . . . Don.' Ron hoped the touch of informality wouldn't be taken amiss. 'Thanks for taking the time to see me. I can see just how busy you are. You seem to have most of the service police in the area in the lobby.'

'Don't mention it.' Ferguson wiped his forehead theatrically. 'The drunks and fights you can expect, but half the deserters and waifs and strays in the south-west turn up here.'

'Never mind, you should be used to it after all these years dealing with journalists.'

The joke broke any ice that was left. 'I hear you're writing a book on great crime mysteries or some such. Have you got a publisher?'

Ron airily mentioned one of the big publishing houses and Ferguson looked impressed. 'Of course no date's been set: shortage of paper and all that. But once supplies have eased or the war ends, whichever comes sooner, they'll want to get back to business. And I want to make sure that this book is ready for them.'

'Of course, of course. George told me you've got the Eastmead crash in mind.'

'Yes. I'd like to pick your brains on how the investigation went. After all, I don't expect there are many left in the local force who were as heavily involved as you.' Ron took out his notebook. 'You don't mind if I take some notes?'

Ferguson seemed happy enough. 'Well, I was relatively junior at the time, but I did a lot of foot-slogging on the case.'

'Did you trace everybody who was on the train?'

'Yes. We even tracked down the woman who got on when the train stopped at the signals at Meldon. We got quite a few leads from that article you did. Unfortunately she was one of the ones killed.'

'What was her name? I think I must have left for London before you sorted that one out.'

'She was Elaine Wilson. At one time she'd been employed as a maid at Carrington House, and she was visiting her mother who was a housekeeper there.'

'Carrington House?'

'Yes, it's that big place up near Stroud.' Bill shook his head. 'It was a bad business. As it happened I was the one who broke the news. She hadn't even been missed. She was living abroad somewhere and everybody had assumed she'd caught a later train.'

'And no chance that . . .'

'Her mother was too upset to see us, but according to the lady of the house Miss Wilson was a single woman with an impeccable reputation.' Bill sighed and shrugged again. 'So we were able to knock that theory on the head straight away.'

The memories were obviously gloomy ones and Ron moved on. 'What about orphanages? Wasn't there one mentioned in Birmingham?'

'Yes, but Maguire dealt with all that and he was happy there was nothing in it.'

'And the Irish dimension, if I can call it that?'

'Don't mention it. I hate to think how many hours we wasted on that.' Bill stopped himself. 'No, that's not fair. It wasn't wasted, and those kids might have been – could have been – Irish. There were too many places to check – Dublin, Belfast and all points west. And that's only across the water. There were all the institutions here with connections to Ireland. It was just impossible. In the end we had to call it a day.'

'What about the sudden deaths you were checking on in the Midlands?' Ron realised he had been firing non-stop questions at the man. 'Sorry, Bill, I haven't given you a chance to amplify on anything.'

'No, that's fine.' He seemed uncertain. 'There was a murder in Leamington Spa.'

'Yes, I remember somebody talking about it at the time. Did they get anyone for it?'

'Not as far as I know. After Maguire took early retirement the acting super detailed me to go up there and check.' There was no mistake; Bill was definitely uncomfortable now.

Ron moved quickly to reassure him. 'I'll go over what I've written at the end, and anything you're unhappy about we'll leave out.'

'It wasn't right.' Bill must have realised the bald statement posed more questions than it answered. 'I mean, they were treating it as murder in the furtherance of theft. But all the detectives I spoke to didn't accept that. They told me it didn't smell right.' He realised he wasn't making much sense to a layman. 'Look, a burglar's rifling a room when the householder disturbs him. Now if he's a professional his main job is finding anything that's valuable in the shortest possible time. If he's disturbed then usually he scarpers, but sometimes there's a fight. Any detective coming to the scene afterwards can easily tell the sequence of events. The trouble was that at this house in Leamington all the signs were that it was the other way round.'

'You mean . . .'

'What I mean is that the detectives thought the murder had taken place first and any theft had happened afterwards. And the man's wife wasn't there that night – the first time she'd been away for a long time.'

'So why did they treat it the way they did?'

'Because the chief super up there was convinced it was a burglar. He instructed every copper to go after every local villain until they got somebody.' Bill sighed at the memory. 'It wasn't a happy station.'

'I won't write up any answer you give, but do you feel there was something funny going on?'

'Maybe. But if it was it couldn't have had anything to do with those kids, now could it?'

They spent the last ten minutes talking generally, but nothing more of value emerged. When Bill looked apologetically at his watch, Ron took the hint and they shook hands. As he turned to leave Ron chanced a final question. 'If you had to venture an opinion about those kids, what would it be?'

Bill pursed his lips. 'Ron, I've been in this job too long. I wouldn't, as you put it, venture an opinion. What I would say, though, is it's a pity you didn't manage to get on to Maguire. He was in charge for a fair time and I think he knew more than he let on.'

'Thanks. Maybe I'll try and get down to Salcombe.'

Bill looked shocked. 'Sorry – haven't you heard?' He almost seemed to be speaking to himself. 'No, of course you wouldn't. We only heard a week or two afterwards.'

'Heard what?'

'Maguire's dead. It seems he fell over one of those cliffs near his house.'

CHAPTER TWENTY-ONE

IT WAS ONLY a quarter to five but already the light from the outside windows was dimming. Kenneth Furniss, the senior clerk, walked over to look out at the gloom before stationing himself near the light switches and shouting instructions to the juniors. 'Right. Look sharp and pull down those blackouts.' Thankful for a break at the end of a long afternoon, the youngsters jumped to it with suppressed jokes and badinage. 'All right. School's not out yet!' Kenneth's expression twitched as his features couldn't quite match the tone of reproof in his voice. As the blackouts came down one by one the room darkened, and for a brief second darkness was complete until Kenneth switched on the lights. It took a further minute or so before everyone was back at their desk. 'Another three-quarters of an hour to go. Evans, I'll be keeping an eye on you.' The last remark was bellowed at a youth who had muttered something to a now pink-faced secretary as she passed. Furniss glared around until, satisfied that all had returned to normal, he walked across to a desk situated in an alcove at the other side of the room.

Jim Thornton looked up. 'He's a bit of a cheeky devil, that one. I'm glad to see you're keeping on top of him.'

'That's the problem these days, Jim.' Kenneth sighed. 'What with all the bombing and everything, people are tending to be a bit casual.' He nodded his head towards Evans, now with his head down and apparently working assiduously. 'And some are most definitely taking advantage.'

'Not much we can do about it, except to keep on reminding everybody that war or no war there's still a business to run.'

'True, but that's why I came over to have a quiet word. We seem to be slipping further and further behind every day. For instance, we didn't really get going this morning until near half ten and this rights issue has to be complete by next Wednesday.'

'Kenneth, there's a war on. I wasn't in myself until nearly ten. Besides, everyone upstairs knows the situation. As a matter of fact I was quite proud of young Armitage. Stepney took a real pasting last night and he'd been up on ARP work all night. You could see the lad was shaken.'

'Jim, I'm not talking about people like him: he's as honest as the day is long. But some of them are swinging the lead.' He responded to Jim's questioning look. 'We were both in the last lot. You can recognise it as well as I can.'

'So what have you got in mind?'

The preliminaries out of the way, Kenneth launched into the main point. 'Well, you know I live in Beckenham?' Jim nodded. 'The wife's moved out to her sister's in Maidstone – at least until the situation improves. So there's no need to go home every night, and I was thinking instead of going up west to Oxford Street or Tottenham Court Road. The shelters are deep and safe and, more to the point, I could be in the office early from there. There's far less chance of there being disruption on the deep tubes, and if everybody knows that I'm going to be in it'll encourage them to make that extra effort.'

'Sounds a good idea to me. Are there any problems?'

For the first time Kenneth looked a little diffident. 'If I'm going up west I need to leave the office a bit early.' Then there was a sudden flash of defensiveness. 'It gets pretty packed up there. I hear people are even starting to arrive mid-afternoon. So if I'm to get any space to sleep I need to be there before six.'

'Don't worry, Kenneth. You go when you need to. I'll sort it out with anyone higher up.' A sudden thought crossed Jim's mind. 'You'd better announce what you're doing to the office and the reasons for it. It might concentrate minds in advance.'

'What about you, Jim? Any chance of getting your wife and kiddie out of it?'

'No. We don't have any relatives down here and Ellen won't hear of going back up north and leaving me here.' He smiled. 'So it's back to Wimbledon and the Anderson shelter in the garden.'

'Ah well, you should all be safe enough in one of those.' Kenneth's tone was optimistic, but it fooled neither of them. As he had said earlier they had both been through the last lot, and knew precisely the effect of high explosive on shored-up underground shelters.

The tube shuddered and came to a halt. Jim could see the expressions of suppressed panic in the eyes all around him, but no one said anything. Then slowly, and with much grinding and shuddering, the forward motion started again. He looked again at the eyes of his fellow passengers; eyes that avoided all contact with others lest they were unable to hide their dread of what the night would bring. Six weeks of the blitz already: how much more could people take? At last the train inched into South Wimbledon and he joined the throng pushing and jostling to get out and get home. The last few nights the sirens had sounded just as he had reached the street and he was half-prepared for that awful sound; but as he hurried through the blackness there was silence, apart, that is, from the sound of footsteps like his own and the occasional shouted warning from a warden. Perhaps they would have a rest tonight.

Jim breathed a little easier and thought of Ellen and Maureen waiting for him. Then it hit him. The letter. The letter that had arrived yesterday, but which he hadn't read until this morning on the tube. The letter that the day's events had driven from his mind. The letter that awakened all the old fears – fears that had diminished since that letter and postcard in the summer.

It had been from Maguire's widow. Jim didn't even know she was a widow until that morning, although he had guessed he must be married. She gave an account of his death. He had taken the dog for a walk and somehow fallen over a cliff into the sea. At the inquest the cause of death had been given as multiple injuries and drowning. Initially the police had been suspicious, but she went on to give vent to her incredulity at the way they had dropped the case. Jim felt the letter in his pocket. He could almost feel the words burning through the envelope. 'Something happened. They didn't want to know. Even the detective inspector couldn't meet my eye.'

Poor woman. It sounded as though she had been kept in the dark the same way Ellen had been until five years before. He had been worried by the first letter back in July. If only Maguire had shown him the photograph all those years ago, he could have told him it wasn't the same children. But no: he had to wait over ten years to find out he had been fooled. The more Jim thought about it, the more convinced he was that it must have been that reporter from Bristol who had somehow alerted Maguire. And what did he do when he found out that the boy he thought was in Eastmead churchyard was alive? He had to rake the whole thing up again. The fool! And then there was the warning to Jim, the hint of something very nasty at the bottom of it all. This conviction was reinforced by the postcard. Despite his resolution always to keep Ellen in the picture, Jim had kept quiet. At the time he had convinced himself that Maguire must be getting paranoid: although he might have seen Lattimer-Williams down in Devon, he now knew he had a legitimate reason for being there. But this? He felt the letter again, and the outline of the photograph inside. Had Maguire found out something concrete? Who knew? But whether it had been an accident or something else, he was dead.

'Put that bloody light out!' The bellow of an irate warden was directed at some unfortunate who had paused to light a cigarette. God almighty. Did the idiot think some German bomb aimer was waiting for some poor sod to light a Woodbine before letting loose. Jim almost tripped over the masonry strewn over the pavement and realised how wrapped up he had been in his own thoughts. It was the bottom of Charnock Road: nearly home now. They had been lucky here the night before last. The bomb had landed in the park and the only damage was to the wall. It had been close, too close for comfort. He had been all for Maureen being evacuated in September the previous year, when the war started, but Ellen wouldn't hear of it. She couldn't bear to think of her girl going to strangers, and her sister's home in Leeds would have been just as dangerous as London.

Ellen had heard him coming up the path and was already putting the meal on the table as he came in through the front door. It was boiled potatoes and sausage. They seemed to have had that an awful lot recently, and the meat in the sausages was becoming increasingly difficult to identify. Still, it wasn't Ellen's fault: everyone had to put up with things like this. Maureen was already busy tucking into the meal; she obviously didn't share his qualms about the sausage. Jim gave Ellen the usual peck. 'Had a good day, love?'

'Much the same as usual. I managed to get a nice bit of mutton for the weekend. We can make some broth out of it for Monday. What about you?' She noticed how tired he looked. 'Everything all right at the office?' He looked up, made as if to reply, but only nodded. She put her arm on his shoulder and spoke quietly. 'It's not all right, is it?'

'What's not all right, Dad?' Despite her concentration on the meal, Maureen's sharp ears had picked up the words.

'Nothing that you need to be concerned with, my girl.' Ellen's tone was sharper than she had intended and she softened it a little. 'If you want to help then get the salt out of the kitchen cupboard. I've forgotten it.' Unabashed, Maureen went through to the kitchen, eyes still glancing towards her father.

Jim patted Ellen's hand. 'Leave it for now. It's not so serious. I'll talk to you later.'

For the rest of the meal the conversation was a bit forced, with both adults half-listening for the sound of the sirens. 'If we don't get a warning can we stay inside tonight? The shelter wasn't too bad in summer, but it's getting chilly now.' Ellen found the Anderson shelter both cold and claustrophobic.

Maureen joined in. 'Yes, Dad. I'm fed up with sleeping in there.'

Jim seemed to be in a better frame of mind. 'My word. Aren't you the one who told me what an adventure it was. Better than a stuffy old room, I think you said.'

'Oh, Dad, I didn't mean every night.' Maureen's indignation with her father's literal interpretation was plain to see, but before she could say any more the warning sounded.

'Come on, the decision's made for us.' Jim led them into the hall, picking up the pre-packed bags of clothing and gas masks as they went. He took Maureen by the hand, switched off the lights and led the way into the garden.

The Anderson shelter was cold. Even fully clothed under the blankets Jim and Ellen shivered. Maureen had been given the extra blankets, and soon the sound of steady breathing indicated that she at least was warm enough. Every so often dull rumblings could be heard.

'Are they near, Jamie?' Ellen's whisper came up from the bunk below, the anxiety plain in her tone.

'Don't worry, love. They're miles away. Could even be as far as Surrey docks.' Just then there came the sound of another explosion, much nearer than before. Jim tried to sound matter of fact. 'I'm coming in with you. It's stupid for us to freeze in separate bunks.' He climbed down and pulled the blanket after him, then carefully arranged it over Ellen and tucked in the ends before clambering in himself. She snuggled up to him and they lay still for a few minutes, letting the warmth slowly seep back. The explosions could still be heard, but now they were further away again.

'What was it you were going to tell me about?' Ellen's question roused Jim just as he was drifting off to sleep.

He didn't answer immediately, debating with himself the wisdom of broaching the subject at this time and in these circumstances. But she would have to know, and there never would be an ideal time. 'You know that letter we got yesterday? I read it on the train this morning. It's from Maguire's widow.'

She took it more calmly than he had anticipated. 'Widow? You never told me he was married.'

'I didn't know either. He never mentioned it.'

'But how can he be dead? He was about the same age as you.'

Quickly Jim recounted the details. His voice came in a sibilant whisper lest he wake his sleeping daughter. There was a long silence.

'Why didn't you tell me everything he had written in July?' Ellen tried to come to terms with the implications of what he had said.

'I should have done, but since you hadn't read through to the end I didn't want to worry you. I know his wife . . . sorry, widow . . . thinks it wasn't an accident. But it might have been. It could be just a coincidence. We can't jump to conclusions . . .' He made as if to continue, but couldn't think what to say.

She interpreted her husband's silence as affirmation of her fears. 'But what do you think, Jamie? You're worried, aren't you?'

He toyed with the idea of being reassuring, then rejected it. Now of all times was a time for truth. 'It's possible he might have been murdered – possible.'

Ellen started to cry softly, smothering the noise in his shoulder so as not to rouse the sleeping girl. Jim hugged her more tightly. 'Don't worry. I'm not dead yet, and I don't intend to be for some time.'

The sobs subsided into a series of sniffs. 'Jamie, why would anyone be murdered? You and Maguire were rewarded for keeping quiet about what you found out. If it ever got out it would be embarrassing for people in high places, but apart from that none of it was so terrible.' Her train of thought led to a comforting conclusion. 'We're not thinking straight, are we? Thinking it's murder is just stupid.' There was a long silence and panic returned. 'Jamie. Jamie! It is stupid, isn't it?'

At last he spoke, obviously searching for the right words. 'We can't keep on fooling ourselves, Ellen. We've talked about this before. There's something more to it. I don't know, maybe Maguire became suspicious and came across whatever it was.'

'But what?'

Jim sounded helpless. 'I just don't know, but it's something connected with what I saw that night.'

They didn't speak for a long while, each turning over the implications of what had been said. It was Ellen who broke the silence. 'So what do we do?'

'You know the plans we made, the bank account I set up? If things get really nasty – and it hasn't come anywhere near that yet – we'll just have to take that option.'

'But they know about the bank account, and how would we live? And what about our house?'

Patiently Jim explained. 'We can move the account, and it'll be just as we planned. We'll sell up here and move back up north. I can always get another job. In any case we're well off. You know how much we've put away.' He stifled Ellen's protests. 'It needn't be for ever. After two or three years we can quietly move back.'

'How can we? If what you say is true they'll be watching for you.'

'It won't last for ever. They'll give up after a while.' He hoped he sounded convincing. 'In any event we need to be making preparations. Not just yet, but within the next few months. There's a firm of solicitors round the corner from the office we can use.' He saw her expression and added hastily, 'Nothing to do with the firm.

She turned the idea over in her mind. 'Couldn't you just go to the police? Explain everything . . .' Her voice tailed off.

'That really would be stupid. You know the people we're dealing with. Do you think the police would take my word against theirs? You know how much influence they have. Look what happened to the investigations into Maguire's death.'

'Are you sure?'

'Certain. And once I'd gone to the police they'd know just how much of a danger I was. No, after that warning I got from Lattimer-Williams they probably think I'll keep my head down. And there's every chance they don't know that Maguire has been in touch.' Jim tried to sound as confident as possible. 'Ten to one they think I'm settled into this new life and have no intention of rocking the boat.'

'Do you think so, Jamie?'

The pleading in her voice was such that he lied for what he hoped was the last time. 'Yes, love. There must be a reasonable chance. We can only wait.'

CHAPTER TWENTY-TWO

'DON'T BE BLOODY STUPID! What do you think is more important, you seeing yourself in khaki or the paper coming out?' The deputy editor made his displeasure plain. 'You're forty now. What difference do you think you'll make to His Majesty's forces?'

'I just feel a bit of a fraud still being here after all the people who've left. I mean, that sportswriter Corbett is forty-two and he's gone.'

'Corbett's an idiot. A patriotic idiot maybe, but an idiot nevertheless. Besides, he isn't married and you are – with two children to boot.' The deputy editor marshalled what he felt was the clinching argument. 'Ron, you're a senior and experienced reporter. We need people like you at any time, but especially now with so many people away. And if you did join up . . . ? At your age and with your experience you'd only end up with a desk job. It's just too easy to get carried away.' He sounded despondent. 'I saw too much of that in the last lot.'

'I suppose you're right.' Ron got up to go. 'But all I seem to do nowadays is write stories – or should I say exactly the same story – about plucky, bloody Londoners keeping their chins up in the blitz.'

'So that's what it's all about; you want a change.' Having worked out to his satisfaction what the problem was, the deputy editor immediately cheered up. 'You know as well as I do that that covers ninety per cent of the home news these days. And, what's more, it's going to stay that way. I hope you haven't forgotten that our beloved proprietor is now a member of the government? I mean, what do you want? That we start telling the truth? He smiled at the picture conjured up by such an outbreak of veracity. 'We'd both be sacked long before the story reached the presses. Followed closely, I imagine, by the granting of your wish to join the army and the realisation of my particular nightmare of having to do a stint as an air raid warden.' He could see that Ron still wasn't happy. 'If it's front line duties you want I'll see to it you get your chance, but you won't like it. All that happens to human interest stories is they get spiked from time to time, but practically any story to do with bombing is butchered. I confidently predict that the country will run out of blue pencils long before this war is over.'

The whole platform shuddered as the bomb exploded somewhere above. 'Sounds like a thousand pounder.' Ron's companion on the left spoke knowledgeably. 'Not directly above, mind; we'd have had a lot more tiles down if it was.'

Ron stared uneasily upwards at the roof of the Piccadilly Line platform at Holborn tube station. He had been granted his wish to report directly on the bombing, but so far the results had been as his deputy editor had so depressingly and accurately predicted: stories cut to the bone and beyond. That being said, it had been a ridiculous and impulsive idea to think of joining up. He hadn't even talked to Rose about it. It must be a reaction to feeling guilty about so many of the younger staff being called up. Another explosion shook the platform, and instinctively people winced and huddled down even further. This was part of the job now: covering the bombing meant he was spending a great deal of time in shelters such as this one. It was safe – at least as safe as anywhere – but it also gave him a great deal of time to think. Rose and the children occupied most of his thoughts. But at least they were safe. Not like Maguire. Once raised, that particular thought couldn't be banished. Ferguson had told him the details of how it had happened, and also the verdict: accidental death. Bill had added that there were some odd features, although 'the man had always been too fond of the bottle'. Accidental death – was it really that? Or had he contributed by telling Maguire how he had been fooled. God knows what transpired as a consequence. He might have contacted Lattimer-Williams . . . And then what? Bribery to hush up a scandal was one thing, but murder . . . ? With an almost physical effort Ron forced his mind onto another track, only to find it was a parallel one. At last he had had a reply from that priest, or at least he thought it was him: the letter had a Malvern postmark, but he hadn't had time to read it yet. He hadn't been home for three nights now, having had to use the office shelters or, like tonight, having to take refuge in a deep tube.

'Did you see St Paul's?' His companion seemed to feel duty bound to keep minds occupied. 'Just a shell now. I passed it this morning.'

Ron, who had spent most of the previous day covering the bombing in the city, had indeed seen St Paul's. It had been a poignant sight. He murmured some remark, only to find himself the target of an officious challenge by another of the company. 'Remember! Careless talk costs lives!'

The response was a stage whisper from the left. 'If the Gestapo ever get here they won't have to look far for recruits.' It produced a collective giggle and, deflated, the challenger subsided.

The sound of the siren was muffled down here, but all along the platform the shout of 'all clear' marked the end of another raid. Ron joined the shuffling throng heading towards the stairways. He had to get back to the office and file his copy. After that . . . he would try to get back home. So far he had been lucky: west London hadn't been as badly hit as the East End and the City. And, providing the house was still standing, maybe there would be a letter from Rose . . .

At last the whistle of the kettle roused him and slowly he came to. He was tired. All those nights in the underground were starting to take their toll. Better do what he needed to and try and get some sleep before getting back to the office. He brought the tea through from the kitchen and settled down to read the post. Rose's letter was a breath of fresh air: both children were now in the primary school choir, and it had reached the finals of a local competition. He read on, momentarily but happily lost in a different world, a snapshot of near normality one hundred and fifty miles away from all this death and destruction.

Reluctantly Ron laid the letter aside and picked up the other one, the one from Malvern. Everything had taken so long that he had forgotten the name of the vicar concerned, so he checked the signature first. Yes, that was it, Mr Beaumont. The writing was copperplate and a thing of beauty in its own right, but although the script was superb the style was abysmal. The first page consisted of a long and rambling explanation of why the reply had taken so long, most of the delay, apparently, to do with changes of address. Ron turned to the next page and skipped through more of the same until a phrase caught his eye, 'I was glad you mentioned the Eastermain Society'. Here, at last, was something of substance. The institution had dealt with several societies, but Mr Beaumont had always felt that this particular one had provided the best future for children in unfortunate circumstances . . . and so on. Ron felt himself switching off again, only to perk up at the next sentence. The vicar explained that Lord Eastermain had telephoned him personally one evening to ask if children destined to leave the institution a few days later could be escorted to Birmingham station. There he was to hand them over to two of his colleagues so they could catch the night train to Taunton. It was unusual, but Eastermain had explained it was necessary to enable them to take an earlier boat from Southampton. He had escorted the two children to the station himself and handed them over to the two men, one of whom he had met previously. He was a Mr Lattimer-Williams from the society.

Ron took a sip of tea, only to find it was cold. Could this be it, the evidence he had been waiting for? The date was crucial: did the man mention a date? He scanned forward. There was no date mentioned, but instead something much better. 'It was the night of that dreadful crash near Bristol . . . when I read about it the next day, I was beside myself with worry . . . happily Lord Eastermain telephoned to assure me that both children were unharmed.' That was it. The proof he needed that they had taken the children on that train. As for Eastermain's assurances . . . well, he had been covering his tracks, hadn't he?

This called for a celebration with something better than cold tea. Now, where had he put it? After some rummaging he uncovered the precious half-bottle of Bell's whisky – still with about a third remaining. Slowly Ron relished the first sip, and was about to raise the glass for a second when an uncomfortable thought struck. Why would someone in Lattimer-Williams's position be acting as escort to children from an orphanage? It just wasn't credible, yet that was what had happened: the letter was proof of that. And why had everything been done so hurriedly? Orphanages, even in those days, must have had to go through certain procedures. Children weren't just chattels to be disposed of on a whim. Even for people like Eastermain and his associates, short-circuiting official procedures could be very embarrassing – if discovered. So embarrassing that it might put at risk the whole murky business of shipping kids abroad. Slowly he realised that, far from solving the problem, the letter only added to the puzzle.

For a moment Ron hesitated. Did he really need to send the acknowledgement to Beaumont along with the letter to Rose? But what did it matter; there was nothing lost by doing it. He slipped the two letters into the box and turned for home. The area had escaped most of the bombing, but the newsagents at the corner had been unlucky. Where it had stood, pedestrians had rapidly established a shortcut between streets. Normally Ron would have stuck to the established route, but the light was already fading and with no street lights the saving of a few hundred yards was useful. Besides, a blast of cold air curling round a street corner reminded him it was late October. He turned up his coat collar and struck off across the waste ground.

At first he thought the uneven shadow lying across the path was masonry brought down by a bomb. Then it moved. What he was looking at was a man. A man, moreover, who was concealing himself from the street. Ron's second thought, following immediately after, was that the street in question was where he lived. But it was the third that brought him up short. The house directly facing both him and the unknown watcher was his own.

Without any conscious decision Ron had come to a halt. Thoughts raced through his mind. Could it be a derelict seeking sanctuary for the night? Hardly: there were many more comfort-able places in bomb-damaged buildings. Was it some sort of police surveillance operation? Perhaps – but these days police were fully engaged in a multitude of other duties. Then the realisation set in that he was clutching at straws. No other dwelling but his own was fully in view. If he had come home by his normal route he would have been unaware of anything amiss. The man was definitely watching his house.

What was he to do? He was tempted to ignore him; pretend he hadn't seen him. After all, that was the English way of dealing with these situations. But something told him he must act. He must do something to transmit the message that not only had the watcher been caught in the act, but also that the subject of the surveillance was aware of what was afoot. Ron approached as cautiously as he could until only about ten feet separated the two men. Then he said something so banal, so commonplace it sounded stupid. 'Can I help you?'

The reaction was electric. In one movement, the figure rose and turned. For a split second the arm lifted and something, he couldn't tell what, was in the man's hand. For the very first time in his life Ron felt sheer, unadulterated terror. Then, just as suddenly, there was a release of tension and the threatening posture relaxed. Finally there was a volley of muttered abuse before the man turned, hurried away and was lost in the shadows.

CHAPTER TWENTY-THREE

JIM STRETCHED IN HIS CHAIR. 'We'd better take a break now. I don't know about you two, but I'm starting to see double.' The others looked relieved: it was after five and they had been checking share certificates since half past two.'

'Think we'll get it finished today?' Tim Dodds, one of the office juniors, spoke up.

Jack Martin, one of the senior clerks, read his mind. 'If Mr Thornton doesn't mind, maybe you can go and help to sort the mail for a quarter of an hour.'

'Off you go, lad, but a quarter of an hour maximum.' Jim gave his consent a little grudgingly and the boy shot out of the door like a rabbit.

'Those were the days when I could move like that.' Martin looked after the departing youngster with envy.

'Come on, Jack, you're not ready for the knacker's yard yet. I bet you can give me a good ten years.'

'Well, maybe I could, but I'm still just old enough to have been in the last war.' He grimaced at the ceiling. 'You remember – the war that was supposed to end all wars. And twenty years later what do we find?' Jack gestured contemptuously. 'Every politician in the land telling us that we can win this one.'

Both men dwelt on the unwelcome thoughts that the conversation had thrown up and a silence fell, eventually broken by Jim. 'That's true, but I don't know why we're both surprised: there must only be about four of us in the office who went through the last lot. All the others are too young.'

Martin jumped in, his tone just a little pedantic. 'Surely you're forgetting Last and all the directors.'

'To be honest, I wasn't counting them. But then I suppose they did their bit the same as everyone else.' Jim's mind went back to the article in the Brighton newspaper and the commemorative plaque subscribed to by brother officers. 'Most of them were in the same regiment, weren't they?'

'Yes, the Wessex Yeomanry. I think that has something to do with why they're all directors here. Mind you, they have plenty of other irons in the fire. They're connected to quite a few Australian companies, I believe.'

Jim found himself suddenly alert. Normally he wasn't one for office gossip, but Jack Martin had worked here since 1920 and no doubt knew a great deal more than he did. He made the effort to sound casual. 'What sort of companies are they?'

Don't know for sure, but agriculture of some sort.' There was a wistful expression in Jack's eyes. 'They say there are a lot of opportunities in Australia. Now if Jane and I had decided to do something different after I came back in 1919 maybe I could have been a cattle rancher in the outback by now. Just think of it. No bombing or rationing.'

'There you go again, writing yourself off.' Jim decided to jolly the senior clerk along. 'There're plenty of opportunities here, you know. And there ought to be more with all the young fellows away.'

'Well, perhaps. But there would have been a damned sight more if Last's brother had survived.' Martin saw Jim's puzzled look. 'I came in on the junior grade and within six years I was heading a section. You see, he was all for promoting from within. Not like this lot.' He broke off in confusion, suddenly remembering the circumstances of his colleague's arrival.

Jim affected not to notice. Instead he recollected his first conversation with Kenneth Furniss and what he had said about Last's brother; this seemed to bear out how he had been regarded in the firm. He decided to be non-committal. 'I've heard he was well liked?'

'He was that. It was a tragedy him being killed in that rail crash.' He decided this was as good an opportunity as any to probe. 'Didn't you work on the railways before you came here?'

Jim nodded and the questioner waited for the anticipated amplification. None came. There was an embarrassed pause before Martin continued. 'I remember round about the time it all happened. I took the trunk call in the office from Lattimer-Williams. The operator asked if we would accept the charge and of course I said yes. It was from somewhere in the Midlands.'

'Don't you mean the West Country?'

'No, it was the Midlands.' Martin was annoyed at being interrupted. 'He asked to speak to Eastermain. Now his lordship didn't come here much even then, but he was here in a meeting that night.' He felt the need to explain. 'That's why I was in working. Anyway, I asked him if he wanted me to get him straight away.' He recollected that Jim had worked there a bare ten years. 'Of course you wouldn't really know Lattimer-Williams; he's hardly been in the office since you started. But during the twenties he used to be here quite a bit.' Martin seemed to be re-living the call. 'I always knew he could be a nasty bugger, but he excelled himself that time. I was as near to slamming the phone down as dammit.'

Jim prompted him. 'But you didn't?'

'No. I interrupted them with the message. I thought I was going to get a mouthful from Eastermain as well, but he turned white and rushed off. I heard him say to Last that he had some arrangements to make.'

Jim was desperately trying to understand it all. 'But surely if Last's brother was dead, then he would have to be told?'

'But that's the whole point. It was almost like a premonition. You see, he wasn't dead when the phone call was made. He didn't die until the train crashed early the next morning.'

'Before he died? Let's get this straight, Jack. When exactly did you get this phone call?'

'It was the night before. Some time just around seven.' He noticed the stunned expression on the other man's face. 'If you don't mind me asking, why are you so interested?'

'Oh, I don't know.' Jim struggled to appear detached. 'I suppose I jumped the gun and got the impression you all had the news soon after it happened.' He picked up one of the share certificates as if he was checking something. 'Did you ever find out what all this business the night before was about?'

'No, but I thought there was something fishy about the whole thing. Eastermain was in quite a state and normally he's quite a cool character – detached almost. But then the news about Last's brother came through and drove it out of my mind, I suppose.' He glanced at his watch. 'Well, I suppose we'd better be getting on with this lot.'

'Yes . . . yes.' With an effort of will Jim forced his mind back to the job in hand. 'Yes, you're right, we'd better get moving. Where's that boy got to?'

At that moment they heard footsteps on the stairs accompanied by a tuneful whistle. The door opened and the youngster saw two pairs of eyes on him. His cheeks flushed. 'Sorry, Mr Thornton.' He added lamely, 'It's called the Lambeth Walk. You must have heard it on the wireless . . .'

Martin winked at Thornton. 'When you're called up, son, and it's likely to be sooner rather than later, the sort of walk you'll be doing won't be called Lambeth and you certainly won't be doing it to music.'

'You're in luck, Jim.' The expression of distaste on Kenneth Furniss's face belied the words.

'In luck? You mean the office pools syndicate has come up?'

'No I do not.' His voice dropped to a confidential whisper. 'They're all here. Eastermain, Lattimer-Williams . . .' He glanced at his watch. 'Even Last, and it's past four now. It must be a record for him.'

Jim felt his stomach lurch. 'Some sort of board meeting, I suppose.'

'No chance. If it was they'd have De Villiers here, doddery though he is. Anyway, these days they're all held in one of the hotels up west. No, I reckon it's some sort of crisis meeting. You know how seldom we see L-W, and as for Eastermain . . . I can't remember when he was last in.' Kenneth nodded towards Last's office. 'They've been bloody quiet. I haven't heard a dicky bird.' Something of Jim's fear must have shown because his colleague's tone became more soothing. 'I don't think we're all due for our cards. If I had to guess, it might be to do with one of their other companies.'

Jim tried to busy himself with some work, his mind churning. Instinctively he knew the meeting had nothing to do with work but very likely everything to do with Maguire and what he had found out. If they were . . . If they had been . . . worried about Maguire, then it was a racing certainty they would be worried about him as well.

Eastermain came out first. He looked neither to right nor left, but as he stalked towards the door his body language spoke volumes. Jim chanced a covert glance at the chairman's features, to find he was looking at a very angry man. Had there been an argument about something? Five minutes passed, then ten, but Last's door remained firmly closed.

Furniss sighed and bundled some files together. 'I'm off, Jim. You coming?'

'No, I've got one or two things to finish.' He watched Kenneth depart. In God's name, why was he waiting? Apart from Last and Lattimer-Williams, he was the only one in the office. But then he realised why: everything must appear normal. There must be no hint of attempting to avoid them.

Finally the door opened and they came out. Last looked surprised. 'You still here, Thornton?'

'Just clearing up, Mr Last.' The two men exchanged glances; there was the faintest of nods from Lattimer-Williams, and Last walked on.

'Some time since we talked, Thornton.' Jim noted the 'Thornton': there was obviously going to be no easy familiarity tonight. 'You remember that little talk we had . . .'

Slowly Jim put down his pen, gripping it hard to avoid any suggestion of a tremble. 'Yes, I do.' He waited. Instinct told him that elaboration could be fatal.

'We were wondering if you had heard from Maguire.'

This was it. Everything depended on how he answered. He could feel Lattimer-Williams's eyes on him. 'Maguire?' He rolled the name around his tongue, putting just a hint of a question into the enunciation. 'I'm sorry, but the name doesn't ring a bell.'

'It should, Thornton. It should.' The voice took on a harder edge. 'Think back to the inspector who was in charge of the police investigation after the accident.'

'Oh, him. I remember his name beginning with a Mac or something, but I wouldn't have recalled it as Maguire.' Lattimer-Williams remained stony-faced. Desperately Jim talked on. 'I only met him a couple of times.'

'Three times, Thornton. Three times. Once after the accident, once when he came to see you in Leeds and once in your hotel in Bristol after the trial.' He moved a little closer to the desk. 'Now I think that if I'd been facing charges of manslaughter I'd have remembered the name of everyone important connected with the case.'

From somewhere Jim found the spirit to fight back. 'Maybe you would, but all I could think about was that I might go down for ten years. There are a lot of details I don't remember about that time. My wife is always reminding me about them.'

For once Lattimer-Williams looked startled, taken aback by the counter-attack. Abruptly he changed tack. 'So I take it you haven't heard from him?'

Jim felt sufficiently emboldened to go onto the offensive. 'No. Is there any reason why I should?'

For just a moment Lattimer-Williams seemed about to answer, then he thought better of it. For the first time Jim sensed he had the advantage. 'No. It's just something that cropped up.'

CHAPTER TWENTY-FOUR

'I HAVEN'T SEEN our house for months now. Whether you like it or not I'm coming back up to London for a few days.' Rose was in her most determined mood, and so far his protests had had no effect. 'It's all fixed. Mother and Christine can look after the children while I'm away.'

'But Rose, the bombing . . . if anything happened to us, what about the children?' He tried to organise all the rational arguments against. 'I know it's hard for you down here, but there are some things we just have to put up with.'

'But you said yourself that West London hasn't been as badly hit as some other places.'

'So far, Rose. So far.' Ron's irritation was beginning to show. It was true that the bombing hadn't been as bad in their area, and quite a few women who had initially gone to stay with relatives outside London were beginning to drift back. In other circumstances it would have been wonderful to have her at home again, but he couldn't tell her the real reason for his reluctance. Try as he might, his thoughts kept returning to the man who had been watching the house. Their house! For a while afterwards he found himself checking to see if he was being followed. Then he realised how stupid that was. If he really was under surveillance, whoever it was knew where he lived. After that he had tried approaching the house from different directions to see if he could surprise the unknown watcher again, but so far there had been nothing. One thing was certain: he was being threatened. Why or by whom was of less importance than the fact that if he was under threat then anyone who was with him would also be at risk . . .

'Ron! Ron, you're daydreaming. I said I want to go back with you tomorrow, then I'll come back to Taunton next weekend.' Airily she dismissed his further protests. 'If you keep on being difficult I'll start to think you have another woman on the go.'

Slowly the train made its way forward in a series of lurches, until the hiss of steam being released heralded a complete halt. From where Ron was standing in the corridor he caught her eye. Rose smiled and glanced upward in mock-trepidation at the sleeping RAF man stretched out across the luggage rack above her. He opened the door. 'You OK, Rose?'

The airman attempted to turn over, then subsided with a groan. 'Don't worry, mate, I won't let him fall on her.' The soldier sitting next to his wife smiled reassuringly. 'Bloody RAF, always want a cushy number.' He went quiet, belatedly realising there were two more airmen sitting in the carriage. Embarrassed, he got to his feet. 'You can have my place for a bit; I'm going out to stretch my legs.' Relieved, Ron sank into the seat.

Rose whispered into his ear. 'Is it always this crowded?'

''Fraid so. And generally late getting in as well.' He put his arm round her and eased her head onto his shoulder. 'Try and get a bit of rest. It could be another hour and a half yet.'

Amid the welcome clank of couplings the train started forward again, slowly picking up speed. He glanced into the corridor, conscious of Rose's steady breathing against his shoulder. She had refused to take no for an answer, and eventually Ron had had to give in. Not that he was any happier about her being in London – even for a week. Apart from shopping she would be alone in the house all day, and there was no way he could guarantee being home at a regular hour. Still, maybe he was being paranoid. It had been three weeks since the incident, and although he couldn't be certain he didn't think the watcher had been around again. Of course it had to be connected to his enquiries about the children. Somehow his seeing Maguire had got back to them and they had reacted: there was no other obvious explanation. About the only thing he could now be certain of was who was behind it. But . . . he had to face it: covering up for shipping kids to Australia was no longer a tenable explanation. It was just conceivable that Eastermain and company might have stooped to bribery to prevent that coming out, but what about Maguire's mysterious death? Then there was confirmation from the priest that Lattimer-Williams had personally escorted those children on the night of the crash. There had to be a reason for that, but what?

The train began to brake and Ron guessed they were approaching the signals at Reading. Rose stirred against his shoulder and his arm tightened round her as she started to slip. Her hair brushed against his cheek and he glanced down at her tenderly. He was a married man with children. Given the circumstances, should he even be thinking of finding out any more?

Once again the door opened. It was the serviceman whose seat he had taken. The man saw Rose snuggling into Ron's collar and winked. 'It's all right, mate, sit down. I couldn't possibly disturb the lady, could I?'

The Piccadilly Line was crowded. These days he found it was getting harder just to squeeze on board. In the evenings it was even worse, with the platforms filling up with people taking shelter for the night. Then he relaxed a little: at least Rose was coping, which was a relief. Today's London was a very different place from the one she had left eighteen months ago. On the first day he had given her instructions about blackout curtains, shelter drill and all of that sort of stuff, but had still been worried: there were always things you couldn't plan for. Ron smiled to himself. She had been nervous when the warning went those two nights, but she seemed to have got used to it. And she was certainly enjoying making contact with the old neighbours who were still left. Still, he had better make the most of normal married life; there were only two days left before she went back to Taunton.

Once out of the station, and still thinking about Rose, he picked his way gingerly through the darkness towards home. Then a voice shook him out of his reverie. 'What the hell are you playing at, Ron?'

Startled, he looked up to find it was the local air raid warden, someone he knew well. 'Denis? Anything wrong?'

'Anything wrong? I'll say there is. It's your house that's wrong.' He peered through the dark at Ron, evidently managing to make out the surprise in his face. 'You don't know, do you?' He sighed deeply at the extent of people's carelessness. 'I think you'd better have a word with that wife of yours. Come to think of it, I'll come round and have a word with her myself.'

Ron was bemused and angry. 'What are you on about?'

'Lights, that's what I'm on about. It was like a bloody lighthouse down there! I hammered on the door until I was blue in the face but there was nobody in. Luckily for you the door wasn't locked, so I went in and switched them off. I say luckily for you because you can be reported for this. If it happens . . .'

Ron finally found his voice. 'Nobody in? And the door unlocked?' He started down the street, but this time at a run, ignoring occasional piles of debris. The house was in darkness. 'Rose! Rose!' He turned back to the street, bumping into the warden who had followed him. 'I thought you said the lights were on.'

'They were, but I switched them off.' His voice rose in panic. 'No! For God's sake don't switch them on again – not until the blackouts are down.'

'But where can she be?' Ron looked up and down the street in bewilderment. He was thinking as he spoke. 'I'd better check with the neighbours.'

'No need to do that.' The warden was squinting up the street. 'I think this is her coming now.'

Ron felt a tidal wave of relief at the sound of high heels on the pavement. It was her, he was sure of it. Why did she always insist on wearing those stupid shoes? 'Rose? Rose, is that you?'

'What's this? A reception committee?' Rose looked askance at the two men on the doorstep. 'I'm sorry ,Ron, but Mrs Grant was showing me photographs of her son . . .'

'Mrs Charteris, why did you leave those lights on?'

Ron joined in. 'And the front door unlocked.'

'I beg your pardon?' Although he couldn't see her face clearly, Ron could picture her cheeks flushing with anger. 'I didn't leave any lights on and the door was certainly locked when I left.'

The warden tried to clarify matters. 'Are you sure?'

'Of course I'm sure!' Rose's tone brooked of no further argument, and the warden subsided with a muttered goodnight.

Ron put his arms round her. 'I was worried.'

She gave him a kiss. 'I'm sorry, but what's all this about lights?'

'I don't know. Let's go inside and get the blinds down, and then we can have a thorough look round.'

Eventually Ron returned from checking upstairs and she handed him his tea. He was preoccupied and his wife was anxious. 'Do you really think we've been burgled?'

Ron pondered his tea for some time before answering. 'Unless you had a brainstorm and forgot to switch off the lights and left the door unlocked then, yes, someone has been in the house.'

'Is anything missing?'

'Not as far as I can see, but we'd better check over the next day or so.' He looked sombre. 'They were experts. The lock wasn't forced and nothing's been disturbed.'

'Then why were the lights left on?'

He shrugged his shoulders. 'Perhaps they were disturbed.'

Rose looked distinctly worried. 'Are you going to report it to the police?'

'I'd better. Not that they'll be able to do much about it – especially as nothing's been taken.'

They drank their tea in silence, each wrapped in their own thoughts. Rose broke the silence. 'Why do you keep saying "they"? Surely it might only be one man?'

'I don't know – just assuming, I suppose.' What he didn't say was that a half-smoked woodbine was lying outside just by the doorstep. As far as he knew Denis didn't smoke, and they certainly didn't. But in the kitchen he had detected the unmistakable whiff of Capstan Full Strength, a distinctive brand favoured by one of his colleagues at work. Most people stuck to one type, which indicated two people. Obviously they must think one man was no longer enough to do the job they had in mind.

CHAPTER TWENTY-FIVE

'MR THORNTON? Can these go into the archives?' Jim looked up to find a secretary staggering towards him with an armful of files.

'Watch it!' He was too late. In a slow but inexorable cascade gravity won and the files toppled over, depositing themselves across the floor.

Her face flushed and she mouthed one or two words. 'I'll pretend I didn't hear that, Janet.' Jim's tone was one of mock-severity. 'I'll give you a hand. With a bit of luck they'll still be in proper order inside the covers.'

'Thanks, Mr Thornton.' She felt the need to explain further. 'Mr Last is having a clear-out. He asked me to get rid of these.'

'Long overdue, by the looks of things.' Jim was checking as he spoke and noted that the most recent file dated back to the early 1930s. 'Has he got many more of these?'

'Another drawer full.'

Jim looked heavenwards in supplication. 'No wonder we can't find stuff when we need it.' Janet smiled in shared understanding. 'Now you take these down to the archives and don't drop them this time. I'll sort out the stuff in the other drawer and put it on my desk. You never know, there might be files in there we've been looking for for weeks.'

Last's drawer was stuffed full; Jim had difficulty forcing it open. All the files were out of date. He reached his hand to the back of the drawer, experience having taught him that it was all too easy for a rogue file to jam there. His fingers touched only a piece of paper jammed down the back. Should he bother? It might be something important. With some effort he forced his arm the length of the drawer and pulled out the hidden treasure. It was a yellowing news-paper cutting, and a quick glance revealed it to be birth announcements – obviously something personal. Jim had a vague sense of disappointment, although what he had expected to find he didn't really know. He stuffed it into his pocket to hand over later.

'Plaice and chips, sir?'

Jim looked up from his paper as the waitress arrived with his order and placed the tray in front of him. 'Thanks.' As she trans-ferred the plates onto the table he glanced around. He really must come to Lyons Corner House more often. It wasn't as well lit as before, but clean and cheerful as always. True, since rationing had started the food had been indifferent to say the least, but the service was still good. He watched the girl in her neat uniform weave her way through the tables, hardly pausing in her stride to transfer dirty dishes to her tray. They certainly deserved the name 'nippies'.

'Don't find you here very often.' A voice at his elbow roused him from his thoughts: it was Kenneth Furniss. 'Mind if I join you?'

Jim waved towards the chair opposite. 'Be my guest, Kenneth. I thought I'd get out of the office for a break today.'

'Same here.' Kenneth followed the other man's gaze towards the waitress, and for a brief moment a jocular comment came to mind – but it was swiftly rejected. Thornton was a bit too strait-laced for that sort of thing. The returning waitress paused in passing to deliver Kenneth's cup of tea and he remembered why he had decided to join Thornton in the first place. 'I was chatting to Jack Martin this morning.' He waited for a response, and when none came decided to plough on anyway. 'He's a bit worried – about your conversation the other night, that is: he feels he might have spoken out of turn.'

Jim hoped his expression gave nothing away. 'Our conversation . . . oh, you mean about L-W and the night Last's brother was killed. That was just Jack filling me in on office gossip. You know what he's like.'

'Yes, you can say that again.' Kenneth smiled his unspoken agree-ment. 'But he thought you were very interested in it all – asked a lot of questions and so on – and afterwards he wondered if . . .' He looked embarrassed. 'Well, he wondered if you had some other motive.' He tried to read Jim's face and failed. 'Not to put too fine a point on it, he wondered if there was anything that was going to rub off on him.'

Jim was not fooled by Kenneth's casual tone. Jack must be worried, and he had conveyed that worry to his colleague. In turn there was now a question mark in Kenneth's mind about Jim, and that could be dangerous. He decided to play it as straight as he could in the circumstances. 'I suppose I must have sounded curious.' He hoped his tone sounded confidential. 'Kenneth, you know me: I'm not one for office gossip. Some people might think me peculiar.' Furniss shook his head, but Jim ignored the impending interruption. 'I'm sure they do – or quite a few at any rate. The point is, the other night when Jack opened up I suddenly realised how little I knew about the background of any of the directors. If any of the questions I asked sounded a bit . . . well intimidating, he'll just have to put it down to me making up for lost time.' He opened his hands in a placatory gesture. 'Jack has no need to be worried, and I'd be grateful if you could pass that on.'

Kenneth looked relieved. 'I'll do that. I know he has a tendency to let his mouth run away with him sometimes, but basically he's all right.' He glanced at the clock on the wall. 'Well, see you back at the office. I feel like a bit of fresh air.'

Once Kenneth had left Jim pushed the empty plate aside and turned to his tea. As far as he could make out he had alleviated any suspicions in his colleague's mind, but there were lessons to be learned. Any behaviour on his part that raised eyebrows might just get back to Last. Perhaps he had been incautious in pushing Jack Martin as far as he had, but the revelations had shaken him. True, there wasn't much to go on, but it confirmed that something else had happened the night before the accident, something that was connected with the fact that 'they' felt he needed to be under observation all the time. He had talked it over with Ellen, of course. She was strong-minded, some might even say stubborn, and certainly not someone who frightened easily, but her reaction this time had startled him. 'You fool, Jamie. Whatever it was, forget it.' He could see her now, face white, voice shaking with anger and, eventually, shoulders heaving as she broke down in tears.

'All right, love. All right.' He remembered his own words as he comforted her. 'If it upsets you that much I'll forget it.' But while Ellen might be able to dismiss the matter, he couldn't. The small persistent voice in his mind couldn't be silenced: it kept asking questions. What was so bad, so damning, that even a scandal about unidentified children took second place? If he did not find out or at least try to find out the truth of the affair, might he not inadvertently be putting himself in greater danger through ignorance?

Jim looked at his watch and picked up the paper. There was another twenty minutes before he was due back at the office, and try as he might his mind kept drifting back to the other business. It was a pointless exercise: whatever the secrets were they must be safe after all this time. Quickly he scanned the city pages, but there was nothing of interest. He beckoned the waitress over and reached into his pocket to get some change, pulling out the cutting along with the money. He had better remember to give it back; no doubt it referred to some relative and was of sentimental value. Idly he glanced at it, to find it wasn't just about births: there was also an 'in memoriam' item. He checked the date at the top, the 28th of October 1938, but it still didn't register. It wasn't until he saw the words 'Wessex Yeomanry' that levers started to click. God almighty, the 28th of October – exactly ten years after the crash! He closed his eyes and tried to organise his thoughts.

'Are you all right, sir?'

He looked up to see the concerned face of the 'nippy' staring down at him.

'Yes . . . yes, thanks.'

Again he scanned down the column: 'In loving memory of Captain John Gould, of Leamington Spa, Warwickshire, ex-officer in the Wessex Yeomanry, cruelly murdered by persons unknown on the 28th October 1928, from his loving . . .' The rest of the text swam in front of his eyes. Gould, John Gould . . . memories came back of that time years ago when Kenneth Furniss had been in such a paddy about being bawled out by L-W. According to Kenneth, Lattimer-Williams had been shouting the odds at Last, something about Gould being a 'wrong un'. At long last the full implications began to dawn. This was the reason for it all. The fact that he had a job with the firm. The fact that Maguire was now dead. It wasn't about unidentified children. It was about murder.

'Are you sure you're all right, sir?'

It was his waitress again. This time he could only nod. He pushed a two shilling piece towards her. 'That should settle the bill.' He made his way to the door, brushing past tables and oblivious to the irritated comments in his wake.

'Your change, sir. Your change.' The waitress shrugged her shoulders at the futility of her plea.

She caught the glance of another customer who smiled sympathetically. 'Never mind him, the rude devil. I'd treat it as a tip if I were you. You deserve it.'

Jim was going to be late back at the office, but for once he couldn't care less: he had to think about this new revelation. The weather was cold and wet, no time to be sitting on a bench in Lincoln's Inn Fields, but he ignored the curious glances. Taking the cutting out of his pocket, he studied it again. What was he to do? He looked around helplessly. First of all he needed time: time to work out what options he had; time to decide on what actions he could or should take.

On the next bench a down and out lit up the remains of a fag. Just for once Jim wished that he hadn't given up. Then like a flash it hit him. The cutting! He must get it back into Last's desk. Without conscious effort he found himself up and moving, jogging almost. It would have to be back in the drawer before Last came back from lunch. The fact that it had been kept secure but hidden indicated the importance that was attached to it. If they found out it was gone . . .

He crashed through the front door. 'Mr Thornton, are you all right?' The secretary looked concerned.

'Perfectly. Perfectly, Janet.' He tried to catch his breath. 'Is Mr Last back from lunch?'

'No, but he should be here soon. I'll mention that . . .'

'Good. I mean, I'll see him later.' Leaving the startled girl in his wake, Jim took the stairs two at a time. Kenneth wasn't there, but luckily his desk wasn't locked and the spare key to Last's office was in its usual place. Picking up a file for camouflage, he deliberately slowed down to a saunter, but once inside almost wrenched the drawer open. For a moment he hesitated, the cutting in his hand. Should he make a copy? A familiar voice echoed up the stairs. Last was coming! Feverishly he pushed the paper to the back of the drawer. It wasn't exactly where he had found it, but it would have to do. He pushed the drawer to, but it didn't move. Christ, it was stuck! Gently, but with increasing desperation, he eased it backwards and forwards. All the time the voice was getting louder. Then with a final massive shove he closed the drawer. He had made it. Just in time, he had made it.

CHAPTER TWENTY-SIX

'SORRY ABOUT YOUR BURGLARY, RON. Were the cops able to come up with anything?' Ellis Grindrod paused to offer his sympathy.

'Thanks, Ellis. No, not really, but then they've got their work cut out.'

'True, but I was speaking to one of the crime reporters the other day and he said that murder has dropped off amazingly. Probably something to do with the war.' The art editor looked reflective. 'But on the other hand ordinary theft and burglary have gone up significantly.'

'Thanks for cheering me up, Ellis. You're making me feel very lucky.'

'He wasn't at all happy. Less juicy copy, I suppose.' Something occurred to him. 'I imagine you're trying to get the locks changed?'

'Yes, but it's a problem: there don't seem to be any locksmiths left. They've all been called up. Mind you, I was lucky. My local newsagent knows somebody . . .' He left the sentence hanging.

'Newsagents always do. I don't know about you, but that's why I always pay my bill on time.' Ellis left, chuckling at his own joke.

Ron tried to concentrate on work, but his mind kept turning back to the break-in. The police had been polite but unhelpful. They had been a bit like Ellis, commenting on the increase in petty theft and the like. He could also tell that they considered the whole thing suspicious in quite another way. It was summed up by the sergeant: 'A very professional break-in with nothing taken – very odd indeed, sir.' No doubt as a consequence they had checked his records thoroughly. What had the unknown intruders been looking for? Almost certainly something about the unidentified children. The first thing he had checked was the file where he kept all the notes he had made over the years. It was undisturbed, but then it was in the attic and he didn't think anyone had been up there. Even if they had how would they have known what they were looking for? It didn't make sense; they had to be looking for something or . . . somebody. He felt numb. That must be it. Break into the house without any obvious sign . . . risk switching on the lights to check for a place of conceal-ment . . . wait for the person or persons to come back. Somebody – maybe Denis – had disturbed them. They couldn't risk being caught or identified, so they had fled. Ron took one or two deep breaths. He mustn't get carried away: this was London 1940, not Chicago 1926. Yet it all made sense. It all hung together. Somebody had watched the house and made to attack him. Somebody – in his own mind the same person – had then broken in. The logic was unavoidable. If they had tried once the chances were they would try again. If he went to the police they would treat him as a lunatic. Thank God Rose was now back in Taunton; at least she was out of danger.

'Ron, I thought you wanted to get away for a couple of hours to check security at your place?' Morris, the deputy editor, shouted to make himself heard over the hubbub. 'Now's as good a time as any, but I want you back on duty by six.'

Grateful for the break, Ron gave Morris the thumbs-up and reached for his coat.

The newsagent indicated that Ron should wait, and it wasn't until the shop was empty that he delved into a drawer. 'The feller I had in mind was fine, but it was bloody difficult finding replacement locks.' He sounded apologetic. 'I'm afraid it's going to cost.'

Ron was philosophical. 'How much?'

'Six pounds, but there's a couple of spare keys for each of them.'

He strode down the road, still seething. Six pounds! It just about cleaned him out of ready cash. Still, he didn't have many options. Once at the house he tried the key he had just been given and after some effort it turned. Obviously six pounds didn't cover oil. He picked up the mail, then put the kettle on: he had time for a cup of tea before rushing back to work.

There were two letters. Rose's was instantly recognisable. The other wasn't familiar, and it was only the postmark that revealed it was yet another missive from that priest in Malvern. He groaned. What he didn't need was an extended and long-winded correspondence stemming from that first enquiry.

He read Rose's letter first and found himself depressed. It wasn't as if there was any dramatically bad news. His son, John, had been in a fight with an evacuee boy at school and the headmaster had been displeased. In addition Christine had had to register to train for munitions work. She would probably need to go up to Bristol and her mother was worried. Wearily he put the letter to one side. No, it was nothing dramatic, just the usual minutiae of family life. The trouble was he wasn't there to share it. Then he shook himself. This was stupid. Here he was near to wallowing in self-pity while millions of men and women were away from their families for the duration.

Finishing the tea, Ron picked up the other letter only to be ready to drop it in the bin after the first few lines. God knows what it must have been like sitting through this man's sermons! 'Interesting news': the words drew his eye down the page, but what followed wasn't just interesting, it was mind-blowing. 'I have had a letter from Basil Tomlinson, in Australia, the boy you were enquiring about. He is well and has joined the Australian army . . .' Firmly Ron placed the letter face down on the table, took a deep breath and turned it over again. There was no mistake. The boy was alive. He read on. 'His sister Heather is still in Carricktown. She is engaged to a local farmer.' The letter ended with the words, 'Basil sent me a photograph of himself in his army uniform. I hope you don't mind, but I would rather not send it through the post. On the other hand, if you are in the vicinity . . .'

Luckily there was enough tea in the pot for a second cup. Ron held it in both hands while he tried to come to terms with what he had just read. Those were the two seen on the platform at Birmingham that night. Those were the ones that the police 'knew' were the dead children. But they couldn't be: they had survived. So who did the bodies found in the wreckage belong to? He shook his head. Better to leave that for the moment. But if they weren't the ones, then why all the subterfuge and bribery from Eastermain and his cronies? Why all the threats and . . . he thought of Maguire . . . maybe murder? His mind was in a whirl. Better put first things first. He was being threatened, and that must be because he was perceived to be a danger. If he was to counteract that, on the basis of the old adage that information was power, he needed to find out more. There was only one source he could think of. Even after all this time, and whatever the risks, he must try to contact Thornton again.

For the third time that week Ron used up most of his precious lunch hour trying to make himself inconspicuous outside the offices of De Villiers and Last. The only cover was a news stand opposite, and the meagreness of this camouflage was demonstrated on the first day when a policeman had demanded his identity card. Thereafter he had let it drop to the newspaper seller that he was trying to meet 'a lady' who worked nearby. No doubt in the vendor's eyes this made him a pathetic case, but it gave him a reason for hanging around.

Anyway, this would have to be the last day. At the best of times it was difficult to be out of the office at midday, even at supposed lunchtimes. As it was, he was not sure if he would recognise Thornton after all this time: he had only seen him once face to face in that hotel in Bristol, with just an indirect glimpse a few years ago in the offices opposite. Even as Ron was coming to terms with possible failure, two figures emerged from the door opposite. Could that be him? Hurriedly he crossed the street and fell in behind them. Yes, he was sure, one of the men was Thornton. But he was going to lunch with a colleague. Damn it! Then the other man peeled off and went down a side street. Ron followed Thornton closely but cautiously. If the moment came to approach him he must seize it: there was unlikely to be a second chance.

Eventually Thornton turned into a Lyons Corner House. Good. If things worked out this might be just the place, but would he be meeting colleagues? Ron needn't have worried: Thornton went to a table in the corner and sat down on his own. He was probably a bit of a loner, and who could blame him in the circumstances?

'Do you mind if I sit here? There doesn't seem to be too much room today.'

Thornton looked up startled, and cast his gaze towards the many gaps on other tables. 'Yes, of course.' He returned to his newspaper.

'Quality of the food has gone down a bit.'

His attempt at conversation didn't go down too well. Thornton was obviously irritated at being interrupted and showed it. 'Don't you know there's a war on?'

The waitress came over, took Thornton's order and looked expectantly at Ron who, remembering the sandwiches left in his desk, made a show of searching his pockets. He smiled winningly at the girl. 'I'm sorry, but I seem to have left my wallet at the office. I'm afraid I'll just have to leave it.'

Once the girl had gone he addressed his companion. 'That was a stupid thing to do.' Thornton didn't take his eyes off the newspaper, but merely grunted. 'You see, Mr Thornton, I didn't really come here for a meal. I came to talk to you.'

The effect was electrifying. The other man turned white. He put down his paper, his fingers trembling. It took some time for the words to emerge. 'Who are you?'

Ron was alarmed at the effect his words had had. 'Don't worry, Mr Thornton. In a peculiar sort of way I think we may be in the same boat.'

'Same boat?' Jim repeated the words mechanically.

'Yes. You see I met you once before. In that hotel in Bristol. The Mallandain wasn't it?'

Slowly recognition dawned on Jim's face. His tone, indeed his whole demeanour, changed markedly. 'You're that bloody journalist, the one that did for Maguire.'

'No. Maguire did for himself, with some help, I imagine, from people we both know about.'

'Don't be bloody clever with me!' Jim's rage was icy. 'I don't know what you want, nor do I care. I just want you to keep away from me. Is that clear?'

He was very near to walking out. Ron's only strategy was to goad him into an indiscretion. 'Yes, quite clear. But I honestly don't know what you're so scared of.'

Their conversation was attracting curious glances, and Thornton's voice dropped until it was practically inaudible. The words came out almost as a hiss. 'Aren't two murders enough for you? Do you want to add more?'

'Two?'

'Yes, two. Gould and Maguire. And just because there was more than ten years between them, don't think you can rely on the same sort of gap next time. Just remember – keep away from me!'

'Oh! Has he gone?' A perplexed waitress was holding a bowl of soup.

Both pairs of eyes followed the receding figure. Ron felt it was beholden to him to provide some sort of explanation. 'Sorry, but I don't think he felt well.'

As an angry waitress made her way back to the kitchen, Jim Thornton's words came back to him: 'two murders' and 'more than ten years between them'. Ron remembered the army museum in Dorset and the photograph with two figures excised: Frobisher and Gould. So Gould had also been murdered, but when and where? A ten year gap would make it the late twenties or early thirties, round about the time of the train crash. The train crash! What was it Ferguson had said about that murder in the Midlands? That he had felt there was something funny about the investigation. That could be it. Hardly able to contain his excitement, he made his way out. Maybe it was a long shot, but a quick check on back issues in the library should prove it one way or the other.

'You never ask easy questions, do you?' The assistant librarian's grumbles continued as he lifted the old copy onto the table. 'We only keep the past five years up here; the rest are in the archives.' He

189

turned the pages until he arrived at what he was looking for. 'This is it: 30th October 1928.'

Ron followed his pointing finger and read the headline. 'Brutal murder in Leamington Spa.' Quickly he scanned the rest of the article. It was exactly as he expected. A Captain John Gould had been murdered at his home in the early evening of the 28th. Police were working on the suspicion that it had been committed in the course of a burglary, and an early arrest could be expected . . . Well, they would say that, wouldn't they? He met the librarian's glance. 'Any chance of seeing the following day's . . .' The look on the face opposite decided the matter. 'No, on second thoughts it doesn't matter. I've all the information I need here.'

'Thanks, Vera.' It had been a long afternoon. Gratefully Ron accepted the cup the tea lady placed on his desk. At last he was able to allow his mind to turn back to what he had discovered. Now it all, or nearly all, made sense. The reason why Lattimer-Williams was escorting the children was explained. It was some sort of alibi, should that be needed in the face of the police investigation. The crash, and the publicity generated by the mystery of the unidentified children, must have complicated matters – particularly since Last, obviously one of the perpetrators, had been killed. So Maguire and Thornton were rewarded for keeping quiet about what they'd found out or seen. As, in a minor way, were people like himself and Rose, who had just stumbled about on the peripheries of the whole thing. No wonder there had been a violent reaction to any threat of re-opening that particular can of worms. Murder was a hanging offence, and there was no statute of limitations.

But given what he now knew, his own position was more precarious than ever. What action should he take: write it all down and deposit the document with a solicitor? After all, that was what was done in the best detective novels. On reflection perhaps not – for despite everything he still felt a vague sense of unease. The police weren't fools. If the original murder had been investigated thoroughly they would soon have come up with the prime suspects. He realised that Ferguson felt the case was steered away from the real culprits: he was a copper and had a nose for these things. It accorded with what the general public felt about people with power and influence: that they could get away with anything. As a journalist Ron knew they could get away with a lot, but there were limits – and murder was way past any of them. And he was almost forgetting the children. None of this threw any light on who they were. Unless . . . unless . . . the two things were connected.

CHAPTER TWENTY-SEVEN

'PASS RIGHT ALONG NOW.' The voice of the inspector was becoming more and more muffled as ever more bodies crowded onto the southbound platform of the Northern Line at Bank station. It had been over half an hour since the last train and the atmosphere was airless. Jostled forward by yet another surge of bodies, Jim cursed himself for not staying in the office for an hour or so, until the worst of the crush was over. And a crush was to be expected, for this was the main underground station for the City. There was a rumble in the distance, setting off a murmur in the crowd. Expectations rose, then quickly faded as it proved only to be the sound of a north-bound train, its passage marked by a rush of hot, stale air. Someone forced his way into the space behind him and he could feel the pressure from the mass of bodies. Surely they would close the platform now: the numbers were getting dangerous.

Jim managed to look at his watch. He was going to be late, very late probably, and Ellen would be worried. Of course the bombing was worry enough on its own, but now with everything else . . . He comforted himself with the knowledge that he had married a strong woman. Whatever happened she would cope.

He had been watchful in the office, but without giving anything away. Now, of all times, he must not draw attention to himself by behaving in any way that was out of character. He thought about the meeting with that reporter. But how could it be described as a meeting? He had been waylaid, nothing more or less! Still, his worry was that something might get back to the office, even though it was hardly likely. He was positive there had been no one he knew in the

Corner House today. Anyway, he had made his feelings plain. Even a reporter as thick-skinned as that one must know there was positively no more information to be had from him.

Jim shuffled uncomfortably as the crowd pressure increased. Murder, that was what was behind it all. Why? He didn't know, but it hardly mattered. That was the reason Lattimer-Williams and Last's brother had been in the Midlands that night. And people were hanged for murder. There had been that case in Pentonville only a week ago. He shuddered. If their necks were at risk no wonder they wanted to be certain of him at all times. He couldn't prove anything, of course, but if the police got hold of that angle then they surely would.

There was a sudden surge behind him as more people crowded onto the platform. Irritated, Jim glanced over his shoulder at those who were pressing behind, then returned to his own thoughts. How stupid he had been to dismiss Maguire's letter as being paranoid. Somehow he must have found out, or at least suspected something. Had he made contact with them again? Threatened something? Demanded more? It didn't matter. Now he was dead. Just as he would be if he gave the slightest cause for suspicion.

At last. The faint rumble in the tunnel was growing in volume. Jim pressed forward as near to the platform edge as he dared, and felt the pressure behind him as others did the same. Deep in the tunnel the lights appeared. Would he be lucky with the doors or would he have to fight to get in? The pressure behind him grew more insistent. The fool, whoever he was! Didn't he realise he would have him over the edge? He pressed back, but the only response was a much greater pressure from behind. The train was nearly on him now, and still he was being propelled forward. Almost too late he realised his danger. Desperately he threw himself downwards, clawing at feet and legs to gain enough purchase to draw himself away from the platform edge. Jim felt the blast of heat from under the engine and thought he was aware of a foot still trying to force him between the platform and the still-moving carriages. He rolled over and, just for a moment, looked directly into the eyes of the man who had been behind: they seemed full of concern. He was just an ordinary man dressed in ordinary city clothes.

'Make a bit of room here.' The same man knelt beside him as passengers crowded round: some to help, some to gawp. His helper looked around. 'I think he fainted. Does anyone here know first aid?'

'You bastard! You tried to push me under!' Jim grasped the man by the lapels and tried to pull himself up, but was restrained by other passengers. The man turned pink and looked embarrassed. Then Jim felt a woman patting his face. As she did so, she turned to address the first helper. 'Don't worry: it must be shock.'

Despite his protests, he was half-carried to the back of the platform and made to lie down on a bench. A few concerned faces lingered over him, but as he recovered they began to drift away.

Suddenly the station seemed empty. He looked at his watch again. It was half past seven. He must get home, but the next train seemed to be an age in coming and all the time his mind was in turmoil. Had someone tried to kill him? He was certain there had been deliberate pressure from behind. But might not the man himself have been pushed by the pressure of the crowd? And why would he stay and try to help? Had it been a clever ploy? The train came in half-empty, and he waited until he could clearly see every person getting on before standing up. He was trembling, but there was absolutely nothing he could do about it. Almost holding his breath, Jim walked quickly to the nearest carriage. Surely everyone must be watching him. Still fearful, he sat next to the door and surreptitiously eyed all his fellow passengers, but none even remotely resembled the man he had seen. As the train lurched and rattled southwards some of the panic left him and rational thought returned. He could have been mistaken. After all, people often went under the tubes – most, it was true, suicides. Then the dark thoughts returned. How convenient if he had gone under: all their worries would now be over. And if it had been deliberate, he now knew they had tried and failed. That placed him in even greater danger than ever. Not noticing the fetid air, Jim found himself breathing deeply.

The train ground to a halt. For ten minutes or so there was silence until the sound of voices came from the trackside. Passengers glanced at each other anxiously, and one or two even started conversations. 'Everybody follow me to the front of the train.' The words heralded the appearance of the guard at the door at the end of the carriage, followed by a file of passengers. The guard didn't reply to the chorus of panicky questions, but merely repeated his instructions. As Jim got up to join the queue one of the men muttered under his breath, 'Power failure. We're all to walk to Clapham South and get out there.'

There were a few underground staff with torches, and by their feeble light they all stumbled their way to the station platform and from there up the stairs to the street. Jim weighed up the options and decided it was best to walk, even though it would be a couple of hours. Gradually his eyes became accustomed to the blackness, and he almost laughed as he realised that walking in the blackout was safer than almost anything else.

He must have been about a mile and a half from home when the sirens went. God, it was early tonight. The explosions started almost immediately, and they were heavy. He must get home. His eyes had accustomed themselves to the darkness and he started to run. From half a mile away he could see the glare and hear the noise of fire engines. Jim's breath came in wheezing gasps as he forced his legs to keep on running, until at last the corner of his street came into view. Already he could see the glare of flames. As he ran he screamed 'Ellen, Maureen', 'Ellen, Maureen', as if it would somehow afford them protection.

The policeman held him back. 'They're doing their best down there. Stay here for the moment.'

He struggled free, only to find someone else holding him. 'Jim! Jim! They're all right. Listen to me. They're all right.' It was Dave, his neighbour from up the street. 'Truly, Jim, Ellen and Maureen are all right. They're with Mavis and me. The bomb landed in the gardens at the back and your house and the one next door are damaged, but no one in the street's hurt.' A few doors down Jim could see the shattered windows and buckled door frame of his home. His instinct was still to get to it, but he allowed himself to be led to his neighbours' house.

Ellen and Maureen were crying, and for a long while they just clung to him. Then it all poured out. The explosion. The house shaking. The windows breaking. He listened with a dreadful feeling of guilt: he should have been there with them. Then Mavis brought the tea and with it came euphoria. They were alive. They had survived. They were together!'

'We can stay with Dave and Mavis for a few nights. I've talked to her and they don't mind a bit.' Ellen tried to put the best gloss possible on their situation. 'The council might be able to help with temporary re-housing. Mavis says that Wimbledon isn't under as much pressure as a lot of places.'

Jim nodded, too busy regarding what was once his home to take in fully what she was saying. From the outside it didn't look too bad, but he remembered the words of the fireman in charge. 'Sorry, sir. It's structurally unsound – a death trap – it's got to come down'. With an effort he wrenched his thoughts away from the house.

'No, love. We're going to go back up north. Back to Leeds.'

All the old arguments – so well rehearsed these last couple of days – came tumbling out. What about his job and Maureen's school and the friends they had made? The bombing seemed to have driven all other thoughts out of her mind. Although he had talked about it, she hadn't once mentioned the threat he might be under. It was almost as if her life had now reached another, more rarefied, plane – where the old concerns, mundane or vital, had no place. He hadn't told her about the incident on the underground platform. At first it had been driven from his mind, and later it seemed like unbearable cruelty to add to her fears. By now his thoughts had clarified. It didn't really matter whether it had been an accident or deliberate. Now Maguire was dead he was their only danger. The only witness who could place Lattimer-Williams and Last's brother in Birmingham that night. There would be another time, and if last night had been planned then it would be soon.

'Ellen, you know why we must go. You come up to the City tomorrow lunchtime and I'll take the afternoon off so we can sort out things with that solicitor. Given what's happened no one will mind.' She didn't seem to be listening, and gently he took her by the arms. 'Look, I'll hand in my notice at work and we'll go as soon as possible. No one will suspect anything. It'll seem a perfectly normal thing to do.' She still wouldn't meet his eye. He gave her a hug. 'I'll even request a reference. If there are any suspicions that should do the trick.'

Her shoulders sank in resignation. 'All right, Jamie. Have it your way. But if what you think is true then you can't run for ever. Sooner or later you'll have to face it.'

CHAPTER TWENTY-EIGHT

'RON!' HE BECAME AWARE of a sub-editor shouting at him. 'A meeting with Morris. He wants all of us over there now.'

'Everybody here?' The deputy editor quickly checked. 'Right, I've got some bad news and some good news. The bad news is that Denton and Smith here', he nodded towards two junior reporters, 'have got their call up papers.'

Over the noise of commiseration a voice piped up. 'And the good news?'

'The good news is that as far as I know they don't owe anybody any money.' Once the laughter had subsided Morris continued. 'Now there's a serious side. We're short-handed as it is, so this will mean a major re-organisation of who covers what. What I'm going to do now is have a quick meeting with the senior people and come up with re-arranged duties.'

'So we're more or less in agreement.' The deputy editor made some final notes. 'I'll get these typed up and circulated.' He anticipated the next question. 'Any mutinies I'll deal with later.' They got up to go, but Ron was called back. Morris was apologetic. 'Ron, I'm sorry about this. I can imagine what it's like having your missus down in Somerset – but it just isn't going to be possible for you to go down there every third or fourth weekend. We need you here. I know you more than make up for it with all the extra hours you put in during the week, but that isn't the point. From now on it's going to be all hands to the pump.'

Ron's mind was already on Rose and how she would take it. He sighed. 'I suppose there's no alternative.'

'Look, we can manage this weekend. Why don't you go down on Thursday night and see what you can sort out? And don't worry, as far as "upstairs" is concerned I'll say it's on compassionate grounds.'

Forlornly Ron checked his watch yet again as the train eased its way into Bristol. It was no good: the last train to Taunton would have gone long ago. Thank God George didn't live far from the station; he would just have to prevail on him again.

He needn't have worried: George was bonhomie personified. 'Nonsense, it's great to see you. Now can I get you anything to eat?'

Afterwards they sat chatting over the two bottles of light ale that George had dug out from deep within a cupboard. Ron hoped against hope they weren't using up his strategic reserves. Once all the personal chat was completed, Ron diffidently mentioned his fresh discoveries. He desperately wanted to share what he had found out, yet at the same time he was worried that the very act of sharing might expose his friend to some of the dangers he faced. 'Thanks for hearing me out. I needed to talk to somebody.'

George was surprised. 'Don't you talk to Rose about it?'

'Maybe I should, but I know her: she'd be desperate with worry.'

For a while they mulled over their conversation in silence. It was George who spoke first. 'I think you need to go to the police.'

'But I told you what Ferguson said. It's been investigated and glossed over already. My raising it again wouldn't be taken seriously. For one thing there's no evidence that would stand up in court, and for another, whatever sort of protection these people have is likely still to be in place.'

'So what are you going to do?'

'I honestly don't know.'

Another silence ensued, but this time it was gloomy rather than reflective, so much so that George became uneasy. He decided to move the conversation on. 'You're no nearer to finding out who those children really were?'

'No. Have you any ideas?'

'Sorry, the Sherlock Holmes thing isn't my forte. Hang on, though, there was something you talked about one time.' George racked his brains. 'I remember. One of the people who died was a woman from Carrington House.'

'Yes. Let's see . . . her name was . . . Elaine . . . Elaine Wilson. Does that mean something?'

'Not the name. No, it's Carrington House. Surely you've heard about it?'

'Isn't it owned by the Omerod family?'

'Was. They lost a packet in the crash of '29. The house was sold, and as far as I know it's an hotel now.'

Ron grew impatient. 'Come on, George. What was so peculiar about it?'

'It's what went on there until the twenties – wild parties, orgies, drugs, you name it.'

'Then why haven't I heard of it?'

'Because I'm a bit older than you and I was still working on the paper when some of it was going on. I suppose it all petered out in the mid-twenties.'

'This is intriguing. Who was at these parties?'

'Practically all the high society names of that era, from film stars to royalty.'

'I see . . .' Scenarios of the weirdest and wildest kind began to cascade through Ron's brain. 'But surely . . . the police . . . I mean . . .' He subsided, still considering some of the possibilities that had been raised.

George shrugged. 'I'm certain the police would have been aware of it . . . so I assume they looked into any possibilities . . .' He too lapsed into silence.

Ron came to a decision. 'Isn't this the place near Meldon station?'

'Yes, about a couple of miles I'd say. Why? Surely you're not thinking of going there?'

'Yes. If I get an early train tomorrow morning I can be back here in time to catch one of the evening connections to Taunton.' He could see the doubt in George's eyes. 'Rose isn't expecting me until tomorrow night, and given what I've told you about the office God knows when or if I'll get another opportunity.'

Carrington village was a dreary little place. The straggle of houses showed absolutely no sign of life. Surely there must at least be a pub? At last he found it, the Bird in Hand. From the outside it looked closed. Ron tried the front door and, finding it locked, he knocked. There was no response. Somewhat at a loss, he stood for a while wondering what to do next, when suddenly the door opened. A burly character appeared and addressed him in none-too-friendly terms. 'Were you the one doing the knocking?'

'I was. Are you open?'

'No, we're not.'

He made to shut the door but Ron spoke quickly. 'I'm a journalist. Are you the landlord?'

The man hesitated, obviously interested. 'I am. What are you after?'

'I'm investigating the Eastmead train crash, and I understand one of those killed came from round here. You see, I've got information on all the other victims but so far nothing on her.' With a flourish he took a notebook and pencil from his inside pocket. As ever it worked a treat.

'You'd better come in.'

He followed the landlord into a dingy bar to be greeted by the sight of a formidable-looking woman in a pinafore who looked distinctly unhappy. 'Kenneth, it's only half past eleven. You'll lose your licence, letting customers in at this time.'

'Oh, do shut up, woman, he's a journalist. Now get us some tea.' Ron braced himself for an argument, but none came. Instead she glared at him, then flounced away. The landlord indicated a chair. 'Sit down. What paper are you from?'

'Thanks. I'm from the *Express*.'

'The *Daily Express*?' The landlord was impressed.

'Yes. I understand an Elaine Wilson from Carrington House was one of those killed. Did you know her?"

'I was a gardener there until they sold the house, but she was before my time.' He turned impatiently. 'The wife will know more. She was an under-housekeeper there. 'Ada! Ada!' The bellow echoed through the bar.

Ada came back with a tray, a teapot and three mugs. 'Kenneth, what will he think, you going on like that.'

Ron sought to defuse any tension by picking up the teapot and offering to pour. The landlord looked horrified. 'Good God, no.' He went to the bar and came back with three bottles. Two, Ron noticed, were India Pale Ale and the third was stout. He proceeded to fill the mugs. He grinned. 'Cheers. Can't be too careful.' Once more Ron attempted to start his spiel but the landlord beat him to it. 'He wants to find out about Elaine Wilson, her who was killed in the crash.'

'Her!' Ada's intonation allowed for all sorts of interpretations. 'She was there when I started.'

'When would that be?' Ron sat with pencil poised.

'It was 1913. She was maybe three years older than me.' Ron sensed a certain evasiveness.

'What sort of person was she?'

Ada looked embarrassed. 'She was . . . popular.'

He persisted. 'In what way?'

It was the landlord who broke the impasse. 'Come on, Ada, you've told me about her before.' He turned back to Ron. 'She had it away with anyone in trousers.'

'Kenneth!' Despite the reproof she didn't disagree with her husband's assessment.

Reminded of what George had told him, Ron decided to probe a little. 'I've heard there were lots of parties at the house.'

Ada's face was a study. At first she tried to look disapproving, but little by little her features creased into a smile. 'Oh, there were. All those people from society . . .' Her voice dropped. 'The stories I could tell you . . .' Both Ron and her husband waited for the revelations, but none came. 'All I can say is we respectable girls had to lock our doors at nights.'

Her husband guffawed. 'And some of the footmen as well, from what I've heard.'

Ron pressed on. 'I take it that Elaine wasn't one of those who locked her door?'

Ada could no longer contain the giggles. 'When she was around it was the men who had to lock themselves away.'

Ron joined in the general mirth. It was going much better than he could have hoped for. 'So when did she leave?'

'It was towards the end of the war, round about 1917 I think. We heard she'd gone to work somewhere in the south of France.' Ada gave him a knowing look. 'It must have been somebody she'd met at the house. I mean, why else would anyone have gone over there when the war was still on?'

'And did she come back much after that? I understand her mother was a housekeeper there.'

'Mrs Wilson . . . now she was a really nice soul. That daughter of hers fair scandalised her.'

'Yes, but did Elaine come back at all?'

'No, I never saw her again.'

But she was at Carrington House the night before the train crash?'

There was a puzzled silence from Ada. 'Yes – that was funny. We only heard afterwards, of course, but hardly anybody knew she was there. She came lateish the night before, after it was dark, and left early in the morning.'

Her husband broke in. 'I knew Donaldson, the chauffeur. He was a close one and no mistake: you could hardly get two words out of him. When the word came out about her getting killed he said he'd picked them up from the station and taken them back in the morning.'

All Ron's senses were alert. 'You said "them".'

The landlord looked put out. 'I expect he meant her mother had gone to meet her and to see her off.'

The beer was going flat and Ron took a final draught. 'That's not bad ale. Can I buy you another one?' The landlord declined so he pushed on. 'And what about her mother? Is she still around?'

This time it was Ada who answered. 'She was in a terrible state when the news came out. Mrs Omerod had her admitted to a nursing home.'

'Committed, more like.'

Ada reacted angrily to her husband's muttered comment. 'How can you say that? Mrs Omerod was kindness itself. It must cost a pretty penny to be in that place, but the money's always been there, even though they've come down in the world a bit.'

'Is she still in the nursing home?' Ron was intrigued.

'Oh yes. She's in the Montfort Grove Home: that's the big place between here and the station. But none of us – and I mean all the old staff who knew her – are allowed to visit.' Ada sniffed in disbelief. 'We're always told she's too ill.'

'Do you think . . . ?'

'Do you think you might get to see her?' The landlord shook his head. 'No chance of that. You have to make an appointment.'

Wearily Ron trudged towards the station. He had managed to catch a bus to the village, but the one going back was too late for his train. On his left he spotted some turrets through the trees, and gradually a big Victorian folly came into view; a sign at the firmly locked gates stated that this was Montfort Grove Nursing Home. Was it worth his while trying to get in? He stood undecided for a while until a chauffeur-driven car slid to a halt by the gates and two men and a woman got out. He was in luck: there were visitors, and this might just be his chance. He strolled in behind them, wishing the porter a hearty 'good afternoon' as he did so. He wasn't challenged; nor was he challenged as he went through the front door into the large hallway. Then his problems started.

The other three visitors were obviously expected, and made their way up some stairs escorted by a uniformed nurse. Through an open door a young woman dressed in civilian clothes eyed him curiously. 'Can I help you?'

Ron strode over putting on his most open and friendly expression. 'I hope so. My name's Davis. I telephoned yesterday. It's to see Mrs Wilson.'

The woman scanned through what looked like an appointments diary, looking increasingly puzzled. 'I can't see any mention of your name. When exactly did you telephone?'

He took a chance. 'It was early evening. I spoke to a very pleasant . . .'

'That would be Adèle; she was on duty then.' Her tone became petulant. 'I keep on reminding her to note down all visitors.'

'I do hope I won't get her into trouble.'

'I expect Matron will have a word with her.' She gave up on the diary. 'You see, Mr Davis, there's a strict rule about not seeing guests without an appointment. Would you be able to come back another time?'

'No – I'm just passing through.' Ron injected what he hoped was just the right amount of hesitation and confidentiality into his next remark. 'War work, you understand.'

Her demeanour became markedly more sympathetic. 'Of course. My brother . . .'

'Then you'll understand. I used to work at Carrington House with Mrs Wilson. I really wanted to see her, and this could well be my last opportunity.'

She reached a decision. 'In the circumstances I can't see why not. I'll get one of the assistants to take you up to her room.'

The nursing assistant stopped at one of the doors. 'Just hang on here, Mr Davis, I'll just see that she's tidy.' Uneasy now at the number of lies he had had to tell to gain entrance, Ron paced up and down impatiently. 'She's ready now.' The assistant ushered him in with a whispered aside. 'She's not too good today.'

Mrs Wilson lay propped up on her pillows. He didn't quite know what he'd been prepared for, but his heart sank. On the bed was a very frail old lady. 'Who are you?' Her quavering voice matched her appearance.

'Hello, Mrs Wilson. I worked at the house in the twenties. I just wanted to see how you were.' The lies flowed all too easily. Maybe there was a special place in hell for journalists.

She held herself up and peered into his face. 'Yes, I remember you.' He hoped his surprise didn't show.

'I'll be going. Have a nice chat. I'll be back in a quarter of an hour.' The door closed behind the assistant, and Mrs Wilson sank back into her pillow.

Ron could see there was a vacancy behind her stare. If she was gaga there was little he could hope for, but at least he had a quarter of an hour. 'I really came to talk about Elaine.' Her eyes filled with tears; it made him feel terrible, but he persisted. 'She didn't stay long at the house, did she?'

The old lady's voice broke. 'It was the first time I'd seen them. Mrs Omerod said they had to be away before the rest of the house was up.' Ron tried to interrupt, but she gripped his arm with surprising strength. 'It was the first time they let them visit, but she told me straight they mustn't come again. They never will now, will they?' She turned her face away.

'Mrs Wilson, you keep saying "them".'

She didn't seem to hear. 'They tried to take everything away. Every little keepsake. But they were my grandchildren too . . . my grandchildren too . . .' Her voice died away.

'Mrs Wilson. Mrs Wilson.' Ron leaned closer, urgency in his voice. 'Were these Elaine's children?'

She ignored the question. 'Elaine gave me something. She said to me, "Look after these, Mum, for the sake of the children."' For a few moments her breathing grew heavy, then slowly it calmed. When she started talking again her voice was weary. 'Afterwards they thought they'd taken everything, but they didn't find it.'

One part of his brain was urging caution, but it was the other part that was in charge. 'Find what, Mrs Wilson? Find what?'

She gestured weakly towards her bedside cupboard. 'In there.'

A clatter of footsteps came up the corridor. He hesitated, but they went past the door. The cupboard door wasn't locked. 'What did you want me to get, Mrs Wilson?'

'The bag.' She sounded very tired.

He pulled out a large old-fashioned leather handbag. 'Is this it?'

She nodded and he passed it over. To his surprise she didn't try to open it, but instead pushed it back to him. 'The end . . . the pocket at the end.'

He checked both ends, but saw nothing. She was becoming impatient, gesturing towards the part he was examining. It was then that he made out an almost invisible compartment that fitted flush with the outside leather. He dug in a finger, prised it open and pulled out the envelope it contained. 'What do you want me to do with this?'

She seemed to be summoning her last reserves of energy. 'Generally she's the only one that comes. But all this time and you're the first one from the house, the first one from the old days to come and see me.' Once again she gripped his arm. 'They weren't bastards! They weren't! You'll see that everyone knows that, won't you?'

A lump forming in his throat, Ron nodded. Perhaps it was his imagination, but she seemed happier, more peaceful. On the other hand it was probably only his conscience over-compensating for the deception he had perpetrated.

When the assistant returned Mrs Wilson was asleep. She exchanged glances with Ron. 'Did she enjoy seeing you?'

Ron smiled his thanks as he followed her out. 'I think so. I think so.'

George wasn't at home. Ron could have caught the train straight to Taunton but he needed somewhere private to check the envelope. Gingerly he tore it open, on tenterhooks lest he also tear whatever documents were inside. Then he emptied the contents onto the table. There were photographs, some documents and a ring – a plain gold wedding ring. He held it up to the light. Although no expert, he could see it must have been expensive. On the inside there was an inscription, 'to Elaine from E'. That was strange: her first name but only the initial of her presumed husband.

He turned to the documents, noting the heading 'Republique Francais'. The first one was a marriage certificate. The bride's name was there, and also the groom's, Edward Brown. The names of the witnesses were difficult to decipher, but looked like Monsieur Dupont and Madame Castaing. The date was October 1917, and the ceremony had been at the mairie of somewhere called Vernet. Where the hell was that? George had an old atlas, and a check through the gazetteer revealed several Vernets. The other two documents turned out to be birth certificates – obviously relating to the two children. The son, Richard Edward, had been born in April 1918. He noted the gap of only six months at best between the wedding and the birth. The daughter, Lucille, was born the following year in July. Both had been registered at different villages, but he was able to establish that both of them were near Biarritz, as was the small town of Vernet. He sat back and tried to think it through. It was obvious that these were the children who had died, but who were they? Brown could well be an assumed name; as for the witnesses, they might be friends, or just a couple of willing locals. Ron grimaced slightly. Whatever had happened, there was no way he was going to find out after all this time.

Carefully he put the documents and the ring together, then turned to the photographs. They showed a series of ordinary family scenes, which appeared to have been taken over a number of years, but there was no obvious clue of who the people were. Then his eyes alighted on one picture and the car that was shown in it . . .

'You here?' George hung up his coat in the hall. 'I thought you'd be on your way home by now.'

'I'm just off.'

'Did you have any luck today?'

'Maybe.'

'Maybe? What sort of an answer is that?'

'I picked up some gossip at the local, but I'll need to check on it.'

'Such as?'

'George, I really have to catch the train. Perhaps we can meet if I'm able to get down in the next month or two.'

'Ron, if I didn't know you better I'd say you were being cagey.' He waited for a response but none came. Instead his friend seemed to be trying to make up his mind about something. 'What's on your mind? This isn't like you.'

'I've got a favour to ask.' Slowly Ron drew something from his inside pocket. 'I hope you don't mind but I've borrowed one of your envelopes.' He pushed the package across the table towards George, who saw it was addressed to Rose.

'What the hell is this for?'

'If . . . I mean in the unlikely event . . .' He stumbled and came to a halt. 'You're my oldest friend. If anything happens to me could you see that this gets to Rose?'

CHAPTER TWENTY-NINE

'THANK GOD YOU'RE ALL RIGHT.' Kenneth Furniss shook Jim's hand. 'And the family too, of course. This bloody war.'

'Thanks, Kenneth.' Jim suddenly found he was exhausted, even though it was just ten o'clock in the morning.

'I'm surprised you've come in. What about the wife and kiddy?'

'Oh, they're fine – staying with neighbours.' For a moment he hesitated about confiding further, then pressed on: Kenneth was the salt of the earth. 'I'm leaving the firm. We're all going back up north – to Leeds.'

Kenneth frowned. 'A bit sudden, isn't it? I know you've all had an awful shock, but it's not generally a good idea to come to quick decisions, especially in the sort of circumstances you're in.'

'It's all right, Kenneth. We've been thinking about it for a while.' He managed a weak grin. 'All that's changed is that Adolf has given us a not-so-gentle push.'

'Well, you know what you're doing. If there's anything I can do to help just let me know.'

'Thanks. By the way, I'd be grateful if you didn't say anything until I've had a word in there.' Jim gestured over his shoulder, towards Last's office.'

Kenneth winked. 'Mum's the word. Mind you, I'd leave it for half an hour or so if I were you.' He went on to explain. 'Lattimer-Williams is in with him at the moment, and Last asked his secretary not to disturb them.'

Jim's carefully constructed confidence began to fall apart. Lattimer-Williams was here. He was in the office this morning of all mornings, and yet now he was in uniform he only put in odd appearances. There had even been talk that he was being sent abroad. He tried to sound off hand. 'Any idea why he's here?'

'You asking me?' Kenneth looked blank. 'As I said before, I think he has a cosy billet at the War Office somewhere. He seems to come and go pretty much as he pleases.'

'Probably something to do with the business, then.'

'I doubt it.' There was a cynical edge to Kenneth's retort. 'You know that meeting Last was going to have with those "very important possible clients"?' He saw the questioning look in Jim's eyes and remembered the trauma he must have undergone during the last few days. 'Sorry, of course you won't, not after what you've been through. He "wasn't at liberty to divulge their names" until he'd cleared it with them.' Kenneth rolled his eyes and imitated Last's mannerism of swallowing his vowels. Jim smiled weakly and nodded. 'Well, L-W turned up out of the blue, had a few quick words and Last cancelled the lot. As I said before, he told his secretary that they mustn't on any account be disturbed.'

Jim didn't know if Kenneth knew more than he was prepared to tell, but he decided to play dumb and see if anything more was forthcoming. 'It's a funny business. After all, Lattimer-Williams is only a director and away most of the time at that.'

Kenneth glanced around to make sure no one else was in earshot. 'Come on, Jim. You've been here long enough to know how things work. Yes, most of the time – at least as far as the day-to-day work is concerned – Last is in charge. But,' Kenneth dropped his voice even lower, 'there are irons in the fire here that none of us know about, and L-W calls the tune.' He didn't bother to wait for a reply. 'All I know is that he was in a filthy mood this morning, and when they got into the office I could hear him sounding off. Then Last must have asked him to tone it down, because they went quiet after that . . .' Kenneth's voice tailed off as a junior came over and he broke off to give some instructions. 'Get young what's-his-name to check it and I want to see it by twelve.' He turned back to Thornton. 'Look, Jim, I'd better get on now . . .'

'Did you catch anything? About what was said, I mean?' Jim didn't care if he was being obvious.

'It didn't mean anything to me. L-W was shouting something about "that bloody Maguire".' Jim was grateful that he had organised his features into a fixed expression, but even so Furniss must have noticed something. 'Does the name mean something?'

'Not really, Kenneth.' He hoped he didn't sound over-casual.

'Then there was something about "who else do you think the bastard blabbed to".' Kenneth shuffled some papers together. 'I really must sort out those youngsters now.' He rose to go, but not before one more confidential aside. 'They were going on about some "bloody journalist" as well, so if you ask me they've squared somebody in the financial press. Ten to one there's some crooked share dealing behind it all.'

Jim watched Lattimer-Williams stride out of the office. Should he call the whole thing off? Try and get re-housed down here after all? But what would be the point? Obviously Maguire had spoken to someone else besides him; but maybe that could work in his favour. Feverishly the thoughts raced through his mind as optimism grew. If some of it was already out in the open, surely the danger was less. They couldn't go round trying to kill everyone. Then another thought occurred to him. Maybe this time they were feeling the heat themselves. But would that make them more dangerous? More ready to strike out? Would they become more cautious? More unwilling to take action that might deliberately throw the spotlight back on them? They also knew about the reporter. Did they know he'd seen him in Lyons Corner House? God Almighty, what was he to do? Jim fixed his eyes on Last's door, desperately trying to nerve himself to take those few steps. Half a dozen times he half-rose, only to sink back. Then one thought began to take precedence over all others: they were worried. At long last they were worried. They were experiencing the same feelings he had had over all these years. The opportunity might not be perfect, but it was probably the best he would ever get. He didn't allow himself to think any more but, instead, got up and made those few final strides.

'So you see we don't have much choice.' Jim tried to read Last's face, but found it difficult. 'The house is coming down. True, we could stay with our neighbours, but that can only last for a week or two.' In the absence of any comment he babbled on. 'Maybe we'd be re-housed, but we'd have to take anything we were given, and it could be anywhere.'

'So you've decided to leave us.'

Last's sudden interjection took the wind out of his sails. 'Yes. Yes, we – that's to say my wife and myself – have decided it would be for . . . for the best.'

'I see. When would you want to go?'

'Soon. We'd like to make it soon. Given the circumstances . . .' His voice tailed off.

'Well, Thornton, how soon is soon?'

Again Jim tried to read the other man's face. 'If possible . . . Friday, next week?'

Last made a grunting noise. Jim didn't know if it was meant to be a sign of agreement. 'Next Friday, you say.' He seemed to come to a decision. 'It's not convenient, Thornton. Not convenient at all . . . But, there's a war on . . . I suppose we all have to make sacrifices.' He managed to make it sound as if the sacrifices were all on his side. 'Yes, very well.'

Jim felt a surge of relief. He had quite convinced Ellen that Last would accept it, but inside there had been a nagging doubt. 'Mr Last, I take it there's no problem with a reference?' Last looked puzzled, as if an important train of thought had just been interrupted. Jim explained further. 'With all the disruptions in mail and everything I thought it would be better for me to have a general reference to take with me.'

There was just a hint of irritation in the reply. 'Thornton, I'm sure you're aware it's not company policy to issue general references.'

'Yes. Yes. Of course.' Jim hesitated. 'There's one other thing. I really need to take this afternoon off.' He realised that Last was waiting for an explanation and he couldn't keep the exasperation from his voice. 'There are all sorts of things I need to see to . . . forms to sort out . . . arrangements to make.'

'If you must, Thornton, if you must.' Last returned to his papers, carefully waiting until the door closed behind his visitor before picking up the telephone.

CHAPTER THIRTY

'WHAT'S WRONG WITH YOU?' Rose seldom lost her temper but she had certainly lost it now. 'You've been mooning about all weekend. You won't talk to anybody – especially my mother: she's really hurt. The children keep asking if Daddy is cross with them.' She was building up to a climax. 'And you refuse to discuss when I can next come up to London. The other time I was joking, but now I'm not so sure. Ron, are you seeing another woman?'

'Don't be stupid, Rose.'

'How dare you call me stupid!' For a moment he wondered if he was going to get the contents of the saucepan over his head. 'Our last weekend together for God knows how long and you behave like this.' She went into the hall and reappeared in a coat. 'I'm going down to the grocer's. Maybe by the time I get back you'll have snapped out of this.'

'Rose! Rose!' It was no good; she was gone. Moodily Ron stared out of the window. She was right of course: the weekend was proving to be a disaster. The trouble was the discovery he had made yesterday. He could neither excise it from his mind or talk about it to Rose.

'Daddy?' Amelia had come into the room and was looking anxious. 'Are you and Mummy cross with each other?'

He put his arm round her shoulders. 'No, not really dear. Grown-ups sometimes get a little bit cross, but they generally forget about it.'

She was still worried. 'Will you and Mummy forget about it?'

'Of course we will.' He gave her a squeeze. 'I'll tell you what, when she comes back we'll all go out and have tea and a bun. We can go to that café on the corner. What's it called?'

'The Old Tea Shop.'

'That's the one.'

Excited, Amelia rushed out to give her brother the news. Ron turned away from the window. He would just have to make an effort to act normally. It was one thing letting this affect Rose and himself, quite another when it came to the children.

The anti-aircraft fire and the searchlights indicated the bombing was somewhere south of the river. Still, you couldn't be lulled into a sense of complacency on the basis that some other poor bastards were getting it and not you. As if to confirm Ron's thoughts the warning wailed out. There was no sense taking chances, and he hurried round the corner to the next tube station. Squatting on the platform he awaited the 'all clear'. Thank God he had been able to pull himself together enough to square things with Rose. But as for her coming up to London . . . Well, he had promised to write this week and at least that bought a little time.

Then what he had discovered at Carrington flooded into his mind, drowning out everything else. No wonder Gould could be murdered with impunity. Of course they were lucky, because they couldn't possibly have known that at the time. But once the accident happened the last thing that was going to happen was a juicy murder case in which that train journey figured so prominently. And having got away with that, no doubt they felt immune to the laws governing ordinary people. The problem was, they were probably right. But just how far down the years did this protection extend? A sense of depression overcame him. The question was academic. If Maguire was anything to go by, it evidently extended at least to the present. He was still firmly and squarely in the firing line.

'Aren't you getting out, mate?' One of Ron's companions from the shelter gave him a nudge. 'The "all clear's" just gone.'

His mind was so preoccupied that he nearly went home by the most direct route. Just in time he turned off and, wending his way through the back streets, managed to approach his house from the opposite direction. He reached for his keys, thinking not for the first time how stupid it all was. Maybe he would look back on this in years to come and wonder how he could have been such an idiot.

It didn't strike him immediately. It was more a gradual awareness, slowly impinging on his consciousness. Someone had been here. Someone had been near the house or . . . in the house. Someone who smoked Capstan Full Strength. Ron's stomach knotted up; sickness rose in his gorge. Then adrenalin fired his whole body. He whirled round, fists balled, ready to fight for his life. The vague shape stepped out from behind the hedge. There must be no hesitation: a second chance was unlikely. Then he remembered the blast debris and in one movement scooped up a brick from the side of the path. One thought and one thought only was in his mind: the temple, that's where he must aim to strike.

His arm was already raised when the figure spoke. 'Mr Charteris? I really wouldn't do that if I were you.'

Adrenaline surging, his arm stayed in the air. He found himself shouting, hearing the words as if from a great distance. 'Keep away. You won't get me as easy as Maguire.'

'Mr Charteris, please drop that. I'm a police officer.'

Slowly his arm sagged. 'How do I know?'

'Because I say so, but if you insist I have my warrant card.' The figure produced a dimmed torch and with his other hand held a document beside it.

For all Ron knew it could have been a cigarette card, but he desperately wanted, needed, to accept the assurance. The brick clattered to the ground. 'What are you doing here?'

'All in good time. Shall we go inside?' The policeman, if such he was, gestured towards the door. Ron's fingers fumbled with the keyring. 'Allow me.' The man produced something from his pocket and unlocked the door. He turned and beckoned to someone and a smaller man emerged from the shadows. He was dragging on a cigarette. Capstan Full Strength, of course.

Ron closed the door. 'What do you . . .'

217

'Let's check the blackouts first and then we can put the lights on.' The first man took charge effortlessly. 'Good. That's better. Why don't we all sit down?' He matched his actions to his words. 'I suppose I'd better introduce myself. I'm Detective Inspector McLaren and this is Sergeant Masters. We're both in the CID.'

The terror that had boiled inside turned to anger. Ron almost screamed at the two of them. 'You weren't so careful about lights the last time you were here. What gives you the right to break into houses . . . to ignore the law . . . to terrorise people . . . to . . .'

'Feeling better?' McLaren sounded almost solicitous. 'I'm sorry about the lights last time. We were interrupted. Now I know you've had a shock, but we really must get on.'

'Get on with what?' Ron's voice was still hoarse with rage.

The second man, Masters, spoke for the first time. He sounded impatient. 'Get on with what we came for.'

'You see, Mr Charteris, we know about the matters you've been researching and have reason to believe you're in considerable danger.'

'You believe that. You . . .' For several seconds Ron was lost for words. 'Oh, that's rich, that's very rich! A murderer has been running round free as a bird for over ten years. He's probably murdered someone else and now he intends to kill others, including me. Let me tell you something. I know I'm in danger. Not only do I know it, but I also know who's threatening me and I know why they're doing it.'

'Mr Charteris, I appreciate you're angry.' McLaren's basilisk-like gaze conveyed menace. 'At the moment we wish to interview a certain person on suspicion of a murder carried out some time ago. We also have reason to believe he may have been involved in certain other . . . offences and, as you say, may be planning more. He's proving elusive but we'll catch up with him. In the meantime we're taking what steps we can to protect potential victims.'

Suddenly Ron's heart lightened. They were on to the bastard. How and why he didn't know, but they were on to him. 'It's Lattimer-Williams, isn't it?'

'Really, I don't wish to go into details.'

He was feeling calmer now. 'Can I ask how, at this stage, you've managed to identify this suspect when the original investigation got nowhere?'

'Being in the newspaper business, you probably appreciate that most detective work relies on information received.'

'So you have an informer?'

Initially McLaren seemed unsure how to answer the question, but eventually there came a reluctant admission. 'Yes we have.' After reflection he decided to be reasonably candid. 'In fact we have an extremely reliable source of information. Of course we treat all information seriously, but when it comes from . . . how can I put it . . . a source at this level . . . it's difficult to think of how much higher you could go.' He could see the expression of perplexity opposite. 'It doesn't come much higher than the ermine, does it?'

'You mean Eastermain . . .'

'Now you wouldn't expect me to reveal details, would you? Sufficient to say that this . . . gentleman has been worried for some time about the activities of another person connected to his organisation. Recently he discovered some very disturbing information which related to a previous offence, together with some other matters. He was appalled and immediately came to the police.'

'I bet he did. It was all getting too warm for him, wasn't it? Whatever protection was there before was dissipating.'

McLaren's tone sharpened. 'You may have your opinions, Mr Charteris, and privately I might or might not agree, but we can only operate on information and evidence.'

Masters broke in. 'The point is we've been keeping your home under surveillance precisely because this is where we feel the person we're looking for might come.'

McLaren looked uneasy. 'And for your protection, of course. For your protection. In fact one of the reasons for seeing you tonight was to advise you of all this and make sure you were aware of the risks.'

Ron nodded. He knew perfectly well why they were having this little chat: to put themselves in the clear should anything happen to him. 'I appreciate the protection, but you scared the life out of me about a month ago.'

'A month ago?' It was Masters who spoke, but both looked alarmed. 'We only received this information the week before last.'

'Then it wasn't you . . .' Ron gestured towards the road. 'On the waste ground over there . . . the man watching the house.' Their expressions said it all. 'He threatened me . . .' The explanation tailed off.

'No, it wasn't us.' McLaren was worried. Clearly this was something he didn't know about. 'All the more reason to take extra precautions until the person we suspect is taken into custody.'

Carefully Ron locked the door behind them. A ton weight seemed to have lifted. Lattimer-Williams was still loose, but it could only be a matter of time. Now where was that whisky? Surely there was a drop or two left. He found it in the larder among the sauces and settled down with the last glassful. So Lord Eastermain had ratted on his chums, or at least one chum. So much for this public school, ex-officer freemasonry. When the chips were down it was every man for himself, with the commanding officer leading the way. But why and why now? Then he remembered the envelope he had left with George and the photographs it contained. Of course, that would be it. That would be why the protection was ebbing. Eastermain had sensed it and got out.

There was only one page left in the writing pad, but it didn't matter: it would only be a short note. He found himself whistling as he wrote. 'My dearest Rose, There should be no problem about you coming up next week . . .'

CHAPTER THIRTY-ONE

THE SECRETARY LED Jim and Ellen up the stairs, turning as she did so to speak confidentially. 'Mr Kroy was the senior partner until last year, but we lost two of the junior partners.' Their startled looks must have registered. 'I mean they were called up. So Mr Kroy's come back temporarily.' She added hastily, 'But don't worry. He's very good.' She tapped on the door and a voice invited them to go in.

'Mr and Mrs Thornton?' The elderly man rose and shook hands, regarding his visitors with interest. 'Please do sit down.' He indicated the chairs at the other side of his desk.

Jim cleared his throat. 'Sorry it's such short notice, but we were bombed out the night before last, so . . .'

'Of course. Of course. We all have to be flexible these days. I suppose we must be thankful that you came through it unscathed.' He peered at some papers in front of him. 'Have you any idea where you'll go now?'

Ellen answered. 'Up north to Leeds.'

'I see.' From the tone of voice and expression it was obvious he didn't see at all. 'I hear that parts of Hampshire and even Surrey are relatively safe – and in easy commuting distance from the City.'

'I won't be working in the City from now on.'

Kroy was about to comment, but saw the expression on Jim's face and decided against it. He went through a few more papers. 'Mr Thornton, I see from the information you gave my secretary that you work for De Villiers and Last?'

Jim was alerted by the note of questioning in his voice. 'Yes. Is there some problem with that?'

'No, not at all, Mr Thornton.' He seemed embarrassed. 'I'm sorry if I sounded somewhat, how shall we say, off hand. It's just that most people prefer to use their firm's solicitor. I'm sure you would receive preferential terms.'

'I'm sure I would. But let's just say that in personal matters I prefer to operate at arm's length.' Jim emphasised his next words. 'And with total confidentiality.'

Kroy saw them to the door and shook hands. 'So, Mr Thornton, just to recapitulate, all correspondence will be forwarded to your neighbour in Wimbledon who will in turn forward it to you. And you will let us have a northern address just as soon as you're settled.' For some considerable time he watched as they walked down the street, before turning to give some instructions to the receptionist.

As usual the tube was crowded, but he was used to it, Ellen wasn't. She mouthed, 'Is it always like this?' He nodded, then guided her back into a seat that had just been vacated. She smiled and attempted to talk, before the impossibility of it all sank in. Eventually the man next to her got up and Jim slid gratefully down. She whispered in his ear. 'What did you think of the solicitor?'

He considered before answering. 'A bit of a City relic. Not my type at all. But then we don't have to like him; he's just got to be competent.'

'Well, is he?'

'Yes, I think so, but more to the point he isn't connected to the firm.'

'Are you sure?'

'As sure as I can be. I've never come across any dealings with them.' The answer seemed to satisfy her. The brakes started to bite and Jim reached up and grasped the strap. 'Our stop next. Let me give you a hand.'

The crowds scurried out of the station and dispersed into the darkness. Each mind focused on reaching home before any warning came. At first they could just make out others around them, but one by one they split off and soon the couple were on their own. The first sirens went as they were trying to negotiate a pile of rubble. 'Quick, Jim. We must get back to Maureen.'

He took her arm to restrain her. 'We won't help Maureen if we break our legs trying to run over this lot.'

Threading their way through the debris of the previous weeks' bombing, Jim tried to remember all the awkward bits, but it was difficult with Ellen pulling frantically. He deliberately stopped and took her by the shoulders. 'Ellen, the bombing isn't anywhere near here. Now take it easy.' Then he saw the terror in her eyes. For the first time in his life he shook her. 'Snap out of it. We'll be home soon.'

'Jamie . . . Jamie . . .'

'What on earth's wrong?' The back of his head seemed to explode and he felt himself falling, falling. He thought he would never reach the ground. A bomb. It must be a bomb . . . but somehow his thoughts refused to coalesce. At a great distance he thought he could hear Ellen screaming. Then there were words. Words he tried to make sense of. 'It's his wife. You never told me there would be a woman involved.' They faded away, then he thought he heard Lattimer-Williams's voice. 'Poor old Jim. What rotten luck that old Kroy was able to let us know when you were heading for home.' He tried to struggle, tried to make his limbs move, but they belonged to someone else. Just for a moment he thought he saw a face, Lattimer-Williams's face, looming above him; then it faded . . .

He could hear the tide. The water thundered and roared inwards and then slowly receded, carrying with it the sibilant drag of a million pebbles. But there was also something else. There was a voice, a familiar voice. 'What are we going to do with her?' He rolled over, reaching for the beach beneath him, but all he could feel was wood. It was a floor.

'Coming round, are we, Jim?' Then the face reappeared above him. 'Strange, I couldn't have hit you as hard as I thought.' He saw

Lattimer-Williams's lips move again. But again the tide came in and he could hear nothing. The sea must be just outside.

'I said, what the hell are we going to do with her?' It was the other voice, but this time starting to break.

He made an effort and formed a word. Lattimer-Williams's face came nearer. 'What was that, Jim? Sea?' There was a laugh. He remembered that laugh. 'So I did hit you hard enough after all. No, we're still in London, Jim. Or at least you are . . . for the moment.'

'For the last time, what are we going to do with her?' The hysterical pitch of the other voice told of a barely suppressed panic.

'For Christ's sake shut up!' The face turned back to him. 'Before we decide anything, Jim and I need to have a chat. After all, who knows who he's been talking to? Who's he taken into his confidence? Maybe he's been a blabbermouth like Maguire. Probably had words with that journalist.'

There was a numbness in his skull, but at least the tide was starting to recede. Then slowly it dawned. The noise must all be inside his head. There was no tide. There was no sea. But with that realisation came other thoughts, other memories. 'Ellen! Where's Ellen? You bastards! Have you touched her? Have you hurt her?'

'The answer, Jim, is no. For the time being, that is. But it depends on you.' He gestured behind him. 'Last was all for finishing you both, but I said no. Didn't I, Last?' He glanced round, but there was no reply. 'Now what I want from you is a full account of everyone you've talked to about those "undertakings", as you described them. We assume, of course, that your wife knows everything.'

For a moment he thought of prevaricating, lying. Anything but the truth. For no one but he and Ellen knew anything. To admit that could be fatal. He started to talk, frantically, desperately. 'There are a lot of people who knew where we were going . . . neighbours . . . relatives. You won't get away with . . . whatever it is you're planning . . .' He broke off as the absurdity of his threats sank in.

Again he saw that gaze on him. 'Jim. Eyes are supposed to be the mirror of the soul. Now I believe that, don't you?' He appeared to be waiting for an answer, and when none came he went on. 'Your soul must be pure, because I can read everything . . . everything . . . in your eyes. You've told no one, have you? No one, that is, except your wife.'

He could only nod, misery seeping through him like water through a sponge. Then, deep down, despair began to be replaced by anger, a molten, corroding anger, an anger that grew and expanded, filling every void, pulsing through every vein. He threw himself at Lattimer-Williams, but grasping only air he felt himself picked up bodily and slammed onto the floor.

'Don't try that again, Jim. Ever.'

Gasping for breath, he tried once more to quell the incoming tide. 'You bastard. You think you're above the law. Just because you got away with murder once, you think you can do it again . . .'

'I can see that you've been doing some delving. But a word of caution, Jim. I don't like the word murder.'

'Then what would you call it?'

'I'd call it justice. Justice administered to a rat. But then, we're not here to talk about that. That's history.'

'You can still hang for it.' Jim closed his eyes and tried to pretend that those last words hadn't emerged, hadn't been articulated. They had. He had to go on. 'It won't be as easy this time. The police will make connections . . .'

He was interrupted. 'It wasn't easy last time. Now if it hadn't been for those children . . .'

Jim's anger returned. 'Those children . . . I've been fobbed off with hints about them all these years. They were just a lucky accident, weren't they? They just helped to muddy the waters.' Lattimer-Williams was now sitting. If there was ever to be a chance it had to be soon.

'The "all clear" will be going soon. We have to get this sorted out.' Last was getting desperate.

'Oh, we can spare a few minutes. After all, Jim kept our secret all these years. Surely he's entitled to an explanation?' There was a muttered curse from the other side of the room. 'In answer to your question, the children certainly were a lucky accident – not for them of course, but definitely for us. You see, the police – or at least certain people in the police – made the connections, they made all the right connections. But unfortunately for them they couldn't even begin to make a case.'

The explosion must only have been a street away. Jim felt the plaster cascading onto him as he heard Last's curses and Lattimer-Williams's coughing. It must be now. He rolled sideways, cannoning into someone's legs and bowling them over. Pray God it was Lattimer-Williams. Last he was sure he could deal with. Lurching along a wall, he feverishly scrabbled for an exit. At last a handle . . .

'I wouldn't step out if I were you.' It was Lattimer-Williams's voice. 'It's a drop of thirty feet. This place was bombed some time ago.' Jim turned towards the voice. 'Don't make me use this revolver. Sit down on the floor . . . slowly . . . and with your back to the wall. That's right. Now where were we?'

Jim sank down, misery flooding back. Last's voice rose again, this time reduced to a whine. 'You fool. We don't have time for all this. Get it over with.'

The snarl of Lattimer-Williams's response cut him short instantly. 'As I was saying, some of the police did make the connections, but their problem was . . . let's just say you were right in your theories about the children, the unknown children, the ones with no identity.' The 'all clear' burst out, the wail rising to a crescendo before tailing away.

'I told you. I told you we didn't have long.' Last's voice was hoarse with fear; but again he was ignored.

'You know the old saying that knowledge is power? In this case total knowledge was total power. You see, I knew . . . that is I know, who those children really were.'

'I suspected as much.' Desperately Jim played for time. 'After all, you were entrusted to look after them.' A sudden, desperate thought occurred. 'If they were such a trump card then, they must still be a trump card now. You don't need to risk your neck for Ellen,' his voice trembled, 'for Ellen and me.'

'Jim, I feel really sorry for you. You went through the last war. Then that accident. And all these years working for us. Yet you're still such an innocent. You still don't see. Twelve years ago the police had an open and shut murder case against us, but it was dropped. Dropped because of pressure from certain quarters. But our friend Maguire wasn't half as discreet as you. Not discreet at all, really. So now I have it on good authority that certain people are determined to re-open the case. I'm told that the police want to interview me personally. Can you believe that? Mind you, I don't think they have enough evidence – evidence that will stand up in court. They don't have any witnesses, you see, but if they did . . . let's just say that those same "certain quarters" who helped us before don't carry nearly as much weight nowadays. They hardly carry any weight at all.'

'You bloody murderer. You're going to do away with us.' In spite of himself Jim's voice was rising in panic. 'To do away with us just because those two kids' relatives don't have as much influence nowadays. You're a madman!'

'The two kids that were with us that night . . . The two kids who were with us that night. Do you really believe they were the ones who died? Oh Jim, Jim. You're even more of an innocent than I thought.' Then Lattimer-Williams laughed.

It was the last thing Jim was to hear.

'Maureen, you have to be a brave girl.' She stared back at the policeman and realised that the words were coming from him. He leaned forward and patted her arm. She could see him swallowing. Maybe he had a sore throat like Dad had the other night. 'Maureen . . . Maureen we think they – your mum and dad – are hurt . . .' He caught the woman's eye as she tightened her arm round the girl. He swallowed again. 'Your Aunt Meg is coming from Leeds to take you back up there . . .'

'But what about Mum and Dad? If they're hurt they'll want me to look after them.'

He started to speak, then stopped, only to start again. 'Maureen, we think your mum and dad are . . .' He looked appealingly at Maureen's neighbour, Mavis Christie.

Mavis held the girl tightly. There was no way round it. It had to be said. 'Now you must be really brave. Your mum and dad are . . . dead.'

'Dead?' She looked at Mavis, puzzled. 'They said they would be back in time for supper.'

'It was a bomb.' She stroked the girl's hair. 'I expect they were thinking about you when it happened.'

Maureen's face began to crumple. 'They can't be dead. They just can't be.' Her crying was muted at first, then she buried her head on Mavis's shoulder and sobbed without restraint.

The policeman, who during the last few weeks had observed more than his fair share of broken hearts, breathed in heavily. 'Maybe everyone could do with some tea.'

Dave roused himself. 'Of course. I'll get some.' The policeman followed him into the kitchen. Dave hardly dared ask. 'Any chance of them still being alive?'

'Not according to the rescue people at Balham station. Everything collapsed.'

'Can we be sure Jim and Ellen were there?'

'No, we can't be absolutely sure. But it's been forty-eight hours now. From what you've told me they're loving parents. If it had been anything else they'd have got in touch.'

Dave lifted the kettle from the hob. 'How bad is it down there?'

There was a long pause. 'Worse than anything I've seen. There could be over a hundred lost.'

From the front room the sobbing was now interspaced with murmurs from Mavis. Dave placed everything carefully on a tray; then it was his turn to breathe in heavily. 'Better get back in now.'

CHAPTER THIRTY-TWO

RON HAD FELT much easier in himself for the last few days, but even so the two figures standing by the car made him jump. 'You again. What's it about this time? And why are you waiting here, outside the office? '

McLaren was definitely uncomfortable. 'We wanted to avoid any embarrassment in your place of work.'

'You've caught him then?'

'Not yet, but I'm afraid we need you to answer a few more questions.'

'But I thought we covered everything on Sunday night.' Puzzled, Ron looked from one to the other. 'I need to get home and get some sleep.'

'Later, Mr Charteris.' The curt response did not invite further delay. 'Could you get into the car, please?'

For a quarter of an hour no one spoke, then McLaren spoke to Masters. 'We'll go over Westminster Bridge. It'll save time.'

'Westminster Bridge? I thought you were based at the Yard.' Ron was feeling distinctly uneasy. 'Just where are we going?'

'To another police station. The bombing has affected all of us, you know.'

'But if you want to talk to me why do we have to go all this way?'

'I don't, but some colleagues of mine do.'

'What colleagues? Are they in the police?' There was a pause before the answer. 'Not specifically.' McLaren hurried on to pre-empt further questions. 'We'll be there directly.'

'The constable will stay here. There'll be someone here soon.' Masters closed the door of the interview room and caught McLaren's glance. 'What's this all about, guv?'

229

His companion shrugged. 'I don't know, but the one who spoke to me on the phone this afternoon is the most senior bloke in Special Branch that I know about.' He lowered his voice. 'Here they are now. The older one is Special Branch.'

Two men strode down the corridor. Special Branch nodded to the detective inspector. 'Any problems, McLaren?'

'No, sir. He's in the interview room now.' Without knocking, the two went in. Almost immediately the constable came out.

'What about the other one, guv? Do you know him?'

'I'm not sure.' There was no doubt: McLaren was worried. 'But if he's who I think he is we shouldn't even be thinking about questions like that, let alone asking them.'

'That's all very well, sir.' The very fact that Masters had dropped the familiar and reverted to the formal indicated how uneasy he felt. 'We haven't arrested Charteris, but we're formally responsible for him, aren't we? We brought him here. He hasn't been charged with anything or formally handed over to anyone else.' He deliberately emphasised the 'formals'.

Master's point hit home. Reluctant as he was, McLaren eventually had to answer. 'You're right. We'll wait here until something is decided.'

'Why am I here?'

'Can't you guess, Charteris?' The answer came from the older man.

There was a flash of anger. 'No I can't, and while we're at it neither of you have said who you are or whom you represent.'

'We haven't, have we?' This time it was the younger man. 'Let's say we're from the security services. I always like that; it's such a catch-all title.'

The older one scowled. He was determined to get down to business. 'Charteris. On Friday,' he glanced at one of the papers in front of him, 'you visited a Mrs Doreen Wilson in the Montfort Grove Nursing Home in Charrington.'

Ron was worried; seriously worried. He played for time. 'Is that a statement or a question?'

'Oh dear.' It was the younger man again. 'Why did you go to see her?'

As options raced through his mind, Ron was aware of two pairs of eyes fixed unblinking on his. Best play it straight, or as near to straight as was possible. 'You probably know already, but for about ten years now I've been investigating the Eastmead train crash. Mrs Wilson's daughter died in the accident and an opportunity cropped up on Friday to visit her.'

'Ten years is a long time.' The younger one was musing almost to himself. 'What do you hope to get out of it?'

'A book, eventually – but not until after the war's over.'

'Wasn't that the crash where those two unidentified children were found?' The questioning had rotated again.

'You know it is, and before you ask, no, I haven't found out who they were. If I had it would be a bestseller, wouldn't it?'

'How did you find Mrs Wilson?' It was the younger one again.

'Not exactly gaga, but not very lucid either.'

'So you didn't get any information or . . . anything else from her?'

Alarm bells started to ring. Had someone at the home discovered something? Did they have information he didn't know about? He would just have to continue the line he was on and hope for the best. 'Nothing . . . nothing that isn't available elsewhere.'

The questioning went on in the same vein for a good twenty minutes; then came a period of silence. It went on so long that Ron began to wonder if it wasn't some sort of interrogation trick. The two men exchanged glances. 'Right, Mr Charteris, we're going to leave you here for a few minutes while we confer.' The older man went to the door and beckoned to the constable.

Nervous now, Ron attempted a weak joke. 'Isn't this the point when I'm offered a cup of tea?' Neither man smiled.

McLaren jumped up as they approached. 'Have you finished with him now?'

He addressed his question to the man from Special Branch, but it was the younger one who replied. 'No.' The response was short and brooked no argument. 'I need a secure room and a telephone.'

The inspector showed him through to an office with an inner one leading off it. 'There's a telephone in there. It's a direct line to the exchange, not a switchboard.'

'Good.' He looked at his companion and nodded towards the door. 'This may take some time. I'm sure you'll get some tea in this place.' He went through to the other office, closing the door firmly behind him. There was an embarrassed pause. Who was senior and who was junior had just been very publicly demonstrated.

Masters took the Special Branch man to the canteen while McLaren waited. The door shot open again. 'How in God's earth do you get through to the exchange?'

'Sorry, there's a special prefix.' The other man wrote it down and hurried back through. McLaren noticed that in his haste the door had only swung to.

'I've said it once. That's who I want to speak to.' The angry tones carried through the door. The decibel level dropped for a few minutes only to rise alarmingly again. 'I can't be sure. That Omerod woman described her as the cat who's got the cream.' The voice dropped again, only to rise abruptly. 'But he can be detained. There are a whole host of regulations. No, I can't accept that! I said it's totally unacceptable.' McLaren found it impossible not to listen, for the conversation now had no *pianissimo*. 'Excuse me, sir, I'm not an idiot! Yes, I know there's a war on. Of course I understand what a propaganda coup it would be.' For quite a while there was silence as the other party held sway. When the voice came again from the inner office its tone was controlled on the surface but underneath there was a boiling, pent-up anger. 'I'll need that in writing, sir.' McLaren realised that the other person was equally furious. 'Sir, you can't expect me to . . .' The voice from the other end broke in again and, though still unintelligible, its tone rose alarmingly. This time whatever was said seemed to have the desired effect. 'There is absolutely no need for . . . Of course, sir! Very well, sir! I said very well!' The telephone smashed down with a force that must have caused damage. Knowing with certainty that discretion was now the better part of valour, the inspector quietly let himself out of the outer office and waited in the corridor.

'McLaren! McLaren! Oh, there you are.' The Special Branch man's face, so calm a few minutes ago, was now flushed and angry, and his hands were trembling. 'Where's my colleague?'

'I'll get him for you.' He hesitated, wondering if this was the moment to ask. 'About Charteris. What's going to happen to him? In a way we're responsible, although he hasn't been formally . . .'

'Charteris is our responsibility now. We're taking him for further questioning in half an hour or so.' He must have noticed the diffidence on McLaren's features. 'Good God, man, he's being transferred into the custody of a senior Special Branch officer.'

'Guv! Guv!' Masters crashed through the door. 'I've just come from the yard by the cells. It's Charteris. He's not going with them at all. There's another car out there.'

'What?' McLaren was on his feet as he spoke. Both of them reached the yard just as a car turned out of the gates and into the lane behind. In a forlorn bid to stop it, the inspector raced to the gates, only to see it accelerating down the road. He turned to find the other two climbing into their vehicle. Furious, he grasped the Special Branch man by the shoulder and found himself shouting, 'What the hell do you mean by that? He was released into your custody. Who are they? Where's he being taken?"

The Special Branch man refused to meet his eyes and started to mumble. 'They were . . .' Lost for words, he appealed to his colleague.

Suddenly McLaren found his hand detached in a none too gentle fashion. It was the younger man. 'McLaren, this is none of your business.' The inspector tried to interrupt, but the sheer venom in the other man's eyes silenced him. 'Now listen to me and listen well. Think very, very hard about your pension, then turn round and get back into that bloody office!'

CHAPTER THIRTY-THREE

'COULD MR MORRIS ADAMS please come forward?' The vicar consulted his notes. 'Mr Adams is a friend and colleague of Ronald from London, and he would like to say a few words.'

Morris looked tired: he had had barely three hours' sleep before catching the first train down. He was silent for a moment as he regarded the packed church, uncertain how to start. 'This is a sad, sad day.' He paused again. 'I knew Ron for nearly twelve years. He was a valued colleague, but he was much more than that. He was also a friend to me and to more people than I could possibly mention . . .'

Rose sat rigidly, her hands closely intertwined with the two smaller ones on either side. Why had this to happen to them? How could her Ron be killed by a bomb? Ron, who always assured her that he knew what he was doing, that he always knew where the nearest shelter was. To one side she could sense Amelia sobbing quietly; on the other John sat as rigid as herself, willing himself not to cry.

'. . . Finally can I say that day in day out Ron reported from the front line – our front line. Wherever the bombs were falling in London he was there.' With a slight break in his voice Morris concluded, 'Ron Charteris wasn't a soldier, he wasn't in uniform, but I can truly say this . . . he died for his country.' He looked directly at the congregation. 'Thank you all for coming.'

They shook hands. 'I'm Rose's sister, Christine. It was good of you to come.'

'Not at all.' Morris looked glum. 'Most of the office wanted to come, but it's wartime and the paper has to come out. I had to turn down an awful lot of people.'

'Of course. Everybody understands.'

Morris was reminded of something. 'I had a word with Rose, of course, and your mother, but in the circumstances it didn't seem appropriate to talk about money and pensions and that sort of thing.' He hesitated. 'In the next few weeks the personnel department will be contacting her, but in the meantime could you tell Rose that the paper will see she's looked after financially. She's not to worry on that score.'

Christine nodded. 'Are you coming back to the house? Only tea and sandwiches, I'm afraid, but you're very welcome.'

'Thank you but no. I really have to catch the next train back.'

'I'm sorry . . . Oh, before you go there's something you might be able to explain.' Morris listened, anxious to help. 'A day after we got the news two policemen came to the house. They were very pleasant and polite, but said they had a warrant to search the premises. Do you know anything about it?'

Morris looked blank. 'No, I haven't heard anything about this.'

'Of course we weren't in any fit state to query any of it and it was distressing, especially for Rose. They searched the house from top to bottom.'

'Did they say where they were from?'

'Not really. They said it was a security matter.'

Morris was as bewildered as she was, but he could see the anxiety in her eyes and the need for some sort of reassurance. 'I can't say for sure, but reporters often come across all sorts of things and make notes about them. Afterwards it may not be possible to publish anything because of security restrictions, but the notes are still there in the notebook.' He hoped what he had outlined sounded plausible. 'So I expect it was something to do with that.'

George gave her a hug. 'Rose, I don't know what to say.' He stopped, unable to go on.

George was Ron's oldest friend: next to her and Amelia and John he must be feeling it as much as anyone. She dabbed her eyes. 'I know. I still can't believe it. It's so hard, but I can't let myself go . . . I must think of the children.'

'Are you coping?'

'Yes, there's Mum and Christine. Don't worry, George, I'll manage somehow. Thousands of others have had to, haven't they?'

He pulled a letter from his inside pocket. 'I don't know if this is the right time, but it might be a while before I see you again.'

She recognised her name on the envelope and looked at him aghast. 'That's Ron's writing.'

'Yes. He gave it to me . . . recently.' George pressed it into her hand. 'He asked me to pass it to you in the event of . . . well, you know.'

There was urgency in her voice. 'Did he know?'

George tried to sound convincing. 'No, I'm sure he didn't. But it's wartime . . . and covering all that bombing . . . it's as that chap from his office said. He was in the front line.'

'Are you sure you'll be all right on your own?' Anxiously, Rose's mother paused yet again to check.

'Mum, I'll be all right. I've got to try living a normal life soon.'

'But it's only been a month.'

'Mum!' She took her firmly by the arm and guided her to the front door. 'John and Amelia are expecting to be met at school.'

She watched her mother and sister go before closing the door. There was something that had to be done; she had been putting it off for quite some time now. But even as that thought came to mind she was distracted by the mess of children's toys thrown down carelessly under the hallstand. Irritated, she tidied the jumble; then she pulled herself up. This was stupid: she was just trying to find things to do. It couldn't be avoided any longer: she had promised herself that the first time she was alone she would open the envelope. Gingerly she pulled it from the bureau. The letter both attracted and repelled her. What could be so important that Ron had left a letter with George? Then from outside there were voices, followed by the crashing of the front door and John's urgent voice echoing from the hall. 'Mum! Mum! Can I . . .'

The rest of what he had to say was drowned by Amelia's aggrieved wail. 'You always get to tell Mum things before me and I was through the gate first.'

Whatever the letter contained would have to wait. Hastily Rose stuffed the envelope back into the top drawer of the bureau as her harassed mother came through the door followed by the two squabbling children. 'Everything all right, Mum?' Her mother nodded wearily and sank back onto a chair. Rose turned to the children. 'Look what you've done! Gran's totally exhausted. Now, whatever you've got to say I want you to say it one at a time. You go first, John.'

'Paul Lloyd wants me to go to his house to play with him after tea.'

That set Amelia off again. 'He always gets invited to go out and I never do.'

Rose approved of Paul. His father owned the garage just down the road and the family lived next door to it. All in all he was a nice boy. 'Of course you can. I'll take you down after tea and come for you.' She brushed aside Amelia's predictable protests. 'You can invite one of your friends over later this week.'

She watched over the garden fence as the boys finished off what they faithfully promised was the very last over of cricket. 'I hope they haven't been a nuisance, Mr Lloyd?'

'Of course not, Mrs Charteris. It's good to see the boys enjoying themselves.' Paul's father clapped as the final ball of the evening was thumped into the shrubbery. 'Lost ball, I shouldn't wonder.' The boys obviously didn't think so as they dived into the bushes. Lloyd sighed. 'This might take a while, but I'll give them a few minutes before I haul them out. Cricket balls are hard to come by these days.'

He came over to where Rose was standing, and she noticed he walked with a slight limp. It appeared he was sensitive about it, because he patted his leg and felt the need to explain. 'Nothing heroic, I'm afraid: just an old rugby injury. The army turned me down because of it, but maybe if this war goes on long enough and they get desperate . . .'

A few people were still ready to accuse ostensibly fit males who were not in uniform of 'dodging the column', and Rose guessed he had been on the receiving end of this sort of treatment. Ron had had a bit of it even though he was over the age limit. She felt obliged to respond. 'We all try to do our bit, and I'm sure your business is absolutely vital to the war effort.'

'It is indeed. Nowadays we have our hands full repairing agricultural machinery and of course I do any essential driving in my Morris Ten. A bit different from before the war – then it was all car repairs and vehicle hire.' He looked wistful. 'I've still got the old Daimler in the garage. Of course we can't use it these days, petrol rationing and all that, but before the war people used to like vintage motor cars for weddings and funer . . .' He stopped himself, conscious of John's mum's newly widowed status.

Rose quickly switched the conversation. 'It's nice that John has made friends with a real local boy like Paul.'

'You couldn't get much more local than our Paul. The family's been round here for more than three generations.' He gestured to the sign above the garage next door, which read 'Lloyd's Motor Cars'. 'My grandfather started the firm and drove the very first car seen in these parts.'

'Mum, Mr Lloyd has this posh car in the garage and he let us sit in it.' John's excitement spilled over. 'And he says that sometime he'll take us for a drive.'

'And so I will, John.' Lloyd smiled at the boy's enthusiasm. 'But it'll have to wait a while yet.'

'I suppose it won't be until the war's over and there's plenty of petrol.' John's crestfallen face said everything.

Over John's head Lloyd smiled at Rose. 'Well, no promises, but maybe not quite as long as that.'

CHAPTER THIRTY-FOUR

'HURRY UP, MUM, or we won't get a seat.' John frantically tugged his mother's arm as they approached the school gates. Rose held Amelia's hand and tried to quicken her step, but it wasn't urgent enough for John. 'Come on! Everyone's going to be there.' Then he produced his trump card. 'Paul's dad is playing Aladdin!'

'Paul Lloyd's dad, you mean? I didn't know he did so much in the school.'

'Of course he does. He was great at sports day last summer. You should have seen him run in the dads' race.' That reminded John of something else. 'There was a mums' race as well, you know. You could have come.'

Rose felt a pang of guilt. Paul's dad had made the effort even though he was a widower and had a responsible job, but there had been so much for her to see to during the last few months. It was no excuse, though; she should become more involved. 'Look, John, I'll have a word with your headmaster and see what I can do.'

By this time they had got into the school hall, and it was Amelia doing the tugging. 'Quick, Mum, there are empty chairs next to Paul.'

The curtains closed for the last time, and when the applause had subsided the headmaster appeared to light-hearted boos. 'Ladies and gentlemen and children. Thank you for coming tonight . . .'

The rest of his thanks were lost on the excited children. Paul leaned across. 'Wasn't it great? Dad said there would be a big explosion when the genie came out of the lamp for the last time.'

'He nearly didn't come out.' Lloyd appeared beside them, still in costume and greasepaint. 'That explosion was a bit stronger than it was supposed to be.'

'Well, I liked it . . .' Paul trailed off as something else took his eye. 'Look, that's the start of the queue for those buns!' The performance became an instant memory as the children hurtled away.

Lloyd settled himself in a chair. 'Enjoy the performance, Mrs Charteris?'

'It was really good. I haven't laughed so much in ages. You must have done this sort of thing before.'

'Well, yes. As far as amateur dramatics are concerned, I plead guilty to being an incurable addict.' He adopted a look of mock-depression. 'Sadly producers don't seem to see me as Hamlet.'

'Don't be so self-deprecating. Before the war I saw quite a few professional shows in the West End, so I like to think I can pick out good performances.' Suddenly she realised she might be sounding a bit precious.' Of course, that's only from my point of view . . .'

'You're being kind, but thank you anyway. Have you tried your hand at amateur dramatics?'

Rose shook her head. 'No. I admire people who do, but it really wouldn't be my forte.' There was an awkward pause, and for a moment Rose wondered if she had been too blunt. She hurried on. 'There's something you could advise me about. John tells me you do all sorts of things for the school, and it made me realise I haven't really been involved at all.'

Lloyd brightened. 'We're always short of school governors. Someone like you would make a welcome change from clergymen and retired bank managers.' He checked himself. 'Mind you, nothing wrong with clergymen or retired bank managers. What I mean is that it would be good to have more parents.'

Rose responded a little nervously. 'But wouldn't that involve being elected and canvassing for votes and all that sort of thing, because I'm not sure . . .'

'Forget about any of that. I'll have a word with the head. You just turn up at the next meeting and I can guarantee you'll be welcomed with open arms.' He got up as shouts from the children indicated that the buns had run out. 'I'd better get cleaned up and change out of this finery. Oh, by the way, the next governors' meeting is on Tuesday night, so I'll look forward to seeing you there.'

'Same here, and thanks for the advice.' She hesitated slightly. 'I hope you don't mind, but Mr Lloyd and Mrs Charteris sound so formal, don't they? My name's Rose.'

His smile indicated her comment had not been taken amiss. 'And I'm Idris.' They shook hands.

'Idris? That's Welsh, isn't it?'

'Yes, it's a family name; my grandfather was Welsh. But I can promise you I don't go in for choral singing – not even at boring governors' meetings.'

Rose's mother put aside the balaclava she was knitting and looked across to her daughter, who was checking John's homework. 'Rose?'

'Yes, Mum.' Somewhat irritated at the interruption, Rose wrenched her mind away from long division. There was a long pause and it was obvious that the older woman was uncertain how to start. 'For goodness sake spit it out, Mum. I've got Amelia's homework to check after this.'

'Well, for a start the way you just reacted. These days you're becoming more and more irritable, sometimes at quite petty things.' Now that the subject had been broached she seized her chance. 'It isn't just me who's noticed it: Christine mentioned it the other day.' Anxious to get to the main point, she pushed on. 'And I think I know the reason.'

Rose didn't often lose her temper, but she was now close to it. 'Oh you do, do you? And what's that?'

'It's your own business, of course, but you're becoming very friendly with Idris Lloyd.'

This time Rose did lose her temper. 'You meant to say too friendly, didn't you? Well, didn't you? But as you rightly said it's my business – and that's the way it's going to stay.' On the point of leaving the room, she saw her mother's crestfallen face and paused. 'Look, Mum, I know you mean well, but I'm an adult, the mother of two children who I have to bring up without a father.' Suddenly she felt tears welling up.

'Rose. Rose, dear, I'm sorry. Maybe I shouldn't have brought it up.'

Rose took the proffered handkerchief. 'No, Mum, it's as much my fault as yours. I've been meaning to talk to you about Idris.' She collected her thoughts. 'It's over a year since Ron . . . since Ron died. He was my husband, and no one can replace him. Nothing will change that. But life has to move on. This war has turned everything upside down. Idris is a good, kind man and we like each other a lot. John, especially, needs a father figure and he gets on well with Idris. Both of them do.'

'But Idris's own family . . . Won't they . . .'

'Mum, he's a widower. His wife died six years ago. His parents are dead and so are Ron's. If we do decide to get married, and for both of us it's still an if, who is there to be hurt?'

Lloyd patiently blew up the football, tightened the lace then bounced the ball experimentally on the grass a couple of times before tossing it over to Paul and John. 'There you are, boys. Now please don't kick it into that hedge again.'

For a while he and Rose watched the boys, pretending to be absorbed in the game. It was Idris who cracked first. 'You know how I feel, Rose, yet whenever I broach the subject you manage to skirt round it.'

'Subject?'

'Yes, subject. And you know perfectly well what I mean. To be blunt, where do we go from here?' You've made it plain you like me, respect me, are fond of me even – but you seem reluctant to go past that point.'

'Idris, we've both been married. We both have children. It isn't just a question of you and me: there are other people to consider.'

'You still haven't answered the question. Is it more than just liking, respect and fondness that you're feeling?'

There was a long period of silence punctuated only by the shouts and shrieks of the boys, until finally Rose answered hesitantly. 'You must know it's more, but I've only been a widow for just over a year. We have to wait.'

It was then that Idris voiced, almost word for word, the same points she had made to her mother a few hours earlier. 'Rose, if we both feel the same, what's the point of waiting? Who's going to be upset?' She didn't answer, so he answered for her. 'A few years ago convention might dictate that we waited, but the war's changed everything.'

'I suppose you're right.'

'Rose, Rose.' Suddenly the absurdity of this response to a proposal hit them both, and once the giggles started they couldn't be contained.

'Mum? Mum! Why are you and Mr Lloyd laughing?' They became aware of two boys looking at them in astonishment.

Idris took it upon himself to explain. 'Your mum is a very funny lady, John, and that's why we're laughing.'

If she had had doubts, then her mother seemed to have overcome them, but Christine still seemed shocked. 'You only met him just over a year ago. How can you be sure? Wouldn't waiting another year be better? That way everyone could . . .'

'Get used to the idea, you mean.'

Christine was flustered. 'No, but it seems so quick.'

'These days no one wants or expects widows to wear black for the rest of their days. Besides there are three children involved, one of whom would benefit from a happier father and two of whom would benefit from the presence of a kind, loving father figure.' She could see Christine was still not convinced. 'Besides, there's a war on. It looks a bit better for all of us than it did a year ago, but no one can tell how it'll finally end. Anything that brings more security into all our lives, especially the children's, has to be a good thing.' Her sister started to interrupt, but Rose was not to be gainsaid. 'Next Saturday afternoon we're going to have a small family party to celebrate at Idris's. There'll be a tea for the children and then we can break the news to them.'

CHAPTER THIRTY-FIVE

'YOU GO ON. I've still got to get changed.' Rose ushered her mother and the children out of the door. 'And tell Idris I'll be about half an hour.'

Christine was still lingering in the hall. 'Do you want me to wait for you?'

'No, I'll be fine.' The shouts of the children, excited at the promise of a special tea, echoed back from the street. 'You catch up and make sure Mum has them under control.'

With everyone gone, the house suddenly felt very silent. Changing took very little time, as there was another reason she wanted a few minutes to herself. Ron's photograph stared at her from the dressing table: it was the one taken on that holiday in Salcombe. She picked it up and sat on the bed. It was the one he had liked, but she had always felt it didn't do him justice. He was looking too solemn; it didn't even hint at his irreverent sense of humour. She felt the emotion begin to well up and quickly replaced the photograph. Today was the start of a new life – a life with a kind, trustworthy man. Ron would have understood. Then suddenly it hit her. The envelope from Ron! The envelope that she had so cravenly avoided opening. The envelope that, for almost a year now, she had deliberately put to the back of her mind. But how could she open it now, today of all days? She stared across at Ron's photo until finally the dilemma resolved itself. She owed it to Ron and she owed it to herself: she must read whatever it contained. Slowly she went downstairs.

Opening the bureau, half-hoping the letter had been mislaid, she quickly rummaged through the various documents. It was still there.

Placing the envelope on the dining table, Rose sat down, aware of her heart thumping furiously. There was a final moment of indecision then, steeling herself, she tore it open and drew out the contents. Inside was yet another envelope, together with a folded sheet of notepaper. Fingers fumbling, she unfolded it.

> My Darling Rose
> If you are reading this the worst will have happened.

She had to stop. Big teardrops were falling on the page. She paused, took a deep breath and carried on.

> I have discovered the identities of the children – the ones who died in the train crash. It may have played a part in what has happened to me.
>
> I have no right to wish this on you, yet I don't know what else to do. You have a choice: destroy the contents of the envelope unread or open it, but remember the information is *dangerous*.
>
> I know you will look after John and Amelia. Give them a big kiss from me. Remember to take care of yourself too. They will depend on you.
>
> All my love
> Ron

Rose found herself weeping in a fit of misery and rage. That bloody crash which had obsessed him so much. Had it been the cause of his death? The other envelope still lay on the table, but was now more menacing than ever. She picked it up and walked towards the fireplace, but even as her fingers grasped the matches she knew she couldn't do it. If it had anything to do with Ron's death she needed to know. She had a right to know.

Quickly she emptied the envelope onto the table. There were some photographs, certificates and what looked like a wedding ring. As Ron had, she picked up the ring first. It was simple, yet of superb quality and craftsmanship. The inscription itself was ordinary enough: 'To Elaine with love from E'. Then she turned to the documents. One was a marriage certificate, while the other two were birth certificates. The French she remembered from her schooldays was more than adequate, but the names and the places didn't mean anything. Could this be the secret that Ron felt was so dangerous?

Briefly she glanced at the photographs, turning them over to see if anything had been written on them, but there was nothing. The first one she picked up showed a mother with a girl as a baby and a boy as a toddler. They seemed happy, but all in all it was an unremarkable family photograph. The second showed only the two children. They looked to be six or seven years old and were sitting together on a settee. In the background a portrait hung on the wall, but the details were unclear. The faces of the children stared out at her: innocent little faces full of childish hopes and fears. The faces of children long dead, and serving only to remind her of her own anguish.

Quickly Rose turned to the third photograph, which showed a picnic scene with a man, woman and baby. In the background was a motor car. She was no good at recognising makes, but even she could tell it was expensive. The only thing that struck her as unusual was that it was a light colour. The woman was the same one and the man sitting next to her on the grass was in uniform: this must be the husband, Brown. The attention of both was concentrated on the child in her arms. Rose felt certain it was the boy: the photo must pre-date the other two. Could it have been taken in wartime? She remembered the date on the birth certificate: April 1918. The baby seemed only a few months old, so that would fit. Her eyes were again drawn to the adults, especially the father. She recognised the uniform as that of a British officer, but his gaze was directed downwards and his features were shielded by his peaked cap.

Ron's letter was still lying there. Again she read the sentence 'It may have played a part in what has happened to me'. Exasperated, she put everything down. There was no way of recognising anyone. These were just family snapshots, so what could Ron have meant by saying they were dangerous? Granted, it wasn't an ordinary family.

Ordinary families didn't have motor cars like that. Ordinary families didn't have picnics using fine china. And as for the picnic basket . . . it was of a size capable of catering for a small army . . . Her interest was pricked and she held up the photo once more, but this time her gaze focused on the picnic basket, or more precisely on an emblem on the interior of the open lid. There was a motto underneath which she tried to read, but it was too blurred. As for the emblem itself, she couldn't identify the three separate elements, but the design was simple and symmetrical; the upright central object supported by a similar one on each side. There was something naggingly familiar about it.

'Rose . . . what's happening?' Christine's voice echoed from the hall. 'It's been nearly an hour. We're all waiting to start and the children are getting hungry.'

Rose started. Since opening the envelope everything else had gone from her mind. 'Sorry, I was just sorting out one or two things.' As she spoke she quickly gathered up the contents of the envelope. Since George had given it to her she had spoken to no one else about it, and given the present confusion in her thoughts now was not the time to start.

Christine came through the door. 'What on earth have you been doing? Aren't you ready yet? Then she saw her sister's face. 'You've been crying.' She came over and put her arms round Rose's shoulders. 'It's not so terrible if you've had second thoughts. I did think it was early to get married again.'

'No, it's not that. In a way I was . . . I was saying goodbye to Ron all over again.' She squeezed her sister's hand. 'Some day maybe I'll be able to tell you all about it.'

'Now stay in the garden!' Idris returned from checking the gate.

Christine chose the moment to voice her opinion. 'Come on, they're all eleven years old and it's not as if it's a main road.'

If Idris was irritated by her intervention he didn't show it. 'If children get carried away they can throw caution to the winds, and even on these roads an army convoy could come along at any time.'

Diplomatically, Rose's mother intervened. 'Does all this traffic mean they're preparing for the second front?'

Idris laughed. 'The last time I chatted to Churchill he still hadn't decided.'

The children raced up, having finished whatever it was they were doing, John got in first. 'We were wondering . . .' He hesitated a moment before blurting out. 'Can we all go to see the Daimler?'

Paul quickly followed up. 'And Dad, can you take us for a drive?'

With a feigned sigh Idris unwound himself from the easy chair. 'The answer to the first question is yes, you can see the Daimler, and Paul,' he turned to his son, 'you're old enough to know we can't use petrol for joyrides. So the answer is most certainly no.' He looked round. 'Who else wants to come?'

Given that neither her mother or sister showed any real interest, Rose felt obliged to accompany them. 'All right, I'll come.'

'Open sesame!' Idris pulled open the garage doors, and there was the prized possession that everyone had heard so much about.

Rose didn't know or care much about cars, but even she was impressed. 'So this is the Daimler.'

Idris explained. 'My dad bought it in 1920. Of course it's a bit dated now, but she's still a beauty.' He flicked an imaginary speck of dust from the bonnet.' Now careful, boys!' He directed his remarks at John and Paul who were clambering between the seats, while Amelia sat decorously in the back.

Rose felt she had to say something. 'As you say, it's a lovely looking . . .' Then she stopped as something jogged her memory. Her mind was drawn back to the envelope she had opened earlier that afternoon and, more specifically, to the photographs. This was the same car, or at least the same make and model. Granted, it was a different colour, but otherwise it was identical.

The boys had now settled into the front seats and Paul thought he would push his luck. 'Dad, can't you just drive out of the garage?'

'It's still no.' He paused in his polishing as the children, realising that Idris was not going to change his mind, opted to return to the house.

Rose took a deep breath. 'Did they make these cars before and during the Great War?'

'Good God, yes. They must have started in the early years of the century.' Idris had resumed his polishing of an imaginary blemish.

She felt a slight tremble in her voice. 'And did they always make them the same colour?'

'Same colour?' He looked perplexed. 'Well, nearly all cars are black and certainly I've only ever seen black Daimlers. You'd need to be one of those American film stars to have a white or cream car, and then most likely it would be a Cadillac.' He looked at her affectionately. 'Remember, I only run a garage in a small county town. Outside wartime it's generally a decent living, but we certainly can't run to white Cadillacs.'

He smiled at his own little joke but she didn't. 'Seriously, Idris, did Daimler ever make cars that were . . . ?' She tried to recollect more details but, of course, the photographs had been black and white. 'Say light grey, or perhaps fawn?'

Idris was puzzled. 'That's a funny question, Rose.' But by now he could see that she was deadly serious and he screwed his face up in concentration. 'If they did it would have been for someone pretty special.'

Some instinct told her she was as near to the truth as she was ever likely to get, and she persisted. 'How special?'

'Oh, I don't know. A prime minister or a president or maybe a royal.' By now Idris had stopped trying to find imperfections on the bodywork. 'Rose, where on earth is all this leading?' Then he interrupted her confused response. 'Hang on, though, my memory must be going. I'd almost forgotten that story Dad used to tell. He was in the Great War, and though he didn't talk about it much, when he did this was one of the things that sometimes came up.' He was now in full flow. 'You see, all the troops in the trenches were terrified and you can understand why.'

'You're not making sense. What stories, and why were they terrified?'

Brought back to earth, he started to explain. 'Apparently the Germans had spotters all over the place, and as soon as they saw anything out of the ordinary the chances were it would result in an artillery barrage. Then everyone around was for it. That's what made the troops nervous.'

Rose was still puzzled. 'What was it that was so out of the ordinary, and what on earth does this have to do with cars?'

For a moment Idris looked blank, then he recovered his train of thought. 'Sorry to get ahead of myself, but a lot of very important people were always visiting the front. As they were generally bigwigs of one sort or another, when they did come they were very careful to stick to the rear echelons. But sometimes they drove or were driven near to the front in their own motor cars.'

Rose was on tenterhooks. 'Idris . . .'

But he was not to be interrupted. 'There was one person in particular who scared them stiff. Dad's language tended to get quite colourful when he talked about him.' Switching into an exaggeratedly posh accent, Idris mimicked his father. 'Of course "one" couldn't possibly use an ordinary camouflaged staff car. It must be "one's" very own grey Daimler.' His voice reverted to normal. 'A car so distinctive that the Germans knew every time it was anywhere near the front, and moreover knew exactly who was in it.'

This time Rose did interrupt. 'Who do you mean?'

When Idris replied there was real passion in his voice. 'Who do I mean? Who do I mean? I mean the Prince of Wales, the very one who abdicated in '36. The monarch whose duty to the nation came a very poor second to his attachment to that floozie.' He paused to draw breath. 'So you can see, Rose, why I will personally always be very happy with a plain old black Daimler . . .'

She started to say something, but the words just wouldn't form. Idris nodded understandingly. 'Yes, I was as surprised as you are when Dad first told me that story.' The sound of childish argument echoed from the house. He took her unresisting arm. 'Let's get back before murder's committed.' Making no reply, Rose allowed him to lead her indoors.

On the eve of their wedding Rose showed him Ron's letter. It was her final adieu to her slain husband, and two tragic innocents who had died in a train crash long ago.